DISCERNING

April 2024

David,

Herein is some philosophy with regard to our education system.

Thank you always for your good work.

Karen

Books by K. N. Proctor

Questions for the Possibilities (non-fiction, 2007)

The Other World (2020)

Tudor Court (2022)

A Blast of Justice (2023)

DISCERNING

K. N. Proctor

ISBN 978-1-7357469-7-5

Printed in the United States of America

Cover illustration: Hannah Wood

". . . even those who by reason of use have their senses exercised to discern both good and evil."

Hebrews 5 vs 14

CONTENTS

Esse quam videri
(to be, rather than merely to seem)

CHAPTER ONE

WE BEGIN

"Helena, do you ever mind your own business?", my mother asked.

"It is my business, and don't you think we should all make it our business?", I replied firmly. "If you don't speak up and take a stand you will be stood on."

Her decisive manner and passionate energy spoke volumes.

"You are always 'on' my dear and you are exhausting to be around", Mom said as she walked out of the room.

I watched Mom leave, and as anger with injustice continued to boil and brew, thoughts began to move. Why should Hong Kong protesters be put in jail and protesters here, throwing bricks through windows, torching businesses, clubbing citizens, get off scot free? Something is very wrong with the world. Standing by instead of taking a stand is wrong, weak. And allowing for such weakness readies one for collapse into the arms of a tyrant.

As I walked down the hall, back to the den desk and my books the thought arrived, I don't quite fit in this world. Not that I want to 'fit' where I cannot respect, I said to myself. I have less and less patience with most people. As a teenager, parties and socializing didn't interest. I thought the things my classmates were doing, drinking, making out, marijuana, was stupid. Ten years and two degrees later I still feel the same. I have little time for people who will not take time to think. And on that thought, it's not that it's been hard to make friends, I just haven't been very interested. They've had to make the effort to make friends with me.

As Helena sat at the den desk in her mother's home, her feet up on a chair staring out at the green park across the street she said to herself, "Most people would rather stand back, stand aside, avoid a conflict than take a stand, and the truth requires more. The truth is one must face reality. Evil exists. One cannot stand by and let evil have its way. I don't respect this passivity, laziness is what it is. This makes it hard to respect people. Without a proper appreciation for one's God given gift of life one will not fight the evil which destroys life. Most won't fight until the hammer comes directly down on their head, and sometimes not even then. Why? Because they won't think, they won't think about what is most important. Why? Lazy? Afraid? Are they afraid of the reality they may find and then of having to face it? If one will not seek the courage required of a human being to live this life, one cannot know who one has been given to be and therefore what life to live. And without this knowledge one cannot be authentic. What relationships can one have without authenticity? Failing to discover who one has been given to be means not fully appreciating life and freedom, nor understanding how easily freedom and the life given can be taken from one. Tyrants have no respect for life or liberty.

Helena, twenty nine, looked twenty four. She had her own residence, an old house she rented, but liked visiting her mom. While at the moment they'd had a disagreement, they were quite close. There was a lot of love in their relationship and it was given by both of them. Helena had also been close to her dad. He had died however years ago, too young. Helena's relationship with her mom was one of two close relationships in life. John was the other. He was the column that held this world in place for her. While Helena was in the unusual position of not really needing anyone, this was not one hundred percent the case. Life on earth would not have held the meaning and appreciation it did without John. He understood her. He loved her. And she loved him very much. They were friends, and nicely, family. John had lived in many different places and for years now they had not lived on the same continent. Time zones and physical distance did not alter their relationship for its strength had been formed when they had married each other quite young. And while they had long been separated neither sought a divorce. Their's was an unusual, and treasured relationship. The strength of their bond had contributed to Helena's unassailable confidence. Where others stepped back or stood still or stepped aside, Helena stood firm and moved forward in confidence in the thinking she had done and in the courage she had found to live life with the classic Greek idea of the good, the true, and the beautiful forefront. While her own personality was a bit dramatic, John's great and steady good sense, great mind and even greater goodness was always there to guide her with wisdom, even with better reason, which helped keep her vision clear. For this she was eternally grateful.

It was Helena's habit of thinking, begun early in life, combined with her sensibility about injustice mixed with the state of the world which caused her to be perpetually 'on' as her mother said. An unusual quality of awareness also allowed for seeing what many missed. Her aware observations of others' actions and the thinking done to understand their reasons and motives, offered her more than glimpses into character. Recently she'd recognized that not once in business had a problem arisen to do with the people with whom she worked. And this Helena knew was due to astute understanding of character. From the time of her first job out of university colleagues had fallen down rabbit holes because they had neither considered human nature nor character. Helena's awareness was an asset likely to steadily increase in worth as she learned more of human nature and character.

Where will I go to find a friend?, she asked herself. Working for myself, with CEO's as clients, where is opportunity to get to know peers? If I feel this way at twenty nine what will the future hold? These conversations with myself are leading me to consider the alternative. My situation is not about having few friends, it is about the lack of a close friend where I live. What then is the alternative?, she reflected.

God has become a great guide, a trusted protector, and beloved father. And this is much more than a friend can be. Like a good mother and father who love their children he loves us, and more than any parent can. Having created us he wants a relationship with us. How can we deny him? I cannot. This relationship is developing, it is hard to describe. A way to think about him is to consider a very large window and a door. One must open a door to let someone in. And, yet unlike a door a window is open to light. He is light. He is light cutting through evil. This evil includes the injustice that gets me in a fury. I have been seeing this window in my mind's eye. It is beckoning me to go through it. And I know that on the other side is God himself. Jesus is silently calling me from the other side of that window. He is letting me know that I can knock at the door or come to the window and enter, be privy to all the light, and, all that lives in the light. If in pricing myself out of the market for good human company I have moved to a new, a holier ground, it will certainly be worth it. Approach.

As I approach I contemplate what may be found. Certainly it must be a closer, perhaps a very close relationship with God. It must then be a new level for living. This would include being without concern for daily worries, obstacles to joy, and any anxiety for the future. Would it also be a gift of strength, a strength which would well suit the fight here against the evils human nature all too often falls to? This could be fun.

Helena had begun a prayer some time ago. Every day she prayed:

Dear Father, I want to serve you. I want more than anything to serve you. I cannot stand by while evil flourishes. Please show me how I can serve in thwarting evil or helping snuff it out when I see it along life's path. Give me the strength needed for the thwarting and snuffing out. Amen.

CHAPTER TWO

HERE WE GO

We started in. I say we because I was no longer alone. From the outside world perspective I was alone. But God was closer now. And I felt strongly that God was watching over John more closely too. He was included in my commitment. In my closer proximity to the source of all good, of life itself, he my husband, though long separated, was under greater protection. It warmed me to know I could in some way be of good help to John who in being so very good, and thus good to me, had been as supporting arms at every fall. Just knowing he was there gave lift to every step.

The first discernment had me puzzling. For a week, at some moment in each day the message came, and always in the form of a young child.

The first day a first grader knocked on my door to sell cookies for a school trip. Hearing the knock my first thought was, who is the cause of this interruption. Then his cheery little face greeted me at my door.

His direct and simple approach, "Will you buy cookies to help us with our school trip?", was not to be refused. He was delighted with my purchase. "It's my tenth sale!", he announced with great excitement and he had me laughing.

The next day it was a young duffer who sat in the grocery cart. His mother was surveying the shelves as I approached. He took immediate notice of me and smiled as I returned his interested gaze.

"Hello, how are you?", I asked the ten month old with interest.

He beamed a wonderful smile right at me.

"I'm Helena. What is your name?", I asked of whom I knew could be a friend.

He stretched out his arm, reaching toward me with his open hand and fingers moving excitedly. His mother turned to look. Then he gurgled something.

I nodded with a big smile saying with energy, "Yes, yes indeed."

This made him giggle joyously. His mother stood staring, apparently not having experienced such response from her offspring and said,

"His name is Henry."

I smiled at her and turning to him said, "Hello Henry. What a good classic name. It is very good to meet you."

He burst forth with, I presumed from the look on his mother's face, many a new sound, laughing, giggling, and bouncing in his little seat. I laughed too. This resulted in a high pitched sound of enjoyment from Henry.

"You be good Henry. Goodbye now", I said giving him a wave.

He had not taken his eyes from me. Now he stared, mouth open, stunned that the fun was to end. Then he waved with all his might both his arms and hands, bouncing in his seat. And we said so long.

The following day the encounter with a little one was subtler though nonetheless poignant. Walking along the street, walking toward me from the opposite direction, was a father with his young daughter of perhaps four years and the family dog.

"Good morning", I greeted them all.

The father responded with a polite, "Good morning."

The dog wagged his tail in hopes I think of more of an exchange. The little girl looked up shyly and a small smile came to her face. As we passed I turned to look back at her. She turned too, and so did the dog. I waved and smiled. Her little smile broadened and she waved. The dog gave a happy bark as though to tell the father, stop. He didn't stop. But I did wait. She looked back three times and each time the dog joined her in turning to look. I kept smiling and waving.

These chance experiences gave me to think. What was at play here? It seemed to be a shared energy and spirit. Each encounter spoke of the joy of life. There was something here to consider. Each of seven days brought a very similar chance meeting of this same spirit, all with young children. I thought sign up to go into the schools to substitute teach. I can do this between my work with clients. And so I did.

In beginning to substitute teach it quickly became obvious high school and middle school would not be a match. Elementary students, six to ten years of age, were infinitely more absorbing, open, and curious for learning than were their elders. This willingness to learn is essential for gaining a true education. And I was interested in offering all I could.

"What is an education?", I would begin asking the children. From the Latin, education is a drawing out or drawing forth of what is within, that which is already there. Rather than a stuffing in of information an education is a nurturing. An appreciative love will help bring out what is there, that the soul may soar to its proper heights. This is my understanding of being a teacher, to be a midwife as Socrates put it.

Arriving in the classroom before the first grade children, I write a quote on the board. Here begins the lesson.

"What are these marks?", I ask and point to the quotation marks. A wee lesson in punctuation ensues.

"Who is this person?", I ask pointing to the name of the person we are quoting, a bit of history is given.

And, "What are these numbers here after the name?" And a little arithmetic determines the number of years the person lived. Then I ask a student to read the quote and I ask the class about its meaning. Thus begins our morning conversation.

Offering another conversation I ask, "Why do we come to school?"

Hand's rise in the air, and we continue our conversation.

Chrome books, an anathema to learning, engendering mind numbing and directing robotic responses are kept closed whenever possible. Given a choice my students prefer personal engagement to mesmerizing, eye tiring, headache inducing screen time.

"Close your chrome books", I announce relief.

No one hesitates, all immediately close the machine and look up for learning.

"Bring out your whiteboards, erase markers and erasers please", and they immediately dive into their desks to be ready for arithmetic.

"Oh boy", I hear one first grader say and his hand goes up.

"Yes, Ashton?"

"Can we do some big numbers?"

"Yes we can", I respond with like energy, smiling.

"Please write the equation

136
+ 46

vertically with the larger number on top and align the numbers," and I show the class on my little whiteboard.

"It is important to line the numbers up", and I show them again.

"Ready, one, two, three, showdown", I call out. And eager minds thrust their boards up into the air over their heads.

Amazingly many of these six year old new first graders have the answer or make a good attempt.

"Your sixes are backwards Nicholas", I tell the responsible little blond boy.

For a young girl who prefers coloring to applying herself to arithmetic I go over to her desk to offer individual help.

"Let's practice together. Write the equation like this", and I show her my white board. Quietly and slowly she copies the numbers out but horizontally.

"Write them on top of one another. This way you can solve the equation. We are adding the numbers one hundred and thirty six and forty six.

136
+ 46

Always begin on the far right side. We are simplifying the addition by breaking the numbers down. We begin by adding six and six and I point to the numbers. What is six plus six?", and I count up with her from six, both of us using our fingers.

"We put the '2' from twelve below the sixes and carry the one over", I show her. We complete the problem. Now she has seen herself do it.

"Do you want a hard or an easy one?", I ask the class.

"Hard", the three math whizzes shout.

"Easy", a few others call out.

"Alright, one easy one and then a harder one."

I prod the girl with whom I was just working saying, "You can do this. You just did a harder one."

She listens and writes out the equation this time as we had done together.

Each morning we practice our numbers. Together we attack arithmetic and I speak with the students about the magic in our number system. The magic of course is the simplicity, the 1 -10 framework upon which all our work with numbers is built.

"Would you like to add 10,000 and 100,000?"

"Yes!", a few shout. Others groan, "Oh, no."

I write the equation on the big board.

"Since both numbers have three zeroes at the end we can just cross them out like this. What is 100 plus 10?"

Someone says, "110!"

"Right!", I respond with equal fervor. "Since we crossed out the zeroes we add them back", and I do so. We do three more examples of how zeroes work.

The ones who love math are ohhing and ahhing. The ones who want to learn are trying it and getting it. The ones who don't like math are even attentive. They may begin to like it better.

We move on to writing. I hand each student a lined paper for their story on the topic, 'What I do When I Get Home.'

"Think about what you do when you get home, and think about the order in which you do it, then just start putting it into words and writing these words on your paper."

Most of them sit looking down at their paper with frustrated expressions and I hear, "I don't know what to write."

"What do you do when you get home?", I ask.

"I play with my brother and my dog, get on my x-box, go outside, play on the swings, and play with Joey."

"Good. Start writing that down."

"How do you spell 'play'?"

"Sound it out", I reply.

Slowly they begin. I walk around the classroom and as they begin writing they look up when I pass, and hands shoot up into the air to have me check on their work or to ask how to spell another word. When I am very present to them most of the students want to work. They want to show me their work. Almost all of them love the attention. And, they find that they very much enjoy their accomplishment.

Then one morning without notice a retired teacher showed up to take over the class for the morning. This relegates me to watching. She commands them with tone and language to dominate and control. Their faces change, no longer curious or eager they are mesmerized into following her direction.

"Everyone will come to the front of the class and sit on the floor."

A few get up from their desks and move toward the front.

"Did I say get up now? Wait until I tell you. Get your white boards out of your desks, and erase marker, and an eraser. When you are ready I will tell you to come to the front." She waits and the children obey.

"Rows one and two take your place on the carpet here." And she indicates the exact place for them to sit.

"Now rows three and four", she commands. She moves to her position of control at the front of the room looking down upon them. "Now hold your board like this, vertically. Seeing a couple of students readying their markers by removing the caps she pounces.

"No one should remove the cap to your marker until I tell you to do so. I will give you an equation to solve. Write it out on your board."

She speaks as to nonthinking creatures. And this attitude of mind is that which is intended from above her station in the hierarchy of the education system. Whether she realizes what she is doing, stamping down young minds and individuality, I do not know. However the intention, if not initiated by her, is there, and it is permeating our education system. It needs to be stopped or America will not be free.

"Johnny has 3 cookies and his mom gives him 5 more. How many cookies does Johnny have now? Now remove the cap to your marker and write the equation. I will repeat it."
And she does and dulls down young minds.

"Draw the cookies like this." And she draws three circles and then five more a little further over. "Now add them together", and she counts by ones all the cookies.

Of course the equation we did the day before, adding 100,000 and 10,000 won't work with the cookie drawing method. They all followed her commanding language but rather than look energized, curious, and challenged, as real learners do, these children looked like sheep. But I knew they were not sheep.

That night I prayed:
Dear Father, please guide me to best serve these children. Please help me to know how to best counter the evil that others do in not following you, in not thinking through what is right and what is true. In Jesus's name, Amen.

CHAPTER THREE

A CONVERSATION

Our first morning of school we had a conversation about why we go to school.

"Let us continue our conversation", I said and paused to learn their readiness for learning. They were with me, listening.

"Why do we go to school?", I asked.

A few hands went up. "Yes, Ryan?"

"To learn", Ryan said.

"Yes, to learn. What is necessary in order to learn? Yes Suzanne?"

"You should pay attention, and not talk when the teacher's talking."

"Yes, listening is essential to learning. Let's write down the tools of learning on the board." I wrote on the big side board the title Tools of Learning. 1. Listen

"Listen. That is our first tool. If you do not listen you will not learn. We will add to this as we go along. Now. Let's go back again to our first day's conversation. What else did we speak about?"

"Yes, Emma?"

"About being human beings."

"Yes Emma, thank you. And as a human being we have a human nature. And that means we must seek to understand our human nature. Who can tell us something about the nature of a human being?"

"Yes, Tom?"

"We talk."

"Yes, we speak. We can speak, and speak with our fellow human beings. We can translate what is going on here," and I place my index finger on my temple, "and share it with another person. This makes us unique and different from all creatures. A dog has a dog nature. We, as human beings, have a human nature and, given this gift have a responsibility to it."

The next day we begin with our Tools of Learning.

"What is another tool of learning?"

"To think", Ashton offered.

"Yes", I replied with enthusiasm and appreciation. "You did some thinking", I smiled directly upon him.

I write under our title Tools of Learning 2. Think then I add number three, 3. A willingness to learn

"No matter how good your teacher is, even if the best in the world, if you do not have a willingness to learn you will not learn. What is this willingness?" I waited. All were listening, no hand was raised.

"It is an openness, a readiness to listen and to take in and consider what is before you. It is to think and another word related to think, reflect. Remember an education is a drawing forth from what is already inside you. You want to develop a great curiosity for what you have inside you, and for what that special something has to teach you about life."

Someone asked, "What do you mean?"

"Imagine an experiment. We put on our gloves and eye googles and a scientist's lab coat. Before us on the lab table is a liquid concoction. We decide to add something to the concoction."

Someone said, "What's a colcockshon?"

"A concoction is something you make from a mix of a few things you put together. Now we pour in another liquid to see what happens. As we pour, our concoction reacts by changing colors. Then it begins to bubble and froth. And maybe it even steams up and overflows the beaker or glass container. Imagine too that your mind will respond to things brought to it from the outside world. Don't you want to learn what your mind will tell you as these things arrive from the outside?", I asked.

A resounding,"Yes!", came from a number of students.

"Who remembers what the most important question is from the first day? Yes, Kate?"

"The 'Who' question."

"Yes, the who question", and I write 'Who' with a question mark on the board. The most important thing for you to know is who you are as a human being, and who you are as a unique person. As Ashton, as Suzanne, as Tom, as Emma, as Kate, . . . then . . . you will begin to know what it means to live a good life. Then you begin to be in position to live a good life."

It is obviously important to give children the opportunity to think in the whole picture because you can see how attentively they listen when you do. For example with our number system, based in 1-10, in teaching that as human beings we have a human nature and, in asking what is our human nature. To help bring forth that which is within one must encourage a child to think about and to begin to register his or her own character, why certain feelings occur when something happens and what one thinks about that, to reflect on what one does and says, what others do and say and what it tells us about a person. To pay attention to our inborn nature and to our conscience is to begin to realize being a human being. The day that retired teacher came to take over my class I was grumpy the entire day. My joy or displeasure shows in my face. The school prefers happy hallways and so that retiree did not return, at least to my class. While the changed look upon the faces of the children during her tutelage may not have been noticed by an onlooker what was obvious was their eagerness to get back to the 'Big numbers', their enjoyment in my attention to their writing, their appreciation for the good books we read aloud, and their satisfaction with our conversation.

It was in these conversations where they would come up and sit on the floor around my chair that we could approach the big, the whole picture. When I had to leave for a two week mandatory virus quarantine their sense of continuity, stability, and of good order had been removed. I sensed something amiss immediately upon return. That night I thought about what exactly was amiss.

The next morning once everyone had arrived I called for them to come to the front to sit together for our conversation. They sensed immediately that this was important and were silent listening to what I wanted to say to them.

"It is important that you know that I did not want to go away and leave you. The school district decides when people must go into quarantine. I love you and want you to know that I am here for you, that we are here together to learn. I seek to offer you what you need to gain the tools of learning to move into your future being able to think for yourself and understand what is important for living a good life."

They listened completely and for the entire time. Quietly they returned to their desks and we began again our work together. This is what they needed. How important to be thinking about the children that one is open to give the message for them when it comes.

The school district has progressive members within its ranks seeking to direct the schools toward the overarching mandate of our education system, steering our youth to the progressive ideal of the better human being. That is, one who behaves uniformly, predictably, controllably. This shows up in efforts to homogenize and mold our youth to follow authority. Respect for and all encouragement of individualism is obviated. This is the reason for a focused effort to erase American history. Rugged individualism helped form the country. The individual tends to think for himself and does not take kindly to dictates and overarching authority. Those seeking power, fame, and position in the world must therefore stamp down this natural inclination in human beings to exercise their God given gifts to live their lives as they see fit. I wasn't going to help them. Witnessing young children moving in just moments from eager energy, absorbing curiosity, and chomping at the bit for challenge ('Big numbers!') to robotic subservience made it a personal responsibility to help stop our education system from ruining our children and the future of our country. I asked for help. What can I do to work for the opposite end? That is, to replace manipulation with good guidance, command with care, and a false man made ideal of what a human being should be with love.

Dear Father, please help me. How am I to best serve you? Why would so many fall in line with what must be a few so evilly intentioned as to wish to see our country cowed to subservience? Please help me see your way, better and better. Amen.

CHAPTER FOUR

HELP ARRIVES

The help for which I asked arrived in a most unexpected way. I didn't notice the alteration at first.

This morning, as usual, I flung back the duvet, got up and opened the louvers on all three windows. An unusually glorious sunny day made her greeting and excitedly anticipating the adventure, I began, as usual, an unplanned Saturday.

It was when eating breakfast I first noticed something. While occasionally I experience an awareness more acute than usual, today I seemed to have more than 20/20 vision. Noticing the chirping birds in unusual detail, I moved closer to the window to see the little duffers. Were the chirping birds, singing a particular song this morning? Was that a melody I discerned? On the bushes out the kitchen window where I leave birdseed on the ground, a cardinal, a large bluejay, and three fat sparrows had gathered. I peered more closely. The bluejay's beak was opening and closing, the cardinal held his beak open in song and all three sparrows were bobbing in time. And yes it was song, a song sung to the music of the morning.

"Well. . .", I voiced aloud with interest and curiosity, yet unable to settle upon any known cause for this heightened awareness. I withdrew from the window and went back to my bowl of wild blueberries, kale, and steel cut oats. As I ate my mind swirled, connecting dots with an unfamiliar quickness. While my mind had always wanted to employ itself on many matters at once, I noticed the speed with which items from its recesses alighted in the forefront, gained clear focus, registered as understood, and then got filed in orderly compartments.

I raced upstairs to change and go for my walk. Everyday whatever the weather I go for a morning walk. As I changed into leggings I recognized a quickness and dexterity beyond the norm. Dashing out the door and onto the path for my walking route, walking seemed too slow a mode to fully enjoy the morning. I began to run. When arriving at the circular track where I normally begin a slow jog, having already run five minutes it was surprising to want to continue without stopping. Something has happened, and I sensed was still happening. Then my request for help came to mind. For what had I asked? Help to stop the slide of our country into an oblivion induced by the domination of young minds through the command and control thinking of our education system.

"Hmmm . . . is this help arriving embodied . . . in my body and in my mind?", I asked aloud, unashamed to voice my thoughts out loud as I always did in my home. From where was I asking for help? Or better, from whom? God. Yes God. Who else? He has always been here. Before me, and after me. He is history. And this is the history they most want to erase. Of course at bottom they cannot. The fact that they do not know this dooms their endeavor from its beginning. However, those who replace God with Man can and are causing a lot of misery as amply shown on the faces of our children. Children who sense the truth and authenticity far better than adults, have their hearts and minds crushed by the lie that human nature can be changed, and into the ideal Man that Man decides upon. What will he have me do?"

Epoch Times writes of parents removing their children from public schools and placing them privately in charter schools and home schooling them. And what of the fifty million American children in public schools? Where to begin? I began to think about the parents I knew, and began indirectly with my landlord. I wrote him a letter.

'Dear Murray,
While I like this old house very much it needs some attention. Are you interested in the following?
1. Placing a mat beneath the bouncing washing machine
2. Replacing the back stoop
3. Stripping the peeling paint and repainting the baseboard in the bathroom
4. Regrouting the three tiles behind the kitchen sink which have come away
Would you kindly let me know your plans for the house? Thank you.'

My landlord is unresponsive. I live alone in this rented house and take very good care of the old hardwood floors, have the windows professionally washed, and keep it clean. He has a good deal with me here. But he won't care until the house is empty for a few months and a couple or family move in and create a lot more wear and tear on the floors, not to mention the old plumbing. His interest in being a landlord is nil. He likes to think of himself as a property owner and neglects the responsibility of being a good landlord. Such lack of personal responsibility wears away at one's character and the fact that he is oblivious to this reality has allowed an arrogance to develop which also shows up in his son. His young son, whom I have encountered in school and through his appearance in this house, has an arrogance most unbecoming in anyone let alone in an elementary school child. It has arisen directly through his father's lack of understanding of what it means to live a good life.

Where is a good example to be set if not at home or in school? And where is a good example to be found in our lives if we allow ourselves and our children to live online? Good books, old books, history is what is needed to see clearly through the modern fog. Humanity has had hard times before. How have we coped? What has been learned before our own time? Open Chrysostom, Hugh of St. Victor, Petrarch, Paul Elmer More, Simone Weil, Dorothy L. Sayers, C.S. Lewis, and Michael Oakeshott.

Consider conscience. Conscience, being within us all, and registering for us right from wrong, at least in most children while children, will guide us to good and away from evil if we listen while young. If we do not choose the good along the journey conscience will dull and die by the time we have not long been an adult.

The discerning did not leave me. Each morning it seemed to be wholly refreshed, and developing. And something else was noticeable. Patience for, laziness, lack of appreciation for this life, which is sibling to lack of personal responsibility to do one's all to live a good life, was dwindling to nothing.

An old friend called. It had occurred to me that a few years back he had wanted more from our friendship, more than another can give. A friendship can be used as a crutch for the effort required for one's own development as a person. He wanted more than could rightly be given and he held this difference between us, my recognition of the fact and his lack of a wish to acknowledge it, likely due to the work required, with resentment. While perhaps the resentment had diminished with time, I did not respect the fact of the existence of its source. Instead of developing a healthier friendship and an ability for one, he spent time and gave his friendship to an offensive, devilish really, man. Over time the time he spent with this man had a bad effect upon my old friend. His call was a surprise. The last time I checked in he subtly rebuffed me. He was on vacation with that devilish fellow and that influence was palpable, and was after years perhaps irreconcilable with his previous self. When I hung up the phone after that call I asked myself is there anything left for a true friendship. The conversation which ensued in his recent call was flat, dulled by a laziness to lift life above the worldly influences of convenience and of ease. Such laziness permeates one's conceptual capacities destroying strength of and independence of thought and then mind. Is respect necessary for friendship? Yes I said to myself. Impatience with laziness of thought is properly justified in the truth that respect should be given as an earned benefit to character development.

All this thinking arrived as Helena sat with her feet up on the ottoman her father had given her. And while her gaze rested on the treed hill and grand old house across the street her mind reflected on who people are. Who were those who gave room to laziness? And who were those who endeavor with life in worthy recognition that time is life? If lazy with any aspect of the gift of life, where is one's appreciation, one's proper love for life? Given that God is the source of love as the classic book tells us then the source of love within us is also connected with being just. God is love and because he is he is a just God. If we allow laziness to creep into life what is the consequence? We don't love as we could. Our children are short changed. Life is short changed. If you give a one hundred dollar bill for something costing fifty dollars and are given twenty five dollars in change would you walk away or request the right change and if need be stand firm for the full amount? How does a child request all the love you can give? It is up to you to find it, and to give it. How much better off would his children be if the landlord had rid himself of his laziness and sought God? Courage is required to be a human being and courage does not permit laziness.

The problem is we do not think enough. What is the cost of reflection? Time. To reflect is to be much more fully human. To reflect is to learn what is most important, to determine for example that having people know you own property is less important than being a good landlord with the property you own is to reflect and decide. Which will develop your character and better benefit your child through good example? To reflect is to face reality. If you are too lazy to reflect or too cowardly to face the reality uncovered in reflection, the consequence to character, and then to the example you offer in the life you live, will be just. It will be equal to who you have become. From where comes one's choice to spend one's time in trivial pursuits, entertainments, many luxuries, retiring one's very self? It comes from a deeply set laziness to life. This laziness speaks of a lack of understanding of life. Life is given and therefore is not ours to merely dispense with as we want. While time is life life is much more than time, that life - in the full - is only to be shown to us through God. Without faith in God the love we give here is majorly mitigated, and means only a paucity of what it can mean with the promise of eternity.

Helena sat waiting in the luxurious lobby of Horvath and Crane, the multinational industrial engineering company where she had a monthly appointment with her client, Wynton Crane. Helena had met Crane's cousin at the University of Edinburgh and he had suggested she call Wynton. Capable and direct on the phone and not to be intimidated, Helena had made a good impression. In particular Crane liked her direct and time appreciating approach and had given her a meeting. Helena, while opinionated, could be quite charming, and her high energy well suited CEO's. Wynton Crane had been a client now for three years.

Crane's secretary, Adele, entered the lobby with a smile for Helena.

"Helena, good to see you, I hope all is well", she said.

"Yes thank you. It's good to see you, anything exciting happening?"

"No, lots of late nights at the office. Wynton is ready for you", Adele said, efficient as ever, and led Helena through the handsome oak doors to the executive offices.

Adele, forty something, pleasant, was most capable in handling any personality in person or on the phone. She was savvy enough to save her own and Crane's time. With well cut brown bobbed hair, she wore, while not so well cut, good quality attire and kept herself fit. Adele was a good example of a focused and productive executive assistant and Helena credited Wynton Crane's good judgment for having chosen his assistant, not merely accepting one from the secretarial pool.

While it had been good luck to meet and get to know the connected cousin in Edinburgh, Helena had handled the meeting with Wynton Crane and the presentation of her dialogue work with professional aplomb and astute insight. Confident in her ability, her presentations invariably impressed. However it was her insight in the moment with a prospective client, insight into character, which resulted in turning presentation into actualizing a client.

As Helena walked the last corridor with Adele they passed fewer and larger offices. Helena always prepared well for her client. As she held that time equals life, she felt a good example essential in the appreciation she showed for the client's time. And this would open the door to a client better understanding that equation. While she shared with clients a good valuation of time, never wasting any, it was the other half of the equation, life, that they most often did not get.

Helena took two deeper breaths as they arrived at the end corner office and reminded herself that today they would move closer to greater appreciation for that simple equation, time equals life. After all, the choices one makes for one's time determine the future and clients were always interested in the future.

"Hello Helena. Come in. Good to see you", Wynton Crane smiled his confident greeting and warmly extended his hand to me.

As I approached his desk I noticed a child's drawings pinned to the wall behind it.

"Thank you. It is good to see you. Are those Matthew's drawings?", I asked, inquiring as to whether the drawings were those of his six year old son.

"Yes, he is giving me all his artwork lately and making his mother a bit jealous", Wynton Crane laughed, relaxing.

"Was your wife the usual recipient?", I inquired.

"Yes. Giving it all to me is something new."

"Why the change do you think?", I asked. My guess was that he had not thought about it and I hoped he would.

There was a brief pause before he answered and by his face I could tell he was thinking now.

Then he said, "I don't know."

One can always work with someone who is honest.

"He wants your attention", I said and paused for a moment to let that simple idea digest. "Why now, more than before?", I kept up the questions.

Wynton Crane, sat down in his large dark brown leather swivel chair, sighed and said, "I've been traveling more, it began a couple of months ago. I'm away more and more days. We have a new Asian client and it looks very promising. I have had to be there", he stopped.

I waited a moment and then said, "Is there someone to step in for you soon?"

"No . . . though there should be", he paused. I kept looking at him. He looked at me and looked away. He came back to me again.

"We've talked about this, haven't we", he said rhetorically. "I have to let go of more rein and let my people develop." I nodded.

Wynton stood and started pacing. After a full minute or more he said,

"It's not that there is no one who could do the job. It's . . . more that . . . I want to do it. I like being in the fray, in the thick of the client getting and grooming", and he laughed.

Yes Wynton Crane enjoyed the pitch and thrust, the fight and the final battle, the sale. I listened and waited.

"I know I need to move on, let someone else, Richard, or Jose, either one could do it well. And they should, they need to develop. I need them to grow. But I don't do it", and he stopped speaking and pacing and sat down on the large crewel work sofa in the middle of his office.

I let his last sentence hang in the silence. And then I repeated his words, "But I don't do it." I paused, then said,

"Why?"

Wynton Crane, rubbing his eyes, stopped, looked up from beneath his thick dark brows and furrowed forehead, his mouth in a tight frown replied softly,

"Why do you think I don't let go?"

I said evenly and directly, "Pride."

CHAPTER FIVE

BACK AT SCHOOL

In taking another maternity leave at school this time I knew all the work entailed. Tonight was the home and school meeting. If all the parents who said they would come, come, which was all but one child's parent, there would be eleven couples and nine individual parents, thirty one people with whom to meet in a two and one half hour period. Only a handful of parents required my making a specific note to remind myself of something that needed to be shared with them about their child. For the rest I would know what to say to help an interested parent help their child learn. One thing I was absolutely determined to ask and encourage was their participation in the school board. At least I hoped to get a good number of them, if not to run for the Board, to attend the Board meetings.

"If you will sit down with Katelyn each evening for fifteen minutes and read to her and have her write one sentence about what was read you will notice quite quickly a significant change for the better in her reading, comprehension, and in her writing", I said to Mr. and Mrs. Belford. They were listening. That was a good sign. We would see if they would do it.

"Thank you. We will try this", Katelyn's father said and looked to her mother.

Mrs. Belford pursed her lips as if to say, 'You mean I will do this with her', though her nod indicated she would likely plan to do it.

"I have a request", I said slowly, looking directly at the two of them.

"Yes?", Mr. Belford replied, stopping his motion to leave.

"Are you aware that our education system is not as it once was?", I paused. A slight nod came from Mr. Belford.

"That is, no longer are we in the business of strictly teaching reading, writing and arithmetic. Rather, our elites at the top want us to direct young minds toward an ideal they see as necessary for a world uniform, and nowhere close to what America has been as a free country, as a Republic."

Mrs. Belford looked befuddled. Mr. Belford looked concerned and furrowed his brow.

"I ask that you attend our school district Board meetings. Listen. And learn what we are teaching our children, of which you may not agree, and which you may wish to fight against."

"Thank you", Katelyn's father said, speaking more quietly than he had done. He guided his wife out the door.

"Roger can be a monkey", Roger's mother, Mrs. Herring said, laughing.

"He can be rambunctious", I replied. "However he is bright and could be quite a good student. If you would speak to him about the importance of listening while I am teaching. I think he would be less frustrated and enjoy his productivity. I think he has a large capacity for learning." I smiled at both Mr. and Mrs. Herring.

"Yes, yes I will", Mrs. Herring responded enthusiastically. And then, looking at her rather reserved husband added in a serious tone, "We will speak with Roger."

"May I ask something else of you?", I said in a likewise serious tone.

This time it was Mr. Herring who responded, "Yes."

"Are you concerned about the direction of our education system?"

"Yes we are. What are you thinking in particular?" Roger's father asked.

His response encouraged me to say more, "Our education system is directed from the top. And has been directed for years by progressive elites who consider human nature to be alterable. They are seeking to mold our young minds away from the individualism that helped found America, to an ideal that would have America fit into a globally accepted mold for humanity." I stopped, hoping I had not gone too far ahead of what they would digest.

A look of calm came over Mr. Herring's face. Where he had been merely attentive he now had a look of appreciative calm as in 'Ah good, the teacher wants to help do something about this quicksand around us'. Mrs. Herring's bubbling acceptance had disappeared and serious consideration of what I had said seemed to show in the slow nod of her head.

Mr. Herring spoke, "We agree with you. I, and I believe my wife, appreciate what you have said. What can we as parents do about this threat?"

"You are right to consider their direction a threat. Please attend the school district's board meetings. And better, run for the school board."

They were both silent for a few moments and kept looking straight at me.

"Yes, I will make it part of my schedule to attend school board meetings", he paused. Then Mr. Herring said, "And, I will think about running for the school board."

"Thank you", I replied, sighing with happy relief.

They both smiled at me and each shook my hand warmly.

With each parent the opportunity presented itself to share my concern, and to ask for their engagement in the system which was working to counter the purpose of an education, to guide one to learn and to think for oneself.

That evening after the school meetings, immediately after dinner I suddenly felt tired and decided to go to bed early. As soon as I lay down sleep arrived. And so did a messenger in my dreams. I was sitting in my room knitting. I don't knit, and do not know how to knit. In through the window came an apparition of light.

He stood before me and gave his message, "Fear not. You will encounter difficulty. Many will oppose you because you will be an obstacle in their way. You will be guided. Continue with your endeavor. You will be given the strength and power to overcome."

When I awoke the next morning the dream came back to me in clear detail. Again I heard the messenger speaking to me in his strong resonant voice his message of assurance and encouragement. I felt wholly refreshed. I was quickly reminded of how I could do what I needed to do in a twenty four hour day all with ease and with extra clarity of mind and thought.

There was now an extra something, a deep warmth or comfort, a confident reassurance that all would, at least ultimately, be well and that I was guided. A thought came to me. 'Be careful not to overstep, that pride should arise out of this feeling of great comfort.'

"Have you been considering 'pride' since we last met?", I asked Wynton Crane.

"I think so. I must say I didn't want to think about it." My client looked at me sideways, not wanting to address pride.

I responded, "Let me share my experience with pride."

Immediately more openness showed in his face.

"A few years ago when reading the Bible I came upon the first commandment. 'Thou shalt love the Lord thy God with all thy heart, with all thy soul, with all thy mind, and with all thy strength.' That is, one should love God first and foremost. I knew that I loved my mom most of all, and then God. But this is not what he asks of us. So I asked him for help. He knew the truth and I knew the truth and I wanted to do as he asked. An answer arrived quite quickly. I was in my apartment and had Beethoven on the Bose. Suddenly his strong beautiful music inspired a dawning of understanding. I fell to my knees in the middle of the living room in gratefulness for this understanding. Of course I loved God most. He had given me my mom. And he had given me everyone I loved and everyone I would ever love. In that moment from standing to kneeling something else arrived. As a ghost that wisps across the stage one must stop to register when this happens, or the ghost is gone, not to be caught again. When you ask wisely in faith (Matthew 7.7) he will give that which you ask, and he may give you something more. In that moment on my knees the gift was a recognition of pride. On your knees it is hard to be prideful. I had too much pride. God hates pride. Pride kills relationships, and most importantly one's relationship with God." I stopped, and waited.

Wynton had been looking at me, listening. Now with a far away look he moved his sight lines out to the skyline. There was a long interval, one that under usual circumstances would be uncomfortable. These moments however were not usual. I knew it was the extra strength in play, that extra something I had been given. I waited. Wynton Crane's mind, and I hoped his heart, were somewhere else at that moment. Then slowly he turned his head toward me and I could see in his face that he was coming back from where he had been.

Slowly he said, "Yes." In that one word and in his voice it was apparent that he understood something more about pride and that along with the effort he had made, he was thinking about God.

The school board meeting began at 6:00PM I arrived fifteen minutes early in hopes of meeting some parents and went over to the closest person to introduce myself.

"Hello, I'm Helena Madison. I substitute teach in our schools", I offered her my hand and smiled.

"Hello. I'm Susan Holk. My son is at Sam Adams in third grade."

"Good for you for coming out", I began, hoping this parent would pick up from there on why she had come.

She jumped right in, "Well, I'm wondering what is being taught. Saige doesn't seem to be interested in studying. He rarely has homework. And he used to be so interested in his numbers, in reading, and in writing too."

"What do you think is missing?", I asked.

"The work I do see is too easy, babyish really. It seems that the teacher teaches down to the worst student in the class. And this seems a poor strategy for the overall well being of the community, of the country, if the system is the same everywhere", she said heatedly.

"Oh yes, it is pretty much the same across the country", I replied, confirming her concern and very happy to be able to voice it to an interested ear.

Just then I saw Mr. Herring, Roger's father, looking at me from across the room. He smiled when I acknowledged seeing him.

"I see a parent of a student, will you please excuse me? It is a very good thing you have come. Be sure to express your concerns", I encouraged her.

"Thank you", she replied.

"Miss Madison, it is good to see you again and here at the Board meeting", Mr. Herring greeted me.

"Thank you. Good for you for coming out", I responded.

He replied, "Your request to participate was good advice. Parents cannot stand idly by while their child's opportunity for an education slips away."

"Parents, teachers, and community members", an official sounding voice was raised above the buzz that had begun over the small group who were standing around in the community hall. Eyes were drawn to the man standing at the front of the room speaking.

"I am Hector Prentice, chairman of the Coberley School District. Thank you for coming tonight. We will begin shortly. Please take a seat. Mrs. Hall will announce our agenda", he finished and a severely thin middle aged woman came directly to the microphone.

"Good evening. My name is Amy Hall, school district secretary. Tonight we will have an open discussion on sex education. The proposal before the Board is to begin sex education in fourth grade. Currently sex education begins in seventh grade. We will take all questions and comments from the floor", she said and apparently finished, returned to her seat.

Tête-à-tête exchanges began between mothers and fathers. The couple closest to me were however silent and looked bored. I wondered if they were going to leave. I knew exactly what I thought about the school engaging in sex education with the students, icks nay! This topic was parental territory. It was up to a parent to discern when their child was ready, and up to the child. A child should be comfortable enough to ask a parent when questions arose.

A hand went up and Mr. Prentice gave the father the floor.

"My wife and I feel that it is our prerogative and not the school's to have the conversation with each of our children when they are ready to have it, and not before. And, importantly, the conversation should be conducted in the way we would have it. It should be a personal conversation, one-to-one with a child and should not be conducted enmasse in a classroom where a child may be uncomfortable asking a question in front of his or her peers", he sat down.

"Thank you", Mr. Prentice said somewhat perfunctorily.

"Yes", he responded to another hand.

"I agree and my husband thinks the same way", a mother said emphatically and sat down.

"Would you give a show of hands, those of you who agree that the parent should be the purveyor of sex education?", Mr. Prentice asked the meeting.

A good majority raised their hand.

"Thank you. Would one of you who did not just now raise your hand offer your view on the subject?", he asked the room. A tall lean man stood and replied, "I would leave this to the schools. There are many parents I'm sure who would be embarrassed and or would not know where or how to begin to explain the birds and the bees. Children are mostly comfortable with their teachers and they would likely do a better job", and he sat down.

A few heads were nodding. I raised my hand.

"Yes", I was given the floor.

"Handing over such an intimate and important question to the school abdicates one's personal responsibility, a personal responsibility attached to the relationship and privilege of parent child. There are only so many opportunities along the path of raising a child where one can seize the privilege to offer good guidance and to understand one's child. Take every opportunity to fully play your part", I emphasized and took my seat.

"Here, here", a man's voice spoke out. It was Mr. Herring, he was smiling at me and then he added, "We agree whole heartedly."

There was silence. And after a few moments Mr. Prentice asked,

"Are there any further comments?"

No one else spoke.

Mr. Prentice spoke again, "Thank you. We will give consideration to your comments. And we will now close the meeting."

Mr. Herring approached me.

"What happens next?", he asked.

"It depends on the Board. We were in the majority tonight. So they may pass on implementing a program of sex education for the fourth graders, at least for the time being. But they may go ahead with their agenda. It is very important that you were here making yourself heard, and to learn what is going on. We will learn more when we learn what they will do", I replied.

CHAPTER SIX

SCHOOL OF LIFE

"Hello Helena", I was surprised to hear a client's voice on the other end of my phone.

Rarely did a CEO call. Hugo Wentworth, whom I had met when living in the U.K., was now working in New York. While he was not a regular client every so often he would call for my time and our dialogue. About a year ago he had flown me to New York for an afternoon session with him. My heart beat a little faster as I wondered if he would again bring me to New York.

"Are you ready for another shot of New York energy?", he asked in his posh English accent, with laughter in his voice. "We've got a lot going on. I'd like you to sit in on a few of our meetings and then give me your opinion on a few people and their ideas", he said straight out.

"Of course. I'd love to help and to come to New York. Thank you for thinking of me", I was smiling.

"Good. I can hear in your voice that you are looking forward to coming to New York again. The meetings are next week. I will put Charlotte on the phone with you and you can arrange the dates as best suits you. I look forward to seeing you again soon. Goodbye Helena", the phone clicked and I was on hold only a few moments.

"Helena, Charlotte here. I hope you are very well", her calm, composed, proper and polite British manner greeted me with sincerity.

"I am very well thank you. I'm already thinking about seeing you and Hugo again. And will shortly think about the museums while there."

"And what shopping you'll want to do no doubt?", Charlotte kindly queried. We laughed.

Charlotte, ever thoughtful, arranged my stay in the old Exeter Regent, a small hotel where charm, character, and quiet attention to a guest's preferences were its raison d'etre. I decided to arrive the evening before the two days of meetings and then to remain the weekend to visit my favorite places and wander New York.

I have always loved visiting New York. Everyone must register her energy in the first few moments of arriving. There is a vibrancy like no other. World class cities tend to have their own charm but New York has her own energy. Her energy inspires one to be more alive to life. The pace means losing a pound or two walking the city and running up and down subway stairs. The smells of the street vendor food stands, the honking horns, and the calls and comments of the merchants hawking scarves, pocket books, hand bags, and sunglasses are trademark New York. But quintessential New York shows herself when it begins to rain and suddenly, before you've walked a block, a man appears with umbrellas. And you smile and thank him as you hand him your $5 bill and he hands you that lightweight compact black umbrella.

Dressed in my navy business suit with matching stockings and navy soft leather low healed sling backs I was suitably unassuming as I sat listening and observing at Hugo's board room table. Hugo first off introduced me to Jack Waters, his senior V.P.. Jack now sat on my right and Hugo, at the head of the table, on my left. The company treasurer, unassuming, sat one down from Jack and beside Hugo's company lawyer. The other key players were across the table.

Trey Harding the president of SonWalt International, the company Hugo's Fielding Enterprises Inc. was planning to partner with on new business in Asia, sat across and one down from me. Mr. Harding was a stocky balding man of about fifty years with ice blue eyes that cut right through you with his swift cold glance. Mr. Harding had not said much, and nothing so far that I could hear. While not looking for another cut from those icy eyes, I was interested to hear his voice. Voices are most revealing.

Next to him sat Sue Langdon, V.P. at the financial house of Hamilton Shey, noticeably eager to help fund the enterprise under consideration. She was younger than Harding, perhaps thirty eight, perfectly blond, coiffeured and manicured, in a tailored suit and blouse with Gucci shoes. Her smile was currently trained on Trey with whom she was having a quiet exchange. She seemed to be scoring points there. I thought I caught a momentary glimmer of a smile across his otherwise impervious expression and a micro warming in those eyes of ice.

Then there was Chandler Fleming, the other lawyer. He sat beside Langdon. He did not appear to be the more typical New York attorney, arrogant with his smarts and knowledge. I hadn't yet sized him up but something did not feel right.

Hugo's executive assistant, Annabelle, sat on Hugo's left, directly across from me. Annabelle had been with Hugo in the U.K. and I had first met her there. I liked her right away, direct and open, a loyal sort one could depend upon. Good for Hugo I had thought when first meeting her.

"We are all here, let's begin", Hugo said in his clear strong voice. Given his warmth of manner Hugo's posh British accent could hardly be held against him even by the most egalitarian of souls. "You have all met before, and I introduced Helena Madison when you each arrived," said Hugo.

Trey Harding gave me another quick icy cut with his sharp glance.

Hugo continued, "On the table is the potential partnering of SonWalt and Fielding Enterprises, along with the partnership arrangement for business in China for American product produced there and for its distribution here and worldwide. Trey has connected us with the Chinese manufacturer in Guangzhou. Sue has jumped in with financing." Langdon beamed her smile of shark white teeth upon Hugo. Boy is she keen, I made a mental note.

"We're ready to move three of our people to Guangzhou to begin operations with potentially another ten to follow. And our team here is ready for the big project of opening distribution channels. All that need be decided is whether we are sold on each other and the partnership arrangement", Hugo finished speaking and looked invitingly at each member of the party encouraging them to speak.

Trey began, "As I said from the beginning I'm in." His statement was curt and felt cold. Hugo's treasurer shifted in his chair. He seemed to respond as I did to Harding's manner. Perhaps Harding says little for good reason and I made another mental note to look out for what that reason might be.

Sue Langdon smiling at the entire table said, "Hamilton Shey has set aside three hundred and fifty million for your project", she nodded to Trey and then tilted her head at Hugo. "We are ready, and simply awaiting your confirmation."

Harding's lawyer, Chandler Fleming, cleared his throat and spoke, "Did we not decide last June for this venture when having gone to China to check out our arrangements we found them in good order and were happy with the Chinese on that end? Have we not already decided that the monies we see coming from this project are substantially greater than what we could do elsewhere? Why I ask is there any hesitation?"

Here is a slick one I thought. I looked at Hugo's face, did he hear what I had heard, someone used to getting his way through oratorical power and persuasion? And someone who likely cared little about what was right and good, and cared most for his own bank account. I wasn't sure, Hugo's face showed only a pensiveness.

Jack said, "Chandler makes a good point. We went to China because we wanted the business and we were checking out the particular arrangement to which Trey had introduced us. We came back satisfied. Is there any good reason for delay?"

Hugo addressed his treasurer, "Sol, do you have any questions or comments?"

This time Sol cleared his throat. I smiled to myself thinking he mimics the lawyer while clearing the air of Fleming's imprint.

He began in a considered manner, "My comment is that yes we have hesitated, and there must be a reason for doing so. We need to see what the reason is."

Smart man I said to myself. I was glad to see Hugo nod, and continue his pensive manner.

Then Hugo said, "Alright. Let's break for lunch", and he stood. Annabelle went to the board room doors and opened them for all present to clear the room.

At lunch I decided to mingle with the other side. I waited for Trey Harding to sit down and I sat down beside him. Hugo gave me an almost imperceptible nod and his eyes twinkled. Harding pretended for a moment not to notice me and reached for his water glass. I sensed he was trying to decide what approach to take with me. He took a sip of water, and I started in before he could land on a strategy.

"I see that SonWalt has been in China since 1990. Is doing business with the Chinese a long-term strategy?", I had turned to Harding wanting to see his face, full view.

He looked at me, not smiling, still deciding what to make of me.

Then he said, "We went in 1990 to scout the lay of the land. Finding the Chinese eager to engage we directed twenty five percent of our new business efforts to China for the rest of that decade. That increased to fifty percent by the beginning of 2000 and now is seventy five percent of all of our business. So yes you can say it's a long-term strategy", his voice had been very even but as he finished a note of self congratulation, pride, and arrogance had asserted itself. He was not looking at me and not dreaming that I would note anything other than his and SonWalt's success. He nodded to the waiter to refill his wine glass.

"Have you found the Chinese demands for their government involvement in your business troublesome?", I persisted.

"Not if you know how to deal with them", he shot back, taking up his wine.

"And how does one deal with them?", I replied.

He shot a sideways glance at me and then said, "Well business is business. You have to know the way one's partners conduct their business."

"What should Fielding Enterprises know about the way SonWalt conducts business?", I asked directly.

"Successfully," he replied in his clipped manner.

The waiter was taking orders, now was a good time to give it a break. And I'd decided that one, I would not do business with this man, and two I would say so to Hugo.

In the nineties bribes were standard fare for doing business in China including with government backed or government involved business. And while the current government had made efforts to curtail corruption it still existed. Harding would not care a jot about the Chinese government condoned live organ harvest, their enslavement of the Uyghurs, their great thievery of technology, and the deception integral to the CCP's machinations for supremacy. I took another look at the man who sat to my left. He ate quickly, steadily, and had the waiter replenish his wine at every opportunity by tapping the lip of his glass with his index finger. I wondered if he had any true interests or pure passions. But the answer came almost instantaneously, no. Here was an example of gluttony for food and drink and greed for money. And I would wager it was all accompanied by a ferocious appetite for power and influence. Greed and gluttony. No, I would not wish to spend time with this example of humanity.

Sue Langdon began a conversation with me in the ladies lounge,

"How do you know Hugo?"

"We met when I was living in the U.K.", I replied, disinclined to be open with her for what I trusted my instincts to be good reason.

Langdon, studying me, taking in my good but simple suit, simple hairstyle, and self manicured nails, said with only a slight trace of sarcasm,

"How fortunate." Then, "Hugo's very bright, very well connected, and . . . single", she had been brushing her hair in the mirror and had not taken her eyes off me.

I replied, "It is fortunate that we met. I very much like Hugo and appreciate time in New York", I finished.

She looked disappointed, hoping I would tell her more that she could gain some gossip.

"We're looking forward to this partnership", she said eagerly. I merely smiled.

Ben Cowan, Fielding's lawyer, was standing at the table in conversation with SonWalt's lawyer. Ben was listening, Chandler was pitching. Ben's expression was even and attentive. Chandler was in high persuasion gear, his gear of habit I guessed. Hugo had the right people in place on his side of the table. Joining with those on the other side would be a mismatch which would cause more than mischief.

That evening Hugo asked me for a debrief. Charlotte ordered in for us and we ate at the company dining table in a beautifully appointed room with expansive windows for bringing in all the available light.

"Well, what do you think?", he asked, his voice filled with the vitality of his interest in life which he possessed in abundance.

"What was your main reason for engaging with SonWalt?", I asked.

"We wanted to take a good look at China. SonWalt has been there since the nineties."

"Yes", I said slowly. "I had learned that. Why is it important to do business in China?"

He replied directly, "There is a lot of business to be had in a country of one billion four hundred million."

"Yes", I said again slowly. "You said 'wanted', and now?"

Hugo waited, thinking. Then he said, "Now I'm not so sure. China represents major concerns. I don't like the idea of doing business with people who have stolen from us, stolen billions of dollars of research and technology. I don't like the idea of handing over technology or proprietary information to them. I don't like their spying one bit. And while I don't say this to most, I don't like their treatment of the Uyghurs and I cannot stomach the live organ harvest in which they engage." The volume of his voice had risen and he was now angry.

"Good for you Hugo", I responded with fervent support.

He looked at me, surprised at himself but perhaps not with me. A moment passed. Then, "What did you think of Harding and his team?"

"I would not do business with them. Harding has assembled people just like himself, completely focused on money. They are proud, and arrogant with what they believe is their success, lost in material pursuit. Harding has likely been practicing the bribery standard for doing business in China for many years. These slippery practices lead to moral corruption that reverberates upon those with whom they have anything to do. All this includes the condoning of the human rights abuses you just named."

There was only a momentary pause, then, Hugo nodded. "Yes that is right." There was a long pause then Hugo said, "We're done with them. And . . . we're not going into China."

Mom, having buzzed me in, waited holding her door wide open. This was her ever so stylish and signature greeting. Upon seeing me turn the corner from the elevator to her condominium apartment her happy smile beamed me in.

"Oh it's good to see you", I enthused as we hugged one another with a strong long embrace.

"You have to tell me all about New York", she said. "How is Hugo and what did you decide together?", Mom asked.

As we moved into the kitchen I asked, "How do you know we decided anything?", looking with a raised brow at my ever perceptive mother.

"Isn't that why he hires you - to help him think things through?", she replied.

"Yes", I said.

"There is some of your food in the fridge, organic raspberries and chia seeds. I've been making those chia seeds and eating them in my cereal. They are quite good", Mom said.

"Good. They are good for you."

"Well tell me how did it all go?", Mom persisted.

"It went well. Hugo did the right thing."

Mom smiled and replied, "Yes, and what was that - as far as you can tell me?"

"He saw that the people with whom he was considering partnering were not his equal in integrity. And that led him to also see, very importantly, that the business he was considering was not a good idea. In fact, that conclusion was very important because it highlighted the essential consideration, the moral consideration."

"This sounds very important", Mom responded.

"Yes. More people need to make these considerations and then they can make the right decisions."

We were quiet. I looked out the big windows to the superb city skyline. This was a city built on the simple hard work and the bold risk taking of entrepreneurs, oilmen and ranchers. And not politics, at least originally. And the air and atmosphere was cleaner for it. But now political interference had ruined the economy. And the city, having lost its vibrancy, had, at least for the time being, lost its character.

"You know Mom, it's really all about character", I broke the silence.

She looked at me and I handed her three washed raspberries.

"Just as the character of this city has been harmed by government interfering, the character of a person is harmed, and potentially ruined by government, as when the education system fails to offer good classical guidance. The removal of

God from the schools and the replacement by a manufactured standard, the preference of an elite group of people, is wrong by definition. Man's nature is fallible and as such man cannot succeed at being the standard. We must look beyond ourselves, to the source of life, love, and good. The truth is not man made."

"You are right. Did you say this to Hugo?"

"In a manner of speaking, yes."

Mom smiled her wonderful loving smile upon me and putting her arm around me kissed my cheek and led us into the living room for a reunion chat.

CHAPTER SEVEN

The Whole Picture

In school I ask the children to consider the question - what is most important. Then I engage them to practice thinking in the whole and not in parts. That is, the subjects of reading, writing, and arithmetic are merely parts to a whole. The whole is the who question - who are we. A human being has a human nature and therefore as human beings we must consider what our human nature is. Then one must consider who one is as an individual. This is our responsibility, a very personal responsibility. It is not the responsibility of any school. It is however the responsibility of the school to ask the individual to consider the who question and they have not only failed to do so they have sought to wholly redirect human life. A true education requires the tools of learning; language, the organization of language in speaking and writing, mathematics, and importantly, thinking to the purpose of helping one become a person of good character able to live a good life.

When one understands that who one is character wise is sacred then one will not succumb to tyrants, to any person or government which would undermine who one is as an individual human being. This is what our children need to learn and we need to know if we will be free.

Reflecting, with my feet up on the ottoman gazing out the window and over to the hilltop treed property across the street I pondered who these people are. Who would instigate and lead toward the dumbing down of minds through control via the media or through pulling the strings in our education system to mold for susceptibility to direction and control over the way we live our lives? Where does this resulting lack of a true education lead? To the narrow horizon of material greed I had just witnessed in the Harding group in Hugo's board room. This dumbing down is evil. Martin Niemöller's quote came to mind, "First they came for the socialists, and I did not speak out because I was not a socialist. Then they came for the trade unionists and I did not speak out because I was not a trade unionist. Then they came for the Jews and I did not speak out because I was not a Jew. Then they came for me and there was no one left to speak out for me."

Adele was away and another assistant led me to the corner office and asked that I wait. The small but luxurious lounge area outside Wynton Crane's office was quiet and to be appreciated. A beautiful marble and brass standing lamp on one side of a mahogany table where a simple fresh flower arrangement sat just off center in an elegant crystal vase, spoke silently to good taste without pretension. I sat down in a firm seated straight backed french period piece brocaded chair wondering who had created this fine, beautiful really, small space. Looking at Wynton's closed door I reaffirmed, today we will address pride.

Wynton's door opened, he smiled directly at me and with a nod stood aside opening wide the door. Still silent he gestured me to the two chairs near a small table. He has not forgotten our last meeting, he is waiting for me to bring up pride.

"How are Jose and Richard?", I asked, reminding him of our last conversation here where he had mentioned them and their readiness to manage and lead.

"Jose has tendered his resignation and is leaving next month", Wynton said dryly. "Richard is fine", he replied briefly, finishing.

I waited a moment and then asked, "How are you?"

He paused, a long pause, leaning forward in his chair, looking at his desk and said, "I guess I'm frustrated. And I'm frustrating myself, not moving on handing a lot more over to Richard and Jose. I won't have the chance now with Jose." He paused again. "I know I'd better act while I can and give Richard a lot more responsibility", he said simply.

"What is holding you back?"

"You told me. Pride.", he replied.

"Do you acknowledge that it's pride?"

"I think I do", he responded.

"Have you been trying to see it, trying to discern where pride plays you up?"

"I don't know. How do I see it?", Wynton asked.

"Pride gets in the way. It shows up by breaking relationships, even with oneself", I said the last bit slowly. His face was pensive and puzzled. "When you told me that Matthew has been giving you all his artwork your response was laughter, enjoyment. And yes one would, should, enjoy one's child's attention, and the results of his efforts. However one should also recognize that your wife might be slightly jealous or even hurt not receiving any attention. I don't think your wife's feelings crossed your mind."

There was only a moment's pause, "No, you're right, they didn't", Wynton's voice gave away that he was disappointed in himself.

"You're disappointed?"

"Yes", he looked at me for help.

"Are you disappointed in yourself for a failure of awareness?" He nodded. "A gap in your attention to Priscilla resulting in not registering her feelings?"

"Why would I miss who she is in this way?", he asked openly questioning himself.

"Prioritizing other things ahead of your wife."

"Yes, I see that", he replied.

"Do you recognize what is most important?"

"What do you mean?", he responded.

"Do you assume that you know what is most important, and therefore do not take the time to reflect on the question?"

A few moments passed this time, then he replied, "Perhaps I do make that assumption. I don't like the idea of assuming things", he was pensive again.

"No, you know very well that assumptions are dangerous."

At this Wynton rose and began to move about his office. He was uncomfortable. But comfort doesn't push us on to greater understanding.

He said, his voice lowered, "Why don't I reflect more?"

"Most don't. It takes an effort we assume unnecessary when things are going fine."

"More assumptions", Wynton's voice held remorse.

I waited now. He was trying to reflect. After a few apposite moments letting him stew I offered, "Reflection is a habit. It needs to be cultivated. Another president, James Madison, wrote, "A habit of reflection is essential for a free people." Wynton stopped pacing and turned to me, his face serious, intent on gaining better understanding.

"What do I need to do?", his question was open, vulnerable.

I smiled at him, thankful. "You have already begun. The vulnerability in your question means you have put a finger on your pride, you have yet to grasp it, but you have recognized pride for what it is, a dangerous intruder."

"Hello, Helena Madison", I responded to whomever was calling on my landline.

A large black old fashioned telephone from the 1920's sat on my mid-brown walnut desk which looked out on the view of the treed hilltop property across the street. I love trees, I really look at a tree. A tree encourages wonder, wonder about all the time its been there, what has gone on in, and who has lived in, the vicinity of where the tree has remained, rooted to the earth. Two of the big trees across the street are oaks. Apparently a Brit brought the seeds across the Atlantic more than a hundred years ago, likely a hundred and fifty years ago. They are not the enormous thick knarred trunks I saw in Scotland, but one day they may be.

"Hello, Roger Merrick. Hugo Wentworth suggested I call you", the same posh British accent made familiar to me by Hugo in a warm clear strong voice met my ear.

"Oh, hello, how nice of Hugo", I replied, pleased.

"He hasn't told you I would call - I can tell", he said.

"No, he didn't. Though that's fine. I would be very happy to help if I can."

"I'm sure you can, from what Hugo says. I'm not in New York though, I'm in the U.K., London", he paused.

"I love the U.K.", I encouraged him.

He laughed, "Good. It would mean your coming across the pond, for a number of weeks and perhaps longer."

"I'm intrigued", I said with an excitement, and energy for adventure.

He laughed again, a clear laugh from deep within, a laughter very different from the mere throat clucking one can hear. His laughter made me smile, he had heard my interest in adventure and responded openly.

"I'll send you some notes first on what we'd be looking at. Make a good read of them and then I'll be back with you to learn your yay or nay. Does that sound reasonable?"

"Yes, it sounds good", I answered.

And he rang off. I still held the receiver a little surprised he had not asked my email address or put me on with his assistant. Replacing the receiver on the phone bed I went over our conversation. With what company or firm was he? Perhaps Hugo had given him my email address when he gave him my number. Well I would soon find out more.

The next day the notes arrived by special delivery to my door. No email, the real thing was handed me by the delivery man once I signed for it. Upon opening the envelope and realizing what it was I sat down at my desk to read. The notes were handwritten. I looked to the second and last page to learn the signature, Roger Merrick. They were dated the previous week.

Dear Helena,

Hugo Wentworth has told me about you. I am hoping that you can be as helpful to us as you are to Hugo. Our assignment, I work with others , is of a very private nature, it is in fact of top security. We can well use your ability to discern character. There are at least two spies within the British government leaking information to the Chinese. We must uncover them and rid ourselves of them. This is of tantamount importance to ourselves and to our allies, and in particular to your own government. We must soon embark on a long planned international project with the United States, and we cannot begin until these spies are removed. We ask that you come, undercover, to work with us. Once you are here, and see the lay of the land, I am confident you will help determine who they are. Then, together we can root them out. We very much look forward to your early response. If it is yes, we will make immediate arrangement for your arrival. My assistant, Eleanor, will contact you and make all arrangements including for your accommodations. We trust you will soon be with us. I very much look forward to meeting you.

Best regards,

Roger Merrick

The first thing to do is reach John and talk with him about this prospective client or rather, prospective assignment. Before calling I paced the house, letting my thoughts and feelings begin to arrange themselves. This assignment would be a challenge. Sort out your thoughts, I told myself, at least a bit first, before blurting them all out for John to put in order.

"What do you think?", I asked John after a barely sorted long blurt.

"That's quite a compliment. Your client Hugo must think a lot of you to speak of you to what must be a very good friend or a very important acquaintance. My guess is that they are good, likely old, friends. Where did Hugo go to school?" John didn't wait for my reply he said,

"I wouldn't be surprised if they were Eton and Oxford. It sounds almost as interesting as you sound excited talking about it", he replied with what I could tell was a smile. "Did you check this Merrick fellow out?", John asked in a more serious tone.

"If you mean on-line, yes. I only found one reference, a charity ball he attended along with a few hundred other people in London two years ago. No photo though."

"If he is involved in top secret work with the government that fits", John said. Then he said, "I'll make a few inquiries with some people in London, see if they've heard of him. What did you think of him after your conversation?"

"I liked the sound of him, open, direct, and I liked his voice."

"You're the judge. That's what he's asking you for."

"What do you mean?"

"To be the judge. They want your powers of discernment. Now you have to discern who they are, beginning with Roger Merrick."

"Yes . . . ," I was thinking. "It seems that I need to take the job before meeting the others."

"Yes, it would seem so," John was thinking too.

Then I said firmly, "I liked him."

"That's a good start. My concern is who they are wanting you to uncover. Someone with connections, close connections to the Chinese.

"Yes."

CHAPTER EIGHT

LONDON

I arrived Monday morning and Eleanor had a driver meet me at Heathrow. My code name for the driver was 'Smythe'. What and how many code names would there be I wondered. Eleanor arranged a house for me in Putney off the Fulham Road. A house! And an old house, just to my taste, high ceilings, hardwood floors, and huge windows, the old kind you draw up and can sit in and lean out to see the whole neighborhood. The entire house was freshly painted.

Every room was eggshell white but for a pale yellow in the main bathroom. All the linens were new, very good Egyptian cotton, towels white, sheets white with a pale yellow and green well spaced flower pattern and textured line, with matching pillow cases trimmed in sunshine yellow. The windows were dressed with white wood louvers and the dishes were all made in England.

Dolby Road is a short quiet street in Putney near the Putney Bridge tube station, a quick jaunt to downtown London. Cozy and quiet, I would be able to feel at home.

Today, Tuesday, I am to meet Roger and the others. These would be the people with whom I would work or, I wasn't quite sure if a better description would be, who would be directing my assignment.

"We've been looking forward to meeting you", Eleanor smiled and extended her hand. "I hope you had a smooth trip. And are you going to like the house?", she asked hopefully in a warm friendly manner. She is not, as I had expected, reserved.

"Oh yes, thank you. The trip was uneventful and I like the house very much", I enthused.

"Good", Eleanor seemed pleased. "Roger and the others are assembled and expecting you to join them for tea. If you're ready I'll bring you in", she waited for my response. What would she say if I'd said I needed to powder my nose first. She would have waited I decided.

I said, "Thank you, I'm ready", though I thought the statement a tad presumptuous.

I followed Eleanor down the hall and we took the elevator to the eighth floor of the wholly nondescript ten story building located off a small side street for which I had not noticed a name. The elevator door opened into a small foyer of somber browns with one large painting on the wall. I paused to note the subject, the original Scotland Yard building, 1829. Eleanor led us down the silent hallway, we passed no one. Then she stopped at a door one could easily have missed. She opened it.

"Follow this hall to the end and knock once on the door. I cannot take you, but they will let you in", she reassured me.

I entered through the door she held and passed into another hall. Eleanor gave me an encouraging smile and a little nod and she closed the door behind her. I walked the length of a long hall to the one door at the end and knocked once.

A tall lean man about forty five years of age with dark hair opened the door. He stood for an extra moment studying me then nodding almost imperceptibly stood aside silently inviting me to enter. I stood in place a moment longer sensing that stepping across the threshold and into what was obviously a most private inner sanctum would commit me to not only the assignment but to serious changes in my life and, to danger. I stepped into the room. And the door closed behind me.

The man who had opened the door now faced me and looking into me said, "I'm Roger Merrick." I was reminded that, as over the phone, I liked his voice and the simple direct manner of his address. His voice was resonant, alive, a voice one could listen to and to which one wanted to listen. This man liked himself. He stood straight and tall, about 6'2, his body in good proportion and his face with good bone structure one could describe as classical Roman.

"I am glad to meet you Helena and happy that you agreed to come."

"Thank you. I'm happy to meet you", I responded in kind.

He paused, allowing for a moment between us before saying, "Let me introduce you to the others." He turned to the room and to the dark wood board room table directly in front of us. The table, positioned in the center of the small windowless room together with its occupants, filled almost the entire space.

"This is Howard Bernard", Roger motioned to the man directly in front of us. Mr. Bernard stood.

He was older than Roger, by ten or so years, he looked at me carefully, in a most reserved manner. He shook my hand with a medium grip and gave me one nod of his head and sat down.

Roger moved on to the woman seated next to Bernard and said,"Evette Eliot".

She did not stand but smiled, extending her hand she took mine gently and shook it longer than had her neighbor. Her smile was genuine and had warmth and something about that warmth surprised me. She was likely about forty eight, a few years older than Roger and more than a few years younger than Bernard. I had seen at a glance that she was the only woman at the table. Impeccably dressed in a tailored Italian suit, feminine in a green and navy wool blend, she was attractive.

As Roger moved forward the next person to be introduced, an elderly man, began to stand. Roger waited until he was on his feet and then said,

"May I introduce Crispin Holtshire, Helena Madison", this time Roger's introduction was more formal, yet warmer.

"How do you do young lady", he spoke in an Etonian, Cambridge, and I guessed Belgravia Square accent. This gentleman shook my hand most firmly, and particularly so for one of ninety odd years. Then after these moments in which deep blue eyes had been intently observing, discerning something, he took both my hands in his and said,

"Welcome." With that one word and gesture I felt comfortable, at home in this room with these people. I caught a slight smile from Roger. These men were discerning. We moved around the table to the other side.

"This is Jonathan Hill." A younger man, thirty six perhaps, as tall as Roger, stood quickly with a bolt upright posture. He wore a gray suit, white oxford cloth shirt, and a nondescript tie. He smiled and shook my hand formally and sat down. I wasn't sure what to make of him but there was something I liked.

We came to the last man. He was perhaps forty three with dark brown eyes and graying hair. I noticed that he had been watching me the entire time we moved around the table. While the others were attentive and noticing, this man was watching. He stood slowly, taking his time, nodding slightly, and as he took my hand Roger said,

"This is Trillian Wortley." His handshake was brief and he did not speak. I would have liked to have heard his voice.

Roger ushered me to my seat, one from the head of the table where he sat down.

"Here we all are", Roger said simply and with energy.

Crispin Holtshire smiled as did Jonathan Hill. Howard Bernard nodded. I managed to see peripherally that Evette Eliot gave a slight smile and almost imperceptible nod and Trillian Wortley was expressionless and continued to watch me. I wondered when, or if, he would let up.

Roger gave a slight turn of his head to Holtshire and Wortley moved his gaze to Holtshire. Oh good I said to myself as a silent sigh of relief.

"We are wanting to include you now in our business. You will be introduced as our secretary. I think your title my dear will be executive assistant", Holtshire chuckled. His words, "my dear" and his chuckle were endearing. He continued in his oh so lovely voice, "You will be at Roger's or Jonathan's side, or anyone of us as we meet with those with whom we do business." I noticed that he had only named Roger and Jonathan.

"Has Roger told you our business?", Crispin asked inquiring most with his eyes while surveying me from over the top of his old style dark brown framed glasses. He was utterly charming.

"Not specifically", I said simply.

Holtshire then looked over to Roger.

Roger said, "Our public business is land management in Evette's case. Howard's business is big business, a multinational corporation dealing in various markets. Jonathan is in shipping, tankers. And Trillian is a banker. Privately we work in his majesty's service", Roger finished, looking at me. I nodded. I noticed he had not mentioned Crispin's business. I thought, Crispin Holtshire is strictly on the private side of things, and likely very privately running the show. The room was quiet. Roger was smiling at me. Crispin Holtshire was looking at me over the rim of his glasses again. The others were looking at me. They were all waiting for me to speak.

So I said, "When do we begin?", and smiled at them all.

My assignment began the next day with Howard Bernard. Perhaps they were thinking that working with CEO's I know something about big business.

"We bought you a few shares of Hudson International so you can attend the shareholders meeting. I'll be there, as will many shareholders. You can sit amongst them. For the purpose of this meeting we don't know one another. I am planning to meet two men there who are business partners, Sam Isla and Trevor Stamos. When you see me with them make your way over. A waiter serving drinks will spill Champaign on you and I'll step in to offer my handkerchief. This will allow for some banter at close quarters with these men. I'll be interested to learn what you notice", Bernard said and stopped.

"Alright", I replied. After Bernard's cool and practical instructional speech I wondered if I'd be able to get to know him.

The room for the shareholders' meeting was a large conference style space with between two and three hundred people attending. Thankfully there were windows. While we were without a view, bushes and trees could be seen outdoors. This made things feel more real. As I sat amongst the shareholders I wondered again about Howard Bernard. I suppose he, all of them, would have to keep a distance between themselves and anyone they meet. This could be a rather cold assignment. Then I thought of Roger and Crispin Holtshire, they were not cold. They were truly interested in me. Certainly they were keenly interested in the success of their project, and therefore in my success in being able to help. But I could feel their depth, they let show some part of who they are. Genuine, yes they are genuine. Evette too showed some warmth, something of who she is. But I didn't know yet who.

"Have you been here before?", the woman sitting next to me said. I was brought out of my own thoughts, I am about to get practice in being reserved.

"No I haven't. Have you?", I responded simply to her address.

"Yes. I'm always at these things. My husband likes me to attend then he wants a run down of the agenda and my impressions of the corporate representatives", she was saying as I nodded, keeping an eye out for Bernard whom I had not yet noticed.

The company speakers proceeded through the agenda. A few shareholders had questions but after about an hour and a half the meeting completed, people began to disperse.

"Are you attending the cocktail party?", my neighbor asked gesturing to a small group who were moving through the secondary group of doors into a smaller room. Just then I saw Bernard moving that way flanked by two other men.

"Yes I am. Are you?", I replied.

"No, I'm pooped and heading back to my hotel. It was nice meeting you. Have a good trip home", she said.

"Thank you", I smiled. Does she think I'm headed back to the States? Perhaps I'll ask Eleanor if I should be trying to cultivate a British accent.

I made my way over to the exiting cocktailers and thought how am I going to learn as much as I normally do without being my more open self. Looking about the smaller more hospitable room I tried to be as nonchalant as possible. There were two bars, one on either side of the room and lots of comfortable looking chairs and a few sofas. I kept Bernard in my line of sight and casually edged my way in his direction. When close enough to hear him I took a champaign glass from a passing waiter and took a sip, cold but not too cold. I was used to the sudden cold of the water when getting into the pool for my regular lap swim. Without warning Bernard was in front of me facing me as were the backs of his two companions. The next moment a waiter passed too closely and a full glass of Champaign spilled over the front of my suit.

"Oh I'm very sorry", the waiter exclaimed loudly in an embarrassed manner, feigned I knew. Looking at him I thought, good actor, he looks contrite. I smiled to myself.

"Let me help you. Use my handkerchief to pat down your blazer", Bernard handed me a large white handkerchief. Bernard's companions whirled round in response to him. "Much better Champaign than red wine", he said charmingly and laughed. Surprised with the charm I tried not to stare, taking Bernard in anew.

In the next moment I said, "Thank you very much", as I patted my blazer with his handkerchief.

Bernard kept up an easy banter in aid of a lady in distress giving me opportunity to learn something of these two men. A sketch of the faces and reactions of these two men, indications of character, was being drawn on my mind.

Handing back the handkerchief and heaping on the charm I said,

"Thank you, your handkerchief I think has done the job. A gentleman indeed," I added smiling at him and then at the other two men.

"You are welcome. Let me introduce myself. I am Stewart Wharton and this is Sam Isla and Trevor Stamos."

"How do you do? I am Sarah Reinholdt", giving them my shareholders meeting code name, keeping up the charm along with a smile.

"Are you a long time shareholder?" Isla said.

"No, quite a recent one", I said easily.

"Trevor and I have been in this game for two years. Their stock has outperformed the market with a thirty eight percent share price increase and a stock split three for one. We've made a killing", he chortled, showing aggressively white teeth and the kind of phony smile a land shark offers. Trevor Stamos gave a self contentedly smug nod and took another glass from the tray of a passing waiter. I was observing and listening.

"Please join us", Bernard, the only gentleman of the group, gestured to the chairs nearby silently asking me to go ahead of them. I sat down in the nearest chair. Bernard unobtrusively let Stamos and Isla go first to sit on either side of me. He sat across from the three of us.

"Are you in your own business?", I asked sounding as naive as possible, turning to one and then the other man.

"Yes, we are partners in some offshore drilling and in import and export", Stamos said almost curtly.

"That sounds adventurous. How do you know one another?"

There was a pause, both seemed to hope the other would jump in, finally Sam Isla said, "We've known each other a long time. And we do like an adventure wouldn't you say old buddy?", he looked to Stamos throwing him the ball or was it a hot potato, as he gulped more Champaign. Stamos began sipping from his glass. I guessed he was thinking, because when he came up for air his reply had a new note,

"Have you ever made the decision to step out, step away from the ordinary, to adventure, to learn what you're made of or to exercise what you know you've got?"

It was a real question he was asking, and he was waiting for my answer.

"Yes. I think I know what you mean", I replied.

Stamos nodded but he didn't say anything else.

"What do you count an adventure?", I asked.

Stamos, looking at me, seeming to recognize a genuine question. Isla was letting his gaze wander the room, checking out the women. Bernard had almost melted into the furniture, indistinguishable from the scene except for his eyes which like a camera were clicking, capturing every moment.

"Learning something new, gaining some advantage that you can use down the road to increase your fortune, improve your position, find your future direction, that's an adventure", Stamos said.

I hoped the surprise at his words was not evident in my face. I decided that his awareness was for situations and did not extend to character, and therefore neither to an attentive conscience.

"And so you found Hudson International and knew it to be a good investment?"

He looked at me more directly, smiled, and replied, "Yes, that's right", appreciating my recognition of his smarts. I was listening and he liked being listened to. He continued, "I decided to meet the key players here and helped a couple of them capture a few opportunities." Bernard was listening too but Stamos hadn't noticed.

"They were very happy and gave us a heads up in good time, ahead of the market. We bought a lot more stock. And . . . as Sam said, we made a killing."

Insider trading? Not quite, but almost. Stamos had relaxed back into his chair and had taken another glass of Champaign. What exactly was I to try and learn I was asking myself. Stamos seemed to be the one to focus on. Moles in the government, I reminded myself. Is he involved politically?

"What gives one the inside track for investments? Is it all a matter of experience, does one have to get involved politically, is it really a matter of who one knows"?, I tried again to sound naive.

Stamos was lazily gazing round the room and responded automatically, "You've got to have a finger in the political pie", he said casually but with certainty.

"Oh politics has never interested me. How would one do that?"

"Cultivating people. Find out where their interests lie and be ready to help them. Move yourself into their network, where possible their circle. With some patience and time you're in place to bait the hook." He was talking now, the Champaign had taken effect. He said matter of factly, “When that doesn’t work, apply pressure.”

Bernard caught my attention, how I don’t know, but he signaled to stop. A moment later he said,

“We’re off to meet some others. Your suit looks immaculate. You can’t tell anything was spilt on it”, he proffered a most attractive smile. And they were gone into the crowd.

I went home that evening and prepared my dinner without conscious attention as my mind was not on food but people. How had Bernard insinuated himself into the Stamos Isla group? As I didn’t know my new kitchen very well I put a spoon on my plate instead of a fork and began to heap a bread and butter plate with mixed greens. When the plate was suddenly overflowing with one handful of greens I had to come back to earth. Telling myself to reverse gears I now methodically took all I needed from the fridge, cut vine tomatoes, applied Italian dressing to the salad, retrieved the quiche from the oven and plumped it down in the center of the salad. Then I allowed my mind to return to digesting my observations on the character of Sam Isla and that of Trevor Stamos. Could there be a connection to a mole in the government? In a nutshell Stamos had more going on. Isla was more content with the moment, immediate stimulus and gratification. Concentrate on Stamos. One had to have a finger in the political pie was his advice. Learn where another’s interests lie, be ready. Hmm I wonder how this might look. And apply pressure if needed. Be ready to help, this likely means to take advantage of any opportunity to put oneself in position for a payback down the road. These two men did not come across as having any degree of sophistication or even perhaps education. Stamos surprised with his semi-autobiographical inquiry about stepping out to learn of what one is made. And then there was his somewhat personal response to my question of what adventure means. As I thought of it he had been open in his answers to my questions, revealing something of himself. Why?

At 8:45 the next morning the landline rang.

"Hello", I responded to my first call at Dolby Road.

"Helena, good morning, it's Eleanor. How did things go yesterday at the shareholders meeting?"

It was interesting that Eleanor was not only abreast of my schedule but interested in the outcome of meetings or at least in my impression of them.

"I'm not sure I know yet, but I can say at least - alright", I smiled.

"I think Howard thought quite well."

"That's good to know. Thanks", I said, pleased to gain a little feedback.

"Evette has asked me to call to have you meet her in Sussex this afternoon. You will be assisting her as she guides some foreign buyers interested in property." Eleanor paused. I think she was kindly letting me register today's assignment.

"Certainly", I replied.

"Your car will drive into Dolby Road at 14:00 hours. Your name is Kate Strothers. There will be materials in the back seat to go over, including a cell phone. You are the assistant of a very busy real estate agent and must field calls for her while she manages the buyers. You will receive a call or two", Eleanor laughed. "Don't worry, someone nice will be on the other end of the call, playing along with you."

"Okay, sounds like fun", it was my turn to laugh.

I was ready in my dress and blazer jacket at the window watching for the car. A black sedan drove slowly past the house and parked a few doors down the street. Is that my car? It might be. I went out the door, locked it, and slowly strolled the little walk to the house gate, keeping an eye on the car. As I stood for a moment at the gate I saw the driver side window come down. It is my car I decided and went over. A young fellow with military posture sat at the wheel.

"Hallo Miss Strothers", he said and gave me a little smile.

"Hallo", I replied, getting in to the back seat.

"I'm Henry," my driver introduced himself directly.

I noticed my photograph beside him on the front seat. Henry had introduced himself in a friendly voice with bounce and yet managed a definitely professional manner. Hmm capable and quick I thought.

"Hallo Henry. How long will it be to get to Sussex?", I inquired.

"Just over an hour and a half Mamam."

"Will you be driving me back later?", I inquired again.

"I don't know yet Mamam", he replied simply.

"I see", saying to myself, the nature of this business is uncertainty.

I drew the mobile phone and folder over and rested them in my lap. Thankfully the mobile was an iPhone and I recognized its face and functioning. The folder was thin, I was thankful for that too, just two sheets. I had to look at them for a few moments before realizing what they were communicating. Evette Eliot was sharing something of the assignment. We would be with a group of three people and today they were deciding upon a four hundred acre piece of land in West Sussex. Their names; Tom Bitmer, Edward Lewes, and Wei Parsons, told me that one of them was likely married to a Brit. Why three of them? What was the likelihood of them buying it together? Unlikely. Perhaps one was representing the buyer, and one was a friend, or two friends. I'd wait and learn. I wonder how my 'bosses' connect with these people? Perhaps I should ask Evette, why these people? Have they singled them out? Is this a dragnet operation?

I looked up from my thoughts and asked Henry, "Have you been long with these people?"

Bright blue eyes met mine in the rear-view mirror. Did I catch a glimmer of a smile?

"Always", he answered succinctly, brevity seemed his modus operandi.

"Right out of school?"

"Yes, Eton."

"Ahh", I said and reflected on his giving me an extra word, when he could have left it at 'Yes'. I wondered now what the surname was to join with the classic Henry.

The green rolling hills out the window caught my attention.

"It's beautiful", I responded aloud.

"Have you been to Brighton, it's not far from here?", Henry asked.

"Yes, as a teenager visiting the U.K.."

"It's one of my favorites. The Scottish Highlands are too."

"I love the Highlands", I replied with enthusiasm. I noted that I was being open with Henry.

"How do you know them?", he asked.

"I was at the University of Edinburgh, I did some exploring."

"Alright", Henry was nodding and smiling. "When we arrive I'll drop you off and Ms. Eliot will meet you. You'll go together from there", he informed me.

"Thank you. Will Ms. Eliot connect with you to pick me up - if that's the plan?"

"I have the number to your mobile. If I'm to pick you up I will ring."

"Very good", I said and nodded. It was a good thing I preferred adventure over security.

Henry pulled into a narrow little alley and said, "This is where you get out", in his best highwayman manner.

I laughed, "Thanks." With my mobile and papers tucked securely in my handbag, I left the folder on the back seat and sprang from the car.

For just about twenty seconds I watched Henry drive down the alley and then out of sight. Then another car, a deep green Jaguar, drew up beside me with Evette in the driver seat.

"Hop in beside me", she said.

After I'd closed the car door she turned to me and asked, "How are you?"

"Good I think", I replied with a smile.

"Good for you. I'm sorry, I was up late with work last night and am a little tired. I hope to be decent company for you." Then she laughed, "It's not easy being the assistant. You don't know where you'll be next, the next day, and sometimes the next hour nor for whom you are working, nor who you will meet", her eyebrows rose as she tilted her head at me. This, I took as her rather covert way of beginning an introduction of the three people I was about to meet and whom I was to nonchalantly scrutinize.

CHAPTER NINE

THE LAY OF THE LAND

We drove from the alley onto the paved road and shortly Evette turned onto an earth road where we were quickly in the countryside.

All she had time for was, "I won't say much more about them, better you take your own impression."

Within less than five minutes she pulled up behind a black Mercedes limousine and stopped.

"Here we go", she said to me in a low voice and then fairly bounced out of the car.

I put on my best serious secretary demeanor, mobile in hand and followed behind her.

"Hallo Edward", Evette said, approaching the very British looking chap.

"Evette, good to see you. You remember Mrs. Parsons and Tom", he turned to the two people standing beside him.

So Edward was the more familiar. And the moniker 'Mrs.' meant what?

"Yes of course. I'm happy to see you again Mrs. Parsons, Tom", Evette extended her hand to Mrs. Parsons and then to Tom. "This is our assistant Kate Strothers." Edward nodded, Tom gave a small smile and Mrs. Parsons remained expressionless. Smiling, I nodded at each of them.

Edward said, "Mrs. Parsons and her husband are very pleased with all the particulars of the property. We wanted to drive in again, sweep through the house and then around the forest areas before the offer."

"Very good. Shall we drive in then?", Evette asked rhetorically.

"You lead", Edward replied.

Mrs. Parsons had not said a word, her face immobile, but her black eyes had been watching. Tom seemed to fade into the background. What was his last name again? Evette had not given it in the introductions.

They followed us, Tom driving, acting as a chauffeur, Mrs. Parsons in the back with Edward, in what I guessed was her Mercedes.

"It's beautiful here, no one in sight, splendidly quiet," I said to Evette when we were alone in her car and she was driving us to the house.

"Yes the property began about half a mile back. It is a very old property owned by the same semi-nobles for the past few hundred years." I wondered what a semi-noble was. Perhaps someone who had been titled long ago and lost influence and therefore the title of nobility. Can one lose title? Perhaps a semi-noble is one for whom title was held indirectly through a distant ancestor or one who was once a full noble and through bad conduct lost some direct access to the title.

"The property was not offered for sale but Parsons approached Edward. Edward is well connected, as are the Parsons who indicated a top price and have connexions useful to both the son and daughter of the owners," Evette said and turned to see my reaction.

I asked, "What does that mean?"

"Well may you ask. It is unclear to me exactly what the connexions offered are but I do know that it was the connexions which made them decide to allow for an offer."

We were driving along what was now a tree canopied road, apparently one no one else used.

"It is splendidly peaceful", I exclaimed. "And the air is heavenly."

"Yes, I like it very much and ask myself what change may be wrought with a change in owner," her voice betrayed concern. "We're coming to the house. I think they will do just as Edward said. They will take one more sweep through the house and then walk and drive some of the grounds. We can take a look in the house if you like when they are touring the grounds. I don't think Mrs. Parsons will want us to accompany her. She likely wants to see things again alone."

A spectacular country house came into view. "Gosh", I exclaimed, marveling at its size and the stunning red brick against all the green of the landscape. "What a long stretch of drive to the house."

"It's a quarter of a mile", Evette informed.

"It looks like the fields come right up to the house itself. Is that a steeple or bell tower rising up mid roof?"

"Both. You like it", Evette laughed at me.

"Yes, it's amazing. We don't have this in America."

Evette steered the car into a long tightly packed pebbled drive. "See what you think of the interior," she said. "It's not as much grand as quirky really. But we will wait until Mrs. Parsons either begins her walk about or her drive around," Evette finished as she slowed up toward the side of the house, went round the corner of the house where the drive narrowed and parked beside what looked to be a gardener's shed built in the same red brick as the house. "We can get out and stroll the immediate grounds and watch to see when they come out," Evette said. I thought this illogically hopeful given the size of the house and, as I imagined, many entrances and exits.

We walked back around toward the front entrance and there Tom had parked the Mercedes. They were not in sight and must have already gone inside.

Evette smiled and nodded knowingly, "They won't be long."

I lowered my voice, "Why are they wanting to buy it?"

Silent, she shook her head slightly, as in let's not talk of this here. She led us to rowed paths crisscrossing a large flower garden set off from one side of the house.

In a whisper Evette said, "Wei Parsons is part of a Chinese family highly connected within the Chinese government. Her husband, a British subject, is very wealthy. A lot of his wealth has come through her connexions. He has partnered with Chinese companies since the 1980's. This means he has long established, by Western standards, relationships there", she paused. In front of us was a mid sized pond beside which stood an ornately carved wood bench.

Evette, about to sit down, hesitated, and then said, "We'd be better to keep walking." She continued, "In other words, Parsons is deeply entrenched with the Chinese. Given the timing, that is with our Western troubles, our financial ties with China, their determination for supremacy, and our long time Western resolve weakened by our inattention to who China is, they are making their move. Parsons is a part of this."

We were at one end of the garden and walking out onto a narrower earth path bordering one of the fields.

I asked, "What part?"

"That's just what we want to learn", for the second time Evette raised one well kept eyebrow at me, as to say, we'd like you to help us with this. I nodded.

Evette and I turned at the same moment to a low and distant sound behind us. We could see the Mercedes moving down the drive and watched as it took the drive to the road and turned in the opposite direction from whence we had come.

"They are taking a drive of the forest. We can go in the house now."

"Are we certain Mrs. Parsons left in the car?", I asked.

Evette hesitated a moment and then said, "You are right to think that way, not make the assumption. The likelihood is that she has left in the limousine. Tom does not act without her direction and usually not without her present."

As we walked up the drive to the front entrance I whispered to Evette, "Are we alone now, and will we be so in the house?"

"Yes", she replied.

Then I asked, "Why can't you stop the Parsons from being able to buy the property?"

"We could. But they would just buy something else. This way we know a little more about them."

We went in the main entrance through a dark oak door and stood in an imposing foyer. The wood, I guessed oak, floors were covered with thick Turkish carpets and the walls were hung with fine multicolored Persian tapestries. Far from my simple taste the richly adorned entrance displayed an opulence obviously meant to impress with not only wealth but with a knowledge of international culture.

Evette led the way into the room immediately adjoining the foyer.

"What an odd room", I exclaimed.

"Isn't it?", she replied rhetorically.

"I begin to see what you mean by quirky."

The room just off the entrance and high ceilinged foyer was a miniature square of deep red walls, without carpet, with one small coffee table and two small matching armchairs of a dull beige color, no overhead lighting and one small standing lamp.

"What do you think they use this room for?", Evette asked me.

"I don't see how anyone could use it", I responded.

She laughed, "I've been wondering and I think you're right."

Evette returned to the foyer and from there we walked the main hallway deeper into the house.

"Do the Parsons have children?", I began my questions, observing the walls of the hall which were chockerblock full of oil paintings.

"No they don't", came my boss's reply.

"What can you tell me about them?" I inquired, noting that all the paintings were of Persian or Asian origin.

"He is a long time politician, was an American, originally a congressman from California. Then, activating his British citizenship, he ran for Parliament here, was elected and ever since has held his seat and gained positions on various committees and organizations. He has a lot of influential connexions", Evette relayed.

"When did they marry?", I continued with my questions.

"This is the second marriage for both of them. Wei Parsons, nee Ho, formerly Chang, was as the name indicates first married to a Chinese. She met Parsons in China while he was on business there about thirty years ago. They were married, if I recall correctly, about two years later."

"What do you know of who Parsons is?", I asked.

"Greg Parsons is an adroit politician, an astute businessman, and now a very wealthy entrepreneur. His chief interest is no longer his elected position. He runs for office when there is an election for his constituency but he takes his election for granted and would not miss the office if he lost. He's chiefly concerned with himself and his bank account and thus cares more about his relationship with the Chinese than with the U.K.. This is why we are involved", she finished.

"Did you show them other properties?"

Evette shook her head and said, "We were notified that they had approached the owner here directly and we managed to have the owner use us to represent them."

"Has Mr. Parsons come out with you to view his prospective purchase?"

"No, only Mrs. Parsons. And she doesn't say very much at all."

"Do you think she suspects . . . your true involvement?"

Evette replied, "I don't think so."

We were standing at the other end of the house before an enormous bank of windows looking out to an extensive back garden and the fields beyond.

"Will they use the house to entertain do you think?"

"I imagine so, business and political associates. I think they are quite directed, he in business and she politically", Evette answered.

"Were the windows, or should I say was this back wall, opened up to create this row of windows?", I asked, appreciating all the light.

"Yes, about fifty years ago. It's unusual and very lovely with all the light."

I stood looking around. We had passed a large drawing room kept in the traditional style and a large modern kitchen and we stood now in the adjoining family room. It was a great open space, high ceilinged, filled with light and dressed far more simply than the front of the house, practical for use by a family.

"What a lovely and expansive open view of sky and nature", I said in delight.

"Yes", Evette responded, enjoying the beauty too.

"Upstairs? Are the bedrooms?"

"Yes, there are eight bedrooms."

"You are welcome to go up to see them. They are not ours yet", came a voice behind us.

We turned simultaneously to see Wei Parsons. She had entered and approached silently, startling us, for neither of us had heard her. She was addressing me.

"Thank you", I managed. "This is my first time to see this lovely property. I can see why you like it", I said covering my discomfort at her arrival. Just then as though sent to relieve my having to say anything else my mobile rang.

"Excuse me", I said and moved to the other side of the room as though not to disturb Evette and Mrs. Parsons.

"Hello, Kate Strothers", thankfully I remembered my name.

"Hallo it's Henry."

"Yes."

"Are you with the client?"

"Yes, sir."

"I am picking you up and will do so in the same place I left you off. Will an hour be about right?", Henry asked.

I looked at my watch, trying to look professional, "Yes that should be fine. Thank you."

"Cheerio", Henry said and rang off.

Evette and Parsons were in conversation. I feigned making some notes and did not join them immediately.

In a few moments Evette said, "Kate, we are going outdoors to walk the periphery of the house. Please join us when you are finished there", and she looked to my note making.

"Certainly. Will do", I responded in a cheery yes boss manner.

They walked back to the front of the house and I heard them go out. What a good opportunity to do a little exploring. I looked around the family room, or what I was calling the family room which would likely be used for meetings of some sort. What were the connections so valued by this family which the

Parsons's could provide I asked myself. Who is Greg Parsons? He values his connections in China most. Is that why he married Wei Chang? She hardly seems the warm loving family type nor a fun loving kind. I went back in my mind's eye to her face in the entryway where she stood watching us in the family room. Her eyes were steely, she had planned to catch us unawares. Given her timing there hadn't been too much for her to hear which didn't fit the conversation of two real estate enthusiasts. Likely Parsons' approach was her standard style. And this said a lot about her. She acted and spoke only with purpose in mind, no spontaneity. I'd guess a calculatedness guides her toward her objective and end. And what is her objective? I think I already know her end.

I headed back down the hallway, this time taking time to better note the paintings. I stopped before one which was Chinese characters in calligraphy. Too bad I don't speak or read Mandarin. Then I felt my mobile in my hand. But I can take a photo and learn what this painting has to say.

Evette and Parsons were in conversation standing at the beginning of the circular drive where her Mercedes Benz was again parked. Parsons had what looked like a contract in her hands. I walked forward but kept a discreet distance. Parsons took her eyes from Evette and glued them to me for what seemed moments too long. Why I asked myself and the answer came immediately, because I am American. After another minute's conversation with Evette, Parsons moved toward her limousine. Her driver, Tom, popped out and opened the rear door for her. In another minute they were off down the drive.

I walked over to Evette but before opening my mouth to speak, waited until the car was far enough down the long drive that Parsons could not see me speaking to Evette. I noted the feeling of a warning to caution that goes off inside when one cannot comfortably or even safely be oneself. While I did not like nor welcome this feeling I was thankful for it. I looked to Evette.

She responded by saying, "They have made their offer. It will be accepted. She is bringing the contract to her husband for signing."

"Most real estate brokers would be elated in this moment", I observed.

"Yes . . . as I said, I shrink from the change that will be wrought when they move in. A neighbor we know will not at all like the idea of the Parsons owning this property."

"I wonder how the connections the current owners - what is their name?"

"Tressler."

"I wonder how the Tressler's will actually end up thinking about where the connections for which they bargained will lead them", I said.

Evette turned to me and then slowly nodded. We had been looking in the direction the black car had gone, and to what was now the empty drive.

That night when checking my email I found one from Mr. Herring, or Tom as I was now using his first name.

Dear Helena,

We hope your absence from our schools is benefiting others.

You were right we had all better be involved in our schools, school district, school board, and education system or our children will not get an education. In fact, it's more than that now, without parents' serious interest in what's happening in schools our children are in peril. Our school board did decide to hold off on sex education for the younger children, at least for the time being. What they are doing may be more dangerous. A group is spearheading an 'history' project to bring to the elementary schools. It appears their objective is to subtly remove mention, let alone study, of George Washington and any other Founding Father or history of our founding, the Declaration of Independence and of our Constitution and replace it with the woke narrative on racism and one of our supposed inferiority.

Just to let you know I am running for the school board. We miss you.

Yours sincerely,
Tom Herring

Dear Tom,

Thank you for being in touch.

Congratulations on your decision to run for the school board. You will be a boon to all who care about education. I'm glad the children are spared the rush to obliterate their innocence. The erasure of history is as you say most dangerous. The lie the woke narrative seeks to perpetrate would expunge the truth of the American story from our memories and minds and ensure it is never planted in young minds. This means of course over time erasing who America is, deadly for us and a tragedy for all who aspire to be free.

Congratulations on engaging in the fight.

Best regards,
Helena

A new recruit to the fight for America, I registered. Slowly but surely. I prayed for help that Lady Liberty would not sink beneath the waves and with her all hope for living a good life.

The Chinese characters I photographed in the home the Parsons were purchasing, sent to my friend for translation, convey the following:

'The China dream embodies five thousand years of culture that we (the Chinese) must with pride direct to take our place, redeem our face, and move to our position of supremacy, superior in knowledge, superior in power above all the world.'

My friend noticed also from the photo I sent him that the artwork was original, not a print. Apparently it was created as a gift, it was unlikely that it had been sold. This means that the Tressler's are connected to the Chinese and this then is how the Parsons found them and knew the connection to offer in order to move them to sell. Who was that connection? Where does the connection lead?

Trillian Wortley made the call himself late that evening.

"Hallo Helena I hope it's not too late to call", he said in an even tone without any inquiry.

"Hello, perhaps you have some work for me?", I inquired.

"Yes. Would you meet me in the City tomorrow morning for 9:30 at Samson's Charter Bank in Threadneedle Street?"

"Yes, of course", I replied.

"Very good. We will be meeting two American bankers. You can walk from the Bank Station. See you tomorrow morning", he said and rang off not wanting to learn if I had a question.

CHAPTER TEN

BANKERS

"Mind the gap", the iconic voice of the London Underground sounded as the underground train pulled up to the platform.

London tube trains are so much quieter, and slower, than their New York cousins. Of course the main reason is their British passengers. Americans are just louder and like to move fast, at least in New York. I sat down, pleased to have a seat at 8:57AM.

Giving myself a minute to look about the car I observed what former experience had taught. The Londoners with whom I occupied the car were at this hour, for the most part, tidily dressed in unassuming colors, there were a number of briefcases and laptops and most passengers had a mobile phone in hand. All were quiet and minding their business. After this observation I continued to think about Trillian Wortley and bankers.

There was something different about Trillian Wortley, something that was either present or missing that singled him out from the others in the group for which I was now working. What was that something? I needed to find out.

Samson's Charter Bank was a four minute walk from Bank Station. As I entered the revolving doors to the lobby I did not see Wortley waiting. He had neglected to tell me whether to wait or to apply at the front desk.

Not being a good waiter I approached the reception desk and said to the man seated there,

"I'm meeting Trillian Wortley at 9:30, Ann Latimer."

"Yes Ms. Latimer. Please meet Mr. Wortley on the tenth floor. I will ring up now to let him know you have arrived", and he politely gestured me toward the elevators.

"Thank you", I replied.

The thought came to me as I entered the elevator, Wortley is testing me. The British are more polite than are Americans and would have had someone meet me. Americans let one fend for oneself.

When the doors opened at the tenth floor a Samson Charter Bank sign and logo, a classical bank structure fronting a globe, announced the lobby reception of their head quarters. A diminutive young man stood waiting in the center of the lobby. I smiled at him.

"Miss Latimer?", he queried.

"Hello", I smiled.

"Hullo, I am Ben Stillingfleet." I registered the appealing resonance of his voice. "Trillian has asked me to bring you to the board room, where your meeting is being held."

"Thank you", I replied.

Ben Stillingfleet, about my age, perhaps five foot five, fit, and of sprightly energy, nodded and led me from the lobby to a pair of glass doors.

Holding the door open for me he said, "We're going just to the left down the hall." I smiled, he is considerate I noted, and headed in the direction indicated. "There is coffee and breakfast on the buffet. Is there anything in particular I can get you?", he asked.

"Oh thank you, no. I've already had breakfast. But should I feel the need for something I'm sure the buffet will be more than adequate", I smiled again at him.

"I eat breakfast too before leaving in the morning. It's a much better start to the day", Ben shared.

Somewhat surprised by the geniality of his manner I responded enthusiastically, "I agree." Then I ventured, "Do you know Mr. Wortley and his American banker associates?"

"Know them, no. I can say that I've met Trillian on several occasions. He isn't an easy fellow to get to know. This is the first time I've seen his two banker associates. I didn't know they were American."

Stillingfleet had just offered an interesting note both with regard to Wortley and his banker associates. We'd arrived at the board room.

Ben said, "Good luck", and smiled kindly, as he reached to open the door for me.

Being younger than those behind the doors we held an openness for sharing information. I nodded, looking at him and taking an extra moment I acknowledged his kind interest.

Once inside my eyes went immediately to Wortley and my instincts went into high gear with regard to him. At the moment I entered he was in a tête-à-tête conversation sitting at the end of the board room table with one of his associates, while the other man, sitting further down the table, looked on uncomfortably. In the next moment Wortley's eye was on me. And something in the look in that eye confirmed my instincts were serving.

"Good morning Ms. Latimer", Wortley said, as he remained seated in his comfortable black leather chair. "I'd like to introduce you to John Blasmore", he introduced the man with whom he'd just been talking, "and Hobart Houston", he gave a nod to the other man at the table.

"Good morning", I said jauntily to each of the men in turn, and the two men just introduced followed Wortley's example and remained seated, staring at me. Though Mr. Houston moved a little in his seat to better face me.

Then they offered a, "Morning."

"Please sit down", Wortley said. "Mr.'s Blasmore and Houston have just come from New York to consummate", Wortley smiled, "our transaction."

He was interrupted by Blasmore.

"You are hoping. We are just working out the final agreement", he said mainly to Wortley though he inclined his head slightly toward the chair where I sat at the other head of the table.

Wortley looked slightly, was it taken aback? Miffed? I took the resulting moment of Wortley's hesitation as my chance to say,

"I'm in the dark about your transaction. Would you fill me in?", smiling at all three men and resting the smile and question upon Mr. Houston.

While Houston smiled back the other two looked put off.

Houston took the cue, "We've hired some high powered international lawyers to create the contract between us. That is, between London and the U.S., and the Chinese for the manufacture, distribution and sale of chips and components for our new technology", he finished having nicely summarized.

While I nodded my appreciation and continued with a pleasant expression for Houston, Wortley's face betrayed anger with both of us. In that moment I got the message that Trillian Wortley was unlikely to choose to work with me again. It struck me that control was of serious interest to Mr. Wortley and that anyone stepping forward without a prod from him would not be welcome in his sheepfold.

Suddenly he said, "Ms. Latimer would you please find Ben Stillingfleet and ask him to contact the lawyers and have them come at 2PM for a conference and late lunch?"

While he had asked a question what he was really doing was telling me under little cover of a polite request that he was done with me. His piercing eyes were messaging his distinct dislike for my bold initiating. He was dismissing me more with this messaging than with his relegating words.

"Certainly", I said, still smiling, though not at Wortley.

I left the room. Gaining the hall I breathed out in relief at the prospect of not having to work with Wortley.

The halls of Samson Charter Bank were wide and unpopulated. Where I wonder does Ben reside? As I recalled there was not a receptionist at the tenth floor lobby entrance. Did Ben occupy an office on the tenth floor? I passed an office with someone at a desk.

Stopping I said, "Hullo, excuse me. Does Ben Stillingfleet have an office on this floor?"

"No. He is on the ninth floor", a woman of about seventy with wizened features but perfectly coiffured and in a fine wool suit answered perfunctorily.

"Thank you", I replied as she immediately redirected her focus back to her computer screen.

I made my way to the elevator bank. Hopefully, from the tenth floor, the elevator would let me out on the ninth floor. It did, depositing me not in a lobby but onto what was more of a half way platform with locked glass doors on either side of the elevator bank. I pressed the call button at one set of doors to try and speak with a person.

"Yes", a female voice responded.

"Hello, I'm Ann Latimer and am looking for Ben Stillingfleet."

"Is he expecting you?", she asked.

"He greeted me earlier this morning and took me to a meeting on the tenth floor", I left it at that.

"Oh. I'll ask him to meet you at the doors", she said.

"Thank you."

Within a minute, not even two, Ben appeared and immediately opened the door.

"Come in", he smiled, inquiring with his eyes and a raised brow asking 'What's up'.

"Trillian Wortley asked me to find you. Do you have an office . . . ?"

"Yes, come on down", Ben responded.

To myself I said, I'm lucky that Ben is such a responsive fellow.

We reached his office. Ben asked, "Would you like to sit down?", gesturing to the small wood circular table off to one side of his desk. He closed his door.

"This is a nice sized office", I commented.

"I've been here a while."

"You've even got a window", I said, moving over to the window to take a look at the view.

"I've been here seven years, straight out of school", Ben responded, joining me at the window.

"That's the Old Lady of Threadneedle Street," he said, pointing off to the right.

"I love London's old architecture", I said slowly savoring the sight.

"Are you done with that meeting?", Ben asked.

"Yes", I said firmly, turning to him. "Wortley wants the lawyers, I assume you know who they are, to come for a 2PM lunch combined conference."

Ben nodded. Going to his desk he sat down and speed dialed from his landline phone.

"Charles, Ben here. Simon and James should come for two o'clock today, a late lunch and conference on the Whittier/Parsons transaction." There was a pause while Ben listened. "Yes, okay. Good", and he rang off.

"Parsons", I reacted aloud to the name, though not intentionally. My instincts worked the other way too, trust these, do not trust those.

Ben looked up at me and pausing only a moment said, “Greg Parsons. Do you know him?”

“No. I met his wife though.”

Ben’s brow rose, inquiring silently ‘Really?’. . . .

“Yes. Do you know Mrs. Parsons?”

Ben replied, “I’ve met her once. She didn’t say a thing. But she watches, and doesn’t miss a thing.”

“Can you tell me more about this transaction?,” I asked.

“I don’t see why not. You got yourself this far”, Ben smiled broadly.

“Horace Whittier and Greg Parsons have done a few deals together. For the last thirty years they have been heavily involved together in China.” Ben had moved to the small table to sit and I joined him. “They are very heavily connected with the Chinese. That is, with big businessmen who are invariably connected with the government. The CCP always has their hand in, or on . . . ”, Ben stopped short.

I picked up with, “You seem to know quite a lot more than merely business.”

“If one wants to understand the consequences of one’s actions, it is essential these days”, he replied.

“Ben?”, I began to ask.

“Yes?”, Ben responded in kind.

“Can we meet for a . . . private . . . conversation?”

“Yes. What do you suggest?”

Before acting on my idea of an informing conversation with Ben a conversation with Roger Merrick was in order. I called Eleanor asking to speak with Roger and was pleasantly surprised to be put through immediately.

“Hullo Helena”, Roger’s cheerful voice came over the line.

“Hullo, thank you for taking my call so readily.”

"I'm glad you knew you could call. Call me directly at any time", he replied and gave me his direct line.

"Trillian Wortley was not too pleased with a question I had for his associate at the bank. When he sent me off as messenger to an assistant it resulted in what may be a good connection for information and possibly insight", I blurted out.

"What was the question Trillian didn't appreciate?", Roger asked.

"I asked the associate he'd left out of the private conversation he was having with the other fellow what the deal was for which they were meeting."

"Good question. Presumably the fellow told you?", I sensed that Roger was smiling.

"Yes. Do you know the Parsons, Greg and Wei Parsons?", I asked.

"I know of them", he replied.

"The Parsons are the first name to appear twice, with Evette's property transaction and with Wortley's banking deal."

"You're thinking in the right directions. You had something you wanted to ask me – about Wortley's assistant?" Roger directed us back to the purpose of my call.

"Yes, Ben Stillingfleet. If Wortley won't work with me I think Ben could be very helpful. May I move forward on conversation with Ben?"

"Ben Stillingfleet does not know who we are. If you can work with him without giving away the ship, go ahead", Roger energetically offered.

"Thank you", I replied, grateful.

Then Roger said, "Are you enjoying yourself", and his voice was gentler.

"I think I am", I replied pensively.

"You are helping us already. Call me again soon", he said warmly and I could hear his smile.

"Thank you. I will", and we rang off.

Ben and I arranged to meet the following day in Bishopsgate, not far from his office.

"How long are you in London?", he asked me after we greeted one another at Tower Hill.

"I'm not sure, it will depend upon my assignment", I answered frankly.

"Ah huh. Well I'm glad you want to talk to me. Opportunity for an open conversation does not come along every day, not even every month", unusually Ben was able to refrain from asking questions. At least he was not going to pry into my assignment.

"Does that mean you're not enjoying working with Wortley or at the bank?", I began.

"No. I always find a way to enjoy myself and meeting you is one of the ways", he laughed.

"Thank you. When things did not go well in the Wortley meeting you were a godsend."

"What would you like to know?", Ben asked directly.

"What can you tell me of the Whittier/Parsons transaction?"

"As mentioned they're in heavily with the Chinese. This transaction is with China and from what I can tell they are pretty unscrupulous characters", he said.

"Why do you say that?"

"I handle a lot of phone calls. Most of the Chinese with whom I deal can speak English. This group are not only uniformly curt they are no longer hiding their aggressiveness and I'd say their assumption of preeminence. They are pushing me, and therefore I imagine everyone they encounter, to look the other way on things honest business people would not consider doing. And they want to skip legalities." I was listening carefully, and thinking.

Then I asked, "What do you think of Wortley?"

Ben took a moment and then said, "I don't know. I've been asking myself that question." We looked at one another.

"Shall we walk?", Ben asked.

"Yes", I responded and nodded.

"Have you seen the Tower of London?", Ben inquired.

"No."

"Do tourist attractions interest you?", Ben asked.

"Not per se. It does interest me to be walking beneath the Tower and on Tower Bridge with you."

"Thanks. I think we see things the same way. The who is more interesting than the what", and Ben smiled.

"So you've been asking yourself about who Wortley is. Is this just lately?", I asked.

"Yes. I guess he seemed fairly straightforward before this," Ben replied.

"Before this deal, do you mean?"

Ben paused, thinking. Then he said, "Yes. I've worked for a few bankers here and Wortley seemed much of a fit with the lot of them. But lately he is more on edge, more driven, anxious, though he keeps it under wraps and I don't think any one else has noticed."

"Why do you think he is in this state?"

"I think he is partnering with Whittier and Parsons on this one", Ben announced.

CHAPTER ELEVEN

ON THE THAMES

It was time to sit and think. Roger has given me just what I need, leeway. Trying to fit in, being reserved, doesn't suit me. I cannot learn what I need in order to see who people are if I don't engage. That's what happened with Howard Bernard - I think I could have chatted up other shareholders if I had just been myself. And too, I might have had more interaction with Wei Parsons. And Wortley? He stopped me cold when I began with my first question. There wasn't anything more I could have done there. What is the connection between Wei Parsons and Wortley? Does Evette know? Did she know that Wortley's current deal is with Parsons before I brought it up with Roger? If not why not? Should I call Roger and ask? Should I ask Evette? What is the relationship amongst the members of this group? While they're all supposed to be on the same team, I'm not sure there is a relationship. If what Ben says is right, that Wortley is a partner with Parsons how can Wortley be working with the team? Of course a partnership with Parsons could be a front the firm has erected for Wortley to learn more.

"Hullo Eleanor. Can you connect me with Evette Eliot?", I asked, having rung the office number.

"Hullo Helena. Yes, one moment please", Eleanor responded.

I waited a few moments and Evette came on the line.

"Hullo Helena, how are you?", there was a little surprise in her voice, and was that a slight impatience or hesitation?

"I'm well thank you. Thank you for taking my call", I paused infinitesimally to learn if she might respond and let me know that it was fine that I was calling. She merely waited.

"When in Trillian Wortley's offices, Greg Parsons's name came up. In fact, Wortley may be doing a deal with Parsons", I finished.

There was a pause on the other end of the phone. Was this surprise, or was she simply waiting to see what else I had to say? I was hoping she would open up and offer an answer.

"Do you have a question you want to ask?", she said.

"I was wondering if you were aware of Wortley being involved with Parsons?"

"Are you wondering if the group works together or individually?", Evette changed the direction of the question.

"Yes, I was wondering that."

"We work individually, and do not introduce each other about", she answered.

There was another pause.

"I hope my call did not cause any trouble. I sought to understand more about Parsons."

"Of course", now her voice sounded warmer.

Evette was not going to say any more. So I said, "Thank you. When do the Tressler's and Parsons move?"

"In three weeks time."

"Thanks again. Goodbye."

"Goodbye", she rang off.

"Whew", I said aloud to myself as I put down the receiver of my landline.

Is this another facet of Evette I had not seen? Was her response surprise at news? Could the Parsons common denominator between Evette Eliot and Trillian Wortley still be news? Roger would surely have informed each of them of the Parsons connection. In which case, it must be that Evette did not wish to divulge her thinking about the connection. This could be understandable, it is likely that they are trained to say little or nothing about the firm's business. Nonetheless as they have hired me to help them uncover a mole it would help to get a clear picture of the workings and possible inter-workings of their individual dealings. One thing was certain, Evette was not being open and she didn't want to be open.

I picked up the phone again. This time I dialed direct using the number Roger had given me.

"Hullo Helena, how are you?", the words were the same as I had just heard from a different voice and the effect was opposite. I was welcomed, he was glad to hear from me.

"Thank you for welcoming my call", I responded.

"You are welcome", he replied with emphasis.

"Would you explain a few things for me? How do the members of the group work together? Or do they work strictly as individuals? I just called Evette and shared that Trillian Wortley was working on a transaction with Greg Parsons. Perhaps I expected her to be more forthcoming about her knowledge of the connection."

"Good for you", Roger laughed.

His response engendered a sense of relief and I began to relax.

"Helena you are doing the right thing in asking questions. Keep it up. Call whomever you think you need to help you with the whole picture."

"Thank you. I appreciate your support."

"You have not only my support, Crispin thinks very highly of you. Even if the others don't have full knowledge of what is happening, Crispin does", he informed me.

Hearing this and hearing Roger's voice I did not feel the need to ask further about the arrangement he and Crispin Holtshire had with their people.

Monday morning began my next assignment with Jonathan Hill at the docks. The Port of London is about thirty miles from London and has full deep sea shipping facilities including warehousing. A driver, not Henry, picked me up at 0800 hours (as Jonathan had phrased it). He was a dour professional and I was missing Henry's fun and helpful manner by the time I was dropped off at Gravesend.

Jonathan was waiting for me outside, "Good morning. I thought we could take a walk along the Thames."

"That'll be lovely", I responded.

"Have you been on the sea? A cruise or perhaps you are a sailor?", he asked with boyish enthusiasm as he guided me closer to the river's edge.

"I have been on a cruise in the Virgin Islands. And I took sailing lessons off the coast of Maine", I offered.

"Well then," he said heartily, "the coast of Maine has the best conditions, tough, for preparing one for what may be met at sea. I love the sea and thought of joining the navy. But I got caught up", and he lowered his voice, "in this work", he continued, "and I've enjoyed being in this world class shipping port."

His enthusiasm, reflected in his stride, was contagious and I found myself striding in pace with him along the path close to the river. Jonathan's genuine interest in life was a personal offering and it caught me. I was walking faster, enjoying listening to him, and was exhilarated by his energy.

"What would you like to know about what we do at the Port?", he asked.

"Oh everything, everything you would tell me. I know nothing of international shipping."

"Alright," Jonathan responded with a lilt of enthusiasm in his voice. "I've been here six years and am still learning. I've gotten to know the dock workers at the wharves, some of whom have been here since they were teenagers. They are the ones who know the most about the actual shipping. I've helped them load ships, watched them repair these monsters of the sea in dry dock, taken orders across the various desks in the office, tracked the voyages and the cargoes, and negotiated contracts."

"Do you know the history of shipping, before, during, and after Aristotle Onassis? He is the only shipping magnate of whom I've heard."

Jonathan laughed, a clear ringing laugh. "I think your curiosity and my interest are going to make a good team. I want to show you a day at the docks. If you follow me about you'll see something of what goes on at the Port. There is a lot of traffic, we were the busiest port in the U.K. last year."

The big barges, moving in both directions along the river, made me feel part of what Jonathan was showing me.

"In Central London there are two main shipments, rubbish going out and sand, gravel, aggregates coming in for all the construction in London. The cargo is mostly non-fuel and the big containers with consumer goods are out of London Gateway on the Essex coast and Tilbury and further out of London, Southampton as example. These containers come from Taiwan, China and elsewhere. With more than forty thousand employees there is a lot happening at any moment in time. How does this sound?", Jonathan asked.

"It sounds great", I exclaimed, almost bowled over with his generosity of spirit.

"Okay", he said simply and led the way to the wharves.

"You asked about history. I like history too. The Port of London dates from the first century A.D. and was the busiest port in the world through Roman times. There were one thousand seven hundred wharves at one time. Now there are seventy, some of which are safeguarded, like Convey's Wharf in Deptford which King Henry VIII commissioned in 1513 to build vessels for the Royal Navy", he paused to learn my interest.

"I'm listening."

"You have safeguarded wharves near you in Fulham, Hurlingham Wharf, the Fulham Railway Bridge. You might want to take a look at Swan and Willowbank Wharves at Putney Bridge. There is a huge sewer being built twenty miles long, the size of the Channel Tunnel, Tideway Tunnel near Putney."

"I will take a look", I replied. Then I asked, "If this is too much off topic please tell me. I find it is most valuable to think from the whole picture, so I would like to get a whole picture perspective on this assignment. Can you tell me what your relationship is with Evette or Trillian Wortley for example?"

Jonathan looked at me for a moment with quite a serious expression then a slow smile arrived. He said, "Yes, I can. I do not have what I would call a relationship with either Evette or Wortley. If you have interest in the relationship between the group members", he paused to check my response. I nodded. He continued, "my relationship is with Crispin Holtshire, and through Crispin with Roger."

"Oh", I paused. "Thank you. Then he guided me along the wharf.

"We are going to take a boat out to that tanker you see further out", he pointed to an enormous red and blue tanker sitting further out on the Thames.

"Whose tanker is it?", I asked.

"See if you can tell me once we're aboard," he replied.

We approached a small motorized boat. Jonathan pulled out from under his jacket what looked like an old CB radio phone.

"Angus, can we use this little motor boat you've got tied in the middle of wharf nine? Pause. "Yes, hold on. It's got a blue cushion at the driver's seat." Jonathan stepped into the boat and reaching into what would be a glove compartment in a car he pulled out a key and said,

"Yes, it's here, thanks. I'll leave it back here when we are done."

And then turning to me he gave me his hand and helped me aboard. He handed me a life preserver, put one on himself, started up the motor and began untying the little boat from the dock.

"Can you swim?", Jonathan asked as he was about to push off from the dock.

"Yes."

I watched as he deftly maneuvered our little craft into the smoky sparkling waters of the Thames. I realized I was grasping the sides of our little dinghy, out of caution. Yet too I tingled with the excitement of our little adventure. In a few minutes Jonathan was on his old phone again.

"Hullo, Jonathan here. Two of us coming aboard off your starboard side." Pause, reply. "About two minutes." Pause, reply. "Yes."

Then to me he said, "They're going to lower a skirt, a hammock like contraption, and we'll get it underneath us and they'll raise us up."

"Can we slide out of the skirt midair"?, I asked, thrilled and concerned.

"I thought of that the first time too", he replied with energy. "Unlikely."

As we approached the skirt appeared over the top edge of the ship and began to descend.

Jonathan waited and once it was in the water maneuvered our little boat between the two arms with chains so that the skirt was underneath us.

"See here, the clamps attached to the arms clamp on either side", he explained as I watched him close the leavers on each side of the boat. Without delay our boat rose up out of the water to the top deck of the ship. Two sailors waiting at the gunnel pulled us in up against the side and held our boat steady flush against the edge.

"Thanks boys", Jonathan smiled at the two sailors.

"Keep your eyes open and tell me who you think owns this ship", Jonathan said as he helped me out of the little boat, and we clambered over the side and onto the deck of the ship.

As he led us along the deck I said, "I haven't seen a flag."

"No, they don't fly it", came his reply.

After we'd gained a little distance from others Jonathan said, "One thing for which I'm always on the look out is foreigners being smuggled in with shipments. The smugglers of today are trafficking in people."

"From where are the smuggled coming?"

"Many places, Africa, Indonesia, North Korea, if they can get out, sometimes China."

"Are they mainly desperate people hoping for a better life?", I asked.

"Mainly. However on occasion we've caught a few sharp operators getting in this way, people who if traveling via the regular avenues would likely be stopped at the border."

"Do you think a mole could get in that way?", I asked.

"A mouse can. Why not a mole?" We laughed.

That night I couldn't sleep. As I lay awake in bed trying to fall asleep my mind kept going back to the group, the four individuals and their relationships with each other. Having spent the day with Jonathan Hill it was easy to see that he, Crispin Holtshire and Roger would get along well. While nothing much came when I rested on Howard Bernard I got stuck on Evette Eliot. Trillian Wortley I summed up as driven by money. He likely could be bought. Perhaps he had been bought. Evette was more complicated. Somehow Evette seemed to be in the middle of it all or was it in the thick of things? I must have fallen asleep because I suddenly realized I'd been dreaming.

I was standing on a street somewhere, somewhere I didn't recognize, and Parsons' black Mercedes was there. It was parked on the other side of the street and there were no other cars around. As I was looking it pulled out slowly and moved along the street past me. I could clearly see that there was no driver. Further along it stopped and Evette got into the front passenger seat and then the car continued along the street. My dream switched scenes. I was with Evette and I experienced a deja vous moment. Evette was talking to me, or rather, as I noted in the dream, saying very little about the people we were about to meet. But what she did say was, "I won't say much more about them, better you take your own impression." This statement seemed as a signal to me, important, very important. And in the dream I went over it in my mind. 'I won't say much more' - she had not told me anything about the people – 'better you take your own impression.' Take? One would say 'make'. Then it came to me. One would say 'make' if one were a native English speaker. But if one were a native German speaker one would say 'take'. I was suddenly wide awake. This is exactly what she had said before we met Parsons together.

I got out of bed, thinking, and went to the kitchen to get something to eat. The black Mercedes sat like a photograph in my mind's eye and the word 'take' which should have been 'make' sat there along side it. I assumed Evette to be a Brit, native born. But if she had grown up in Britain she would not have used 'take' in that sentence. My dream had just told me this was important. If she was a German native how did she get her job and position with the firm? As I buttered some bread I remembered something. She had told me she'd been up late the night before working and that she was tired. And so she had slipped. If she had, some years back, been working her way up in the firm, perhaps having been given a foot in the door through some contact or other, she would have been on her toes, no slipping. So what was the German connection? Parsons had a big black Mercedes. Henry picked me up in a black Mercedes. Mercedes was a common choice for governments and people with money or pretensions to money. But did this simple coincidence carry some meaning? Or, perhaps simply the coincidence awakened me to a German connection.

CHAPTER TWELVE

THE PUZZLE

The first thought that came when I awoke was that I must spend more time around Evette. Where was her office? I could ask for an office near her's. She would wonder why I was there. Roger might provide a project as facade for my being there.

Roger agreed without hesitation and Eleanor set it up for me. Part of my office wall which included the door was glass and I could see Evette's office from mine. I laid out lots of papers, set up my Mac, placed my water bottle, and brought in some of my books to make it feel like it really was my office. It all felt a bit clandestine and covert but that's the business I'm in at this time.

Thanking Eleanor for her help I had asked, "Does Evette have her own assistant?"

"Yes, Sabine. She is just down the hall from you", Eleanor had replied.

Sabine is a German name I said to myself as I walked down the hall to introduce myself to Sabine.

Only one person, a young woman, sat at a desk at the end of the hall and there was only one desk.

"Hello, I'm Helena Madison and I've just moved into the office four down on the right", I smiled.

"Hello, I'm Sabine", a sturdy bobbed haired blond woman of about thirty offered her hand. Firm grip, full eye contact, I noted. Accent?

"Do you know everyone here? I'm quite new", I made my foray.

"Yes, I can show you around if you like", she responded.

"Thank you, do you have time now?"

"Yes, I work mainly for Evette and she is out of the office at a meeting just now."

"Very good", I smiled.

"Are you familiar with your own hall?", she asked.

"I know Evette a little, no one else though and no one has made an appearance yet."

"Let's start here", she said and efficiently moved toward the offices.

"This is Evette's office", and she gestured to her left and continued walking. I glanced inside. There was zero clutter and not much at all but the furniture, not even a computer.

"This is Nigel Wilkinson's office," Sabine indicated the office beside Evette's. "He is almost always on assignment and unlikely to return for another month or so." Sabine did not stop and gesturing to the next office on her right said,

"This is Charlotte Summerhay's. She is rarely here." The room, absent a desk, had a small sofa and three comfortable lounging chairs, looked more like a place for conversation than an office.

We had left the hall and entering an open area like a lobby reception with a number of chairs, Sabine said,

"This is an open conference area and through this door", she pointed to two dark wood doors, much larger than the office doors, "is a private conference space."

"There aren't too many people about", I commented.

"No, but this is pretty much the usual for our floor," Sabine replied.

"Do you work on other floors?"

"I do sometimes. Most of the time however I'm here. If you need anything please ask. Only occasionally does Evette keep me busy," she offered. She had not a trace of an accent.

"Are you from here?", I asked casually.

"No I was born in Berlin. However I grew up here", Sabine replied.

Check, I said to myself.

She had efficiently brought us back to our hall. I stopped at my door and thanked her. She nodded and headed back to her desk. I glanced briefly at Evette's office and wondered what, if anything, went on there. Was all her work done outside the office?

Just as I entered my office, contemplating Evette's Berliner assistant, I heard a phone ring and then Sabine's voice, "Evette Eliot's office."

I moved to my door to listen.

"Yes Mrs. Parsons." Then there was a long silence on Sabine's end, getting thorough instructions I surmised.

"Yes I will", and she hung up.

I heard her get up from her desk and head my way. I moved to my desk. Sabine entered Evette's office and placing a key in what must be a locked desk drawer opened the middle drawer. She removed a file folder like the one that was on the back seat of the limousine the day I met Parsons. Sabine opened the file and scanned two or three papers. Then she locked the desk and left the office with the folder. So, Mrs. Parsons directed people even inside the firm. I decided that I'd like to take a good look at that folder and the rest of the contents of that drawer.

I stayed all day, stepping out of my new office a number of times to glance Sabine's way in hopes of seeing the folder on her desk and Sabine absent. The folder was not in sight and Sabine was always there. What time did she leave?

At 6PM Sabine tidily closed up her desk and left. The entire floor appeared empty and I decided to take a good look at that drawer. While I was pretty sure the folder was not there I was very curious as to what else might be there.

The middle drawer was locked, but the other two were not. The top drawer held only a pen and a pencil in a pen tray, and personal stationery. The bottom drawer was a little more interesting. It too held a few file folders, far less interesting I guessed than the one Sabine had sought after Mrs. Parsons's call. I took all three folders out, closed the drawer and returned to my desk.

The folders were unnamed. The first one had a number of loose papers which I began to read. There were names and addresses which I did not recognize and which appeared to be clients and respective properties. The second folder had, as mine had, only two loose sheets of paper with instructions including directions to a townhouse in London. The third one held two bound contracts, one for a Mr. and Mrs. George Albernathy, and the second for a Mr. and Mrs. Gregory Parsons. My pulse quickened as I began to scrutinize the Parsons contract. Why did the Parsons need another manor house, and in Kent? The date on the contract was one month before the one with which I had familiarity. Evette had been silent on this Parsons' purchase. The price paid was £39 million. Evette was getting some hefty commissions. People can do almost anything for money my instincts reminded me. What does Evette think of their purchasing a second manor house? Or perhaps this is one of a number? What is the German connection? When this question arose in my mind I knew that my instincts were telling me there was a German connection. After studying the contract for any telling detail, including other names, I noted that there was no loan, no mortgage broker, the Parsons were paying all cash. I returned the file folders to the third drawer and left the building.

After a quick dinner I called Ben Stillingfleet.

"What do you know of the Parsons? Are they connected with the Germans in some way?"

Ben was laughing at me over the phone, "You're funny. You call up out of the blue and start right in with what you want. Your directness is charming."

"I'm glad you think so."

"Now that you mention it there was something. At one point Wortley had me place a long distance call to Frankfurt to a", there was a pause as Ben sought the name, "to a Karl Wiechert."

"Do you remember anything else, any one else with regard to a German connection?"

"That is the only German I recall. And what are you thinking - when you say a German connexion?"

"Wortley's colleague is Evette Eliot, and Evette I have discovered is not a native Brit rather she is a native German", I hazarded using Evette's name in case Ben had heard it before.

"Okay. I'm not going to ask what your interest is in this or what work you are doing. So how can I help you?", Ben asked.

"Can you get access to more information? Can you research this Karl Wiechert for example?"

"Yes. I'd be happy to. This is the most fun I've had in a while", he replied enthusiastically.

"Thanks Ben."

I approached Eleanor again, "May I obtain information through Roger's office on Trillian Wortley's actions, travels, and anything out of the ordinary? And also may I have anything the firm would be willing to give me on Evette's background, and on Greg and Wei Parsons and a Karl Wiechert in Frankfurt?"

"Your request is out of the ordinary, particularly with regard to one of our own. But I will ask Roger and get back to you", Eleanor replied.

"Thank you very much."

Before the end of the day Eleanor called to say that they would provide me with all the information they could.

Eleanor began, "Surprisingly we have very little information on Evette." She continued to say that the firm had nothing on Karl Wiechert and nothing more they could give me than what I already had on the Parsons. However there was information on Wortley. Wortley has been spending much more time on banking transactions that involve the Parsons. His first contact with the Parsons was a year and half ago when Evette Eliot introduced them at a charity ball. Since that time Wortley has increased travel expenses of about fifty percent, time out of the office on work related matters has increased fifty percent and Wortley has been unavailable for firm meetings twice in the last year and never before.

"Helena, it's Ben", I heard Ben's steady confident voice on the other end of the phone.

"Hi Ben."

"Today Karl Wiechert called Wortley. This is the first time Wiechert has called here. About half an hour later Wortley asked me to reserve a table for three at La Scala for tomorrow at 1PM."

"Good work", I enthused over the phone. "Who is the third person?", I asked.

"I don't know. And I don't know if Wiechert is a party for lunch", Ben replied.

"How can I hear their conversation? I've got to be there."

"If you go they will see you, I will be fired, and you may be too", Ben shot back.

"Perhaps another plan is in order. I'll let you know what happens."

"You'd better", Ben said, and I could tell he was smiling.

"Are you getting tired of me calling for your help?", I asked Eleanor.

"Not at all. You're giving me some fun. Who do you want to know about now?"

"Does the firm have nondescript employees in back rooms no one ever sees whom you can call on to do some undercover work?"

"I think we could manage something. Run it by me", Eleanor replied valiantly.

"Could we have someone sit at the table next to Wortley and his two lunch partners tomorrow for 1PM at La Scala, listen to the conversation and later provide me with a recording?"

"I think we can find someone happy to have lunch on the firm at La Scala", Eleanor was smiling.

The next evening I sat in my living room in Dolby Road listening to Trillian Wortley, Karl Wiechert and Evette Eliot discussing plans they had with Parsons that sounded decidedly unpatriotic, un-American, considering Greg Parsons had been American, and anti-British considering Wortley and Eliot are British citizens. Their plans, revealing their intentions, were far more pro Chinese than pro Western. After preliminary greetings and having ordered their meals the conversation was:

"How long can we continue with Parsons undiscovered?", Evette asked.

"As long as we have to", said a male voice in a German accent. This was Karl Wiechert, as confirmed by the firm's employee who listened and recorded from the neighboring table.

"The Parsons have purchased three manor houses in three months. If the firm notices this, or at least notices my enormous commissions we will be discovered", Evette said.

"We can help you with that. I can have monies directed to a German account", Wiechert said.

"We should have considered that idea earlier. And, I may have to use the money", Evette replied.

"You can get it with a day's notice", the German responded.

Then he asked, "Are you having any trouble?"

"No. The Parsons have cut me in on their business with China and they're handling the money." It was Wortley speaking. Then he chuckled rather sickeningly, "Though I've got quite a bit so far."

Wiechert spoke again, "We haven't had any trouble because she seems to be quite capable of providing an impenetrable shield."

"Yes. And it's important that efforts continue toward a more organized and directed order, not merely a Western way", Evette replied.

"You will get to meet him. And then you will be comfortable with directions you will receive", Karl said.

"When and through whom will that happen?", Evette asked.

"She will let you know", Karl answered.

I placed a call to Roger leaving a message that I had important information and would be in to see him first thing in the morning.

The next morning I went directly to Roger's office to report my discoveries.

"This is quite serious", Roger stated in understated British style. This was the note he had been sounding the last few minutes after my report.

"You and I are about to work more closely together", Roger had been making up his mind. He pressed an, invisible to me, button on his desk and Eleanor's voice came immediately in response from some unseen recess.

"Please order in lunch for two - one moment. Do you have any requests for lunch or anything you do not wish to eat?", Roger asked me. After my response in the negative he resumed with Eleanor. "Helena and I will meet over lunch here. Thank you Eleanor."

Roger led us to the end of his office. As he pressed on the paneling one panel opened into an adjoining room with a lovely view of the park across the street. The table was laid with linens and silver.

"The table is kept ready like this?", I asked spontaneously.

Roger nodded. "As we are only two let's move the extra place settings to the other end of the table." And suiting the action to his words we moved the extra five place settings.

Whomever supplied the firm with food was very efficient. Fresh, nourishing, tasty food arrived in minutes, simply and aesthetically presented. Apparently it was impermissible for unknowns, even a regular supplier, to enter this sanctum as Eleanor brought in the food, laid it before us and left. I felt privileged.

The recording of the previous day's lunch at La Scala of the three cohorts in crime, for to my mind and to Roger's the collusion with Wiechert bordered on treason, was playing as we ate.

Roger was listening carefully.

"Our mole is 'She', in this conversation", Roger said once the recording finished. Then he said, "Wortley and Evette are moles of a type, worker moles, more like worker bees. The master mole is on the other end, commanding our queen bee, commandeering all the honey from here and digesting it in China, for China's advantage and our detriment. We have a lot of work to do", Roger looked at me with a stern and serious expression. "We've kept you for over a month now?", he asked, and I thought it rhetorical. Roger was an astute fellow, surely keeping every detail in mind or memory. I nodded.

"We'll have to up your pay", he said and laughed, though I knew that my next pay check would show a noticeable increase.

"It would appear that while there is at least one mole within, there is a master mole on the outside, and that the external interference is Chinese. Parsons knows the master mind on the Chinese side of this business. While I'd like you to tail Parsons, and perhaps through Evette, that method may be too direct and dangerous. Since Wiechert doesn't know you, tailing him may be the way. We will run an all points check, like an APB, on Wiechert which should make your job easier. This will provide his whereabouts, where he lives and spends time, with whom he deals, when he is most available. I understand we don't currently have anything on him, which is concerning. You will have to help us determine what he is doing, and why. Though the why we can in a general sense guess. He is employed by the German or Chinese government, perhaps both, to connect connexions here with the Germans and the Chinese. He is connected with Parsons and I think he connected Evette with Parsons. Wortley is connected through Evette. What do you think is the modus operandi for each of them?", Roger asked me.

"I think Wortley is in it for the money. Evette appears to have a cause of sorts. Wiechert didn't give much away. 'She' is likely here - in the firm somewhere, somewhere inconspicuous. And Parsons - she is inscrutable but will be fascinating to uncover", I replied.

Roger let out a good laugh.

"Good for you. I agree with what you have said. The one thing I would add is that we will need Crispin's help to nab Parsons", Roger said and paused. Then he continued, "I am going to be seen with you tomorrow in your new office. Eleanor will arrange that Evette be at her desk and phone at 10AM to receive a call. I will come by to see you at that time. If I'm not mistaken, Evette, seeing me there and in conversation with you will become very curious and will engage you afterwards. And hopefully sooner than later. Respond to her curiosity by seeking to spend more time with her. We need to find 'she' and either 'she' or Parsons has to lead us to the director mole in China."

Roger can be quite funny.

"Jonathan tells me that you learned to sail off the coast of Maine", he offered as we began our conversation in my office at 9:59AM.

"Yes, I took an intensive course arranged by my alma mater over a long weekend. While it was a good experience I'm not sure how much I retained."

"Jonathan probably didn't tell you of our little adventure together off the Guernsey coast", he paused momentarily for my response. I shook my head.

"We were out on the water one weekend, using the quiet and solitude for a good chat and had docked on shore for our lunch. We heard a lot of giggling and realized we had landed near a spa resort. Soon the giggling became loud laughter which continued unabated. A woman's voice said, "We're going to need help getting out of here." Jonathan and I, responding instinctively to those words, moved into shore and then closer to the bushes that hid us from the other party. Through the bushes we could see an enormous mud bath with a man and a woman nude struggling in ludicrous fashion to get out of the tub. The woman was no taller than five feet and the man but two inches taller, both of them roly-poly figures. Any attempt to swing a leg up and over the side of the tub met with a slippery descent down one side of the tub and up the other side. As they both were making their attempts the two would collide in the middle and capsize face down in the mud. Both were greased and caked in clumpy mud. It was all we could do not to laugh out loud. Jonathan called over asking if we could help. "Yes please!", came the simultaneous and immediate response from both. We clambered through the bushes. I covered the woman with a towel and held her forearms steady as she stepped over the side. She fell into me and I lifted her over the edge. Jonathan rescued the man. They proceeded to relate their adventure of sliding down one end of the tub and up the other side as they attempted to extricate themselves. They had us laughing and this fed their tale with exaggerations and their enjoyment in playing off each other each topping the other as in a farcical relay match."

As I imagined this scene I began to laugh and then Roger joined me, our regaling each other laughing made each of us laugh all the more until for a minute or more we could not stop and our laughter became uproarious. As I threw back my head in enjoyment and came back up I caught sight of Evette staring at us from her office, a look of disbelief and curiosity on her face. When we gathered back our normal demeanor I said in a low voice,

"You were right, we have caught her interest."

CHAPTER THIRTEEN

AN INVITATION

Evette poured out the tea as we sat in the luxurious living room of one of her real estate clients, whose name I was determined to obtain. I gathered, given her invitation for a private tea, that Evette desired to make friends and that in these impressive surroundings she desired to impress.

"What do you think of this house?", she asked.

"Impressive. Are you always surrounded by such luxury?", I inquired, wondering why exactly she had brought me here.

"Well, you saw the Parsons' Sussex manor house. Yes, I suppose most of my clients are purchasing large and luxurious estates."

Had she purposefully mentioned Parsons' Sussex house? Seeking to answer a question regarding Evette's openness with me I asked, "Do the Parsons's own another house other than the Sussex one?"

Evette smiled and raising her perfectly shaped brow and lowering her voice to a velvet purr she slowly revealed, "There are two others", making eye contact.

"Goodness, and are they large estates too?", I asked another question, withholding the why inquiry for later.

"The one in Kent", she revealed, "is smaller, only about two hundred acres. But the one in Northumberland is larger than the one in Sussex."

"Goodness", I repeated sounding awed, hoping she would continue in her efforts at friendship.

And she did.

"I know. What spenders they are and what commissions I am garnering", she replied with an obviously feigned childlike glee meant to convey a sense of fun rather than an interest in money.

I nodded with an expressive face in response to the direction she had taken.

"In fact", she paused, encouraging an attentive ear, "I'm invited to a party in Kent this weekend. Would you like to join me?"

As I dressed for what was a somewhat formal party, I reflected on why Evette had chosen a client's home for our tea. I also wondered at her invitation. The client's home would make the impression she desired, and I thought, keep her own residence from spy's eyes. And I could relate to this latter reason. Like Evette, I was, if only temporarily, a spy too. That she was seeking a closer relationship with me was evident. Why had she invited me to the Parsons' party? Given that Evette had sold three manor houses to the Parsons's and I am invited to Parsons' party – they must know who I am - and who Evette is. Evette would not bring her assistant Kate Strothers to the Parsons' party. Was it an American connection that interested? And, my first question remained yet unanswered. Why were the Parsons buying up English manor houses?

A perfectly mannered British servant took my coat as I stood in the enormous entryway of Connaught House. Scanning the foyer, the hall before me, and the spacious parlor on my right, this house was furnished with more classic taste than the Sussex house. But then it was not the Parsons's choices I had seen in the Sussex house. Were the paintings, tapestries, and vases I could see here Parsons personal choices, or were they a result of decision to create a certain impression? Suddenly, as before, Wei Parsons appeared, this time with a smile for me.

"Hello Helena, thank you for joining us." My thinking was confirmed, she knows who I am. Her voice, flowing like a full bodied burgundy was meant to intoxicate.

"Thank you for including me", I replied with a sincere smile. After all I was pleased to be here, this evening would help me do my job well.

"Our guests are in the Great Room. Come with me", she said, that fluid voice was now almost seductive and I found myself moving without hesitation of thought, forward, following Parsons. Be careful, came my internal warning.

As we approached the Great Room it struck me that the sound emanating from the room, rather than the noisy chatter of happy guests enjoying themselves, was a subdued, almost restrained, group of conversations conducted a few decibels above whisper volume. Were these people, subconsciously sensing the motives of their host and thus seeking to retain some privacy? Or were they used to living under the shadow of spying eyes and prying ears?

"I will introduce you to an old friend", Wei Parsons said, in a tone meant to sound as though she was bestowing a valuable gift.

"Shasta, this is Helena Madison, Evette has invited her and we are delighted she has come", she messaged. And as she spoke I observed the face of her old friend. The friend had stood expressionless staring at me and when Evette's name was uttered there was a momentary flicker of her eye and flex of her brow as if in expression of the thought 'oh one of those'. Now, in full receipt of her marching orders, Shasta launched into what was, on the surface, a most amiable conversation. As I listened to cute comments about "Wei's" parties, funny anecdotes about a few of the guests, and knowledgeable remarks on the classical architecture of the house, I wondered what was meant by the moniker 'friend' given my interlocutor by our hostess. Was Shasta a friend or, and I thought of Roger's name for those who follow the leader, a worker bee? While I continued to nod along to Shasta's monologue I managed to glance around the room at the faces. And yes, there were a number of faces where the character lines read - 'I follow, I am a worker bee'.

Wei Parsons had disappeared as silently as she had arrived and I hadn't noticed when. Be more aware I told myself. This is a group of people I could not enjoy I thought as I continued to observe. I spied Parsons across the room and angled myself a bit better for the view. Her face, as I had seen it the day of our meeting, was wholly immobile. And, I noted, not as it had been minutes ago for the few moments when she greeted me with the smile made for me. She was speaking with two men and a woman, all of whom appeared delighted to be talking with her. Here was a woman with money and power, and the power resided not solely in the money. Looking around for her husband, I realized I didn't know what Greg Parsons looked like. The old friend was still talking. I waited for a pause.

"Do you also know Greg Parsons?", I asked innocently.

"Oh yes, I've been to any number of Wei's parties and he is usually on the scene."

I looked about, dramatizing my interest in seeing him, hoping she would point Parsons out. It worked.

"There he is. Do you see him standing by the piano with the woman in a long teal blue gown?"

Then I saw him. His face stunned me, incomprehensibly so for a moment. If I had been rifling through television channels to see if anything worthwhile was on and this face appeared I would likewise have been struck, stuck for a moment, staring, not knowing what it was that stunned me. And then in the next moment I would have emphatically clicked the television off in order to rid my mind's eye of the image. The face at which I now forced myself to continue to look was characterless. For a man in his late sixties this spoke of a serious and significant void. I was instantly reminded of Plutarch's wisdom that character shows most in the face. This man was devoid of anything resembling character. Here was something evil. I looked away.

And then I was able to reply, a bit late, "Yes, I see him."

Another worker bee arrived and began to talk with the woman who had been talking at me. With an inner sigh of relief, I said to myself, now I can seek out Evette. I made an escape and felt better. If I could not find a good soul with whom to speak, at least in being able to move away I could explore.

In a perfectly fitted sleeveless fine black silk full length gown with beautiful Italian black and gold heels Evette looked a celebrity. Evette was making money and spending it. She was engrossed in conversation with a man of about sixty years, fit, handsome in a manly way, with a strong chin and a full head of light brown hair. I approached and stood just off from their space so that Evette would see me. In a moment she did see me and it took her only a few beats to pause in conversation.

"Helena, are you enjoying yourself?", she did not, thankfully, wait for answer. "This is Karl Wiechert, Helena Madison."

Disappointment and intense curiosity simultaneously flooded me. Now I was no longer anonymous to Wiechert and now I would learn something about him first hand.

"How do you do?", I said and smiled.

He extended his large hand and looked intensely at me with calculating blue eyes. His handshake did not match his intense gaze for it was, rather than a good grasp and shake, a touch/slide and go. He repeated my words,

"How do you do?"

Of what had they been speaking? Evette's demeanor had not changed upon seeing me. She had not hesitated to introduce me to him. Would she continue and include me?

"How do you know Evette?", he asked.

This would be telling. I looked to Evette and she nodded ever so slightly.

"We work together", I answered simply.

Wiechert nodded. He kept looking at me. He took a sip of his Champaign, looked for a moment to Evette and back to me.

"Karl's in the business of connecting people, here, there, and everywhere", Evette said and laughed.

She had had too much to drink. But I didn't think she was drunk. She wanted to test me, and the drink was making her a little more bold than she may have intended. If I was closer than she had imagined to Roger, perhaps I could be useful to her, and now I realized too, to Wiechert. And I surmised that could be very useful to Evette. I smiled charmingly, interestedly, and moved slightly closer in to the circle.

And in my best tell me more manner said with an excited lilt in my voice, "Here, there, and everywhere . . . ?" Karl Wiechert smiled. My response was just right.

"You are a world traveler - yes? Do you enjoy adventure, and the high life?", and he gestured with his Champaign glass to the luxury all around us; the resplendent room, the sumptuous food, the expensive clothing and jewelry, and the guests where power was making its presence felt. I let my eyes be riveted upon him.

"Well, it isn't that difficult to take a piece of the pie", he laughed. I noticed again the word 'take', though in this context it wasn't wholly out of place. Laughter is revealing and I did not like his laugh.

"Evette can tell you more", he had finished.

I gave Evette an open look as in - I could be game. She smiled, satisfied, and her slight nod told me she was pleased with her invitation. A waiter came by with more Champaign. Evette and Wiechert replaced their empty glasses with full ones. I excused myself to the buffet table.

Thankful to remove myself from the insidious conversation and the selfish greed and gluttony which seemed to be the fare here, I wandered to survey the party-goers. As I scanned the faces of the guests I sought an unusual face. Here, that meant one with character lines. I noticed that Wortley wasn't here. He likely doesn't get invited at this level. Hmm, Roger's idea of association was bang on, Evette had moved on it and invited me. Was 'She' here? If so, who might she be?

I took a plate from the buffet and unseeingly placed bits of food on it. While I couldn't eat a thing if need be I could nibble and avoid being conspicuous. I eyed all the guests and casually strolled out to the terrace. The terrace stretched the length of the house and the view at 10PM on a clear June evening at Connaught House was spectacular. It was apparent that only a few, five people, three women and two men, were, like me, seeking refuge and had come alone to be out of doors. Yes this would be the choice for someone wanting to remain inconspicuous or who sought relief from decadence. I moved to the edge of the stonewall of the terrace. An expanse of open meadow with a dozen horses grazing on lush grass with rolling hills in the distance and all the way to the horizon - green and nothing but Nature in sight - offered a feast for the eyes. Nature's spectacle immediately, gently, engaged me removing me from the man made ugliness from which I sought release. One of the women was enjoying the sunset about twenty feet from where I stood, she returned my glance and we smiled, acknowledging the shared appreciation of the beauty before us.

I took a few moments to savor the gift. Someone passed behind me. Involuntarily I glanced left and but glimpsed the departure of one of the other women wisping away.

Only that night after getting home and showering off the shivers from the after reflections of the party did that wisp of a moment on the terrace return to mind. She must have been quite close as otherwise I would not have noticed at all. Only my instincts had sensed her, almost as though a ghost had wisped across the terrace.

Roger and I discussed my meeting Wiechert.

"You learned something about him. What were your adjectives? Cold, calculating, sharp, pragmatic, likely cunning." I nodded.

"I understand you have the information we gathered on him", Roger paused for my confirmation. I nodded again.

"I think our original idea of your observing Wiechert need not change. He is unlikely to suspect you of being assigned to him", suddenly Roger paused and looked more intently at me.

Slowly he said, "It seems that we have recruited you, in a most unusual way I should add, to be almost one of us,", he stopped and waited for my response.

As I didn't quite know what to say I just smiled. Roger kept looking at me and a cautious hint of a smile arrived on his face. Was there a drop or two of sadness in the smile for the state of human character which required action necessary from those of good character? A thought came, The only thing necessary for the triumph of evil . . .

Roger suddenly quoted, "The only thing necessary for the triumph of evil is for good men to do nothing." And then he asked, "Is that Edmund Burke or was it put together from John

Stuart Mill who said something about bad men need do nothing more when good men look on or do nothing?"

I shook my head, "I always thought it was Burke. It certainly could have been." Roger nodded.

"Have you thought about what you would like to do?", he asked kindly.

"I have been thinking . . . it is all only half baked just now", I replied.

Roger was listening, "Go on."

"Your idea about Evette being interested in your coming and chatting with me was bang on. She will be, at least for the time being, open to my overtures for friendship. She appears to be spending a lot of time with Wiechert, it should be fairly easy to learn more about him directly or indirectly through Evette. Given that Wei Parsons directly broached me, she too must think I may be interested, useful, in their furtherance of breaching British security."

"Yes", Roger responded pensively. A few minutes passed while Roger continued to think. Then he said, "Alright, do as you see fit. But be careful."

This time I invited myself. Henry delivered me to another manor house in Kent to which Sabine had given directions. It was good to see Henry and again we chatted enroute.

"How are you doing?", he asked kindly.

"It's all rather a whirlwind. I'm not always sure what I'm doing. But Eleanor and others, including you, are very helpful and supportive."

"I'm glad to hear it", he replied enthusiastically.

"Can you trust me Henry?", I was thinking of Roger's increased trust and that perhaps a signal had been given along the ranks.

Henry looked at me in the rear-view mirror for a couple of moments, nodded his head slightly and said firmly,

"Yes."

"What can you tell me of Evette, Wortley, or anyone at all associated with them?"

Henry did not respond for a few minutes, he was thinking.

Then he began, "I have driven Evette many times and Wortley a few times, and once together. Twice Evette had someone else with her, Wortley never. Once Evette had a man with her, and once a woman we picked up along the route." Henry paused to learn my response.

"Please, tell me anything, anything at all that you remember about the conversation Evette had with Wortley, and, about the two people she was with."

Henry nodded. Again he paused and I waited as his undoubtedly excellent memory went back over the facts.

"The conversation with Wortley, and it was Evette's conversation, was short and in staccato fashion. The timbre of it was as Evette directing. I did not hear all they said. What I do recall is that Evette was giving Wortley an assignment, there was someone he was to meet and obtain something from, a file, note, or message. I do not remember Evette naming the person and I think I would have if she had mentioned a name." I silently agreed.

"Do you think it was a woman or a man Wortley was to meet?"

This time the pause was brief, "A woman."

'She', I thought. Why? Why did 'She' come to mind? My mind snapped back to Henry as he continued.

"The first time Evette was with someone, a man, I picked them both up together in Threadneedle Street. He was German as I heard his accent, though I could not hear their conversation as they kept their voices low."

"Thank you Henry", I said, grateful.

He looked again at me in the rear-view mirror and let himself smile.

"The second time, I picked her up in the Hurlingham Road, not far from where you are. She has had me pick her up there a number of times. I think she lives nearby. I've been trying to count the number of times I've driven Evette. I'd say it is ten or a dozen times. That time we picked up a woman and I drove them to Heathrow. Evette had a carryon and the woman a larger suitcase."

"Did you drop them at the same terminal?" I asked, butterflies were beginning flight in my stomach.

"Yes, Terminal 5. But it's strange, I wasn't sure the woman was actually flying from Terminal 5. I had a feeling Evette was flying locally, and the woman internationally.

"Why?", I asked with urgency.

"I'm not sure, it was just a feeling. Of course Evette could have been flying to Aberdeen or Edinburgh, and the woman to Shanghai, from Terminal 5."

"Why did you say Shanghai?", I shot back.

Henry paused, as he was wont to do while thinking. This time it was a very long few minutes.

"It was something that was said."

I waited, staring at him in the mirror.

"The year of the snake", he said.

"What?", I asked, trying to understand.

"The woman said, "That will be the year of the snake."

"Henry. Your memory deserves applause. Tell me everything you can about this woman."

"She is hard to describe. I would say by the way she moves she was in her early forties. But her face lines, there were more lines than one would expect for a healthy forty two or forty four", he replied. "She was very thin."

"Go on."

"Her hair was a nondescript mousy brown, I don't think she colored it. She was about five foot six, she wore flat shoes. She wore a suit, it was pretty nondescript too, a lightish gray with a dark, dark navy I think, blouse. She wore her hair in an average style, shortish, not too short, well cut. And, glasses, she wore glasses."

"Nondescript?", I offered.'

"Yes", Henry replied.

CHAPTER FOURTEEN

DISCOVERIES

The Bradford's, this time Evette offered the client's name, had dug up the garden adjacent to the house and built a pool and tennis courts. We sat by an enormous pool in the heated and covered portion. The pool had a deck area comparable to that of a luxury hotel.

"Where do you find such wealthy clients and why do we get to be here?", I asked.

Evette replied with a broad grin, "Once you have one wealthy client they just start showing up. And when I have something to check on for them I take advantage and enjoy the luxury."

"Are they like the Parsons, buying more than one property with you?"

"The Parsons, my dear, are special", Evette lowered her voice in a conspiratorial manner. I offered an eager expression.

"The Parsons are my best client, most lucrative and most . . . interesting", she added the last bit after what I felt was a quick decision, as bait.

"Why are they most interesting?", I asked, accepting the bait.

"Because with them I can further my interests", she offered and waited to learn my further interest.

I turned fully to her. We were sitting stretched out on the chaise lounge chairs by the pool and now I faced her alight with attentiveness. Evette poured herself another cocktail from the pitcher which stood on the table by her lounge chair.

And taking a long draft Evette said, "My grandfather resented the poverty, hunger and destitution in Germany after the Second World War. And vivid in his mind were his father's stories of the treatment Germany received by Britain and her allies after the First World War. My grandfather talked often of his experience and his father's experience. It sits with me." She looked at me, her cocktail glass in hand, and after a few more swallows it was almost empty again. Her face was bitter with a long brewing resentment.

"What do they say - to the victors the spoils?", she spoke in a cynical tone as much to herself as to me. And lifting her glass high she then gulped down the rest of her drink.

"Wiechert understands how I feel. His family suffered too, losing their land after the division of Germany following the war", she said.

"Is he an old friend?", I ventured.

"Our families knew one another. When he learned that I felt as he did about Germany he said he could help. And then he introduced me to Parsons", she refilled her glass again. "Parsons has the contacts one needs these days. If there is another war it is going to be very different", she stopped speaking but continued to drink.

"When you say Parsons, do you mean Wei Parsons?", I asked. She was in her own world now, not really paying me attention.

"Yes, Wei. Greg is always busy with business. He likes his power to make deals. It's Wei who makes all the connexions."

"Deals, deals with China?"

"Hmm? Yes, China, that's where the power is and will be", she pronounced.

"How do you feel about that thought? Does that thinking scare you?"

"I don't think about it. I just see how things are going. And I go that way. Don't you?", she asked.

"I just try and do my job", I replied, evasively.

Evette, attempting a smile, made a lopsided line with her mouth and then said, "Wei can get you in on this, if you want."

"This? What exactly?", I asked directly. I was hoping that in chatting she'd reveal the mole on the inside.

"Wiechert and Parsons have a good thing going. They do a lot of work with China and China pays."

"Do you mean business?"

"Business, contacts, information, all kinds of information", she looked at me now, her brow raised in a 'you know what I mean' expression. She was waiting for me to jump in, to give her the full go ahead. How was I to learn what I needed?

I asked a question, "How does she", I paused to let register my knowledge, "help your objectives?" I'd used the word Wiechert had used on the tape. I had used, 'she', as a name.

"She smooths the way with her counterpart in China", Evette answered without hesitation.

"I haven't met her. What is she like?" I was holding my breath now.

"I'd introduce you, but she doesn't do things that way. But I am going to meet him soon. I don't know about your meeting him, not immediately anyway."

"You're living the high life Evette. It's all quite exciting", I said with energy.

She held up her glass, now almost empty again, and I held up mine, still almost full. She clinked her glass to mine.

Evette had gotten in deep. I could see the change in her in the two months I had known her. She was beginning to look dissipated. She was certainly drinking too much. My mind's eye moved back to the firm's board room and Roger's introduction. Her face, pretty, and her smile warm as she extended her hand with energy to shake mine. And I recalled her face today at the pool, her mouth a lopsided line and dark patches under her eyes.

She was in trouble and more so because she didn't know it. She had been baited with money and power and what they had sold her, a lie. They had enticed her with a lie about helping her cause, helping right the wrong Germany had suffered twice at the hands of the West. Why hadn't Evette fully assimilated to the West? What held her to her grandfather's world view? Who had Evette become, or failed to become? She needed help. Was she too far gone down the rabbit hole?

I invited Evette to tea, this time at my home. If she was open to help I was going to offer it. Perhaps I could learn about 'She'. And if not, I would still try to learn something.

We sat together in my dining room, Evette quiet, subdued compared to my experience with her on social occasions. I had offered her wine before dinner, which I had decided upon instead of tea, she declined the wine, I think in recognition of my abstention. We both drank water, her's with lemon, mine with ginger root. The moment Evette had stepped into the house I'd noticed a reticence. Was she wary? I thought no, it's not a wariness. We'd been talking about local news, a bombing in the Piccadilly Circus tube station. And how, fortunately, the terrorists had mistimed it. The train had emptied, refilled with passengers from the platform and had left the station. The platform was almost empty when the bomb went off. The few passengers there, were on the platform at the opposite end from the blast and while frightened were unharmed.

"It was a surprise, you inviting me . . . to your home", Evette suddenly said.

"Oh, - I'm glad you accepted. Why was it a surprise?", I responded.

Evette paused, then, "I don't know, you don't seem interested in the regular fare, in entertaining yourself or in mixing in. You're more on your own, your own person."

She'd noticed. I said, "Thank you. I will take that as a compliment."

"Do. I think it is", she laughed and raised her glass. Then remembering it was water, took a single sip.

Was she humbled?

"Do you enjoy your work?", Evette asked me.

"I do, very much." What does she know about me? She knows Roger hired me and that he obviously brought me over from the United States.

"I envy you", Evette said and taking her eyes from me gazed out the window, seeming to let herself travel in mind.

Waiting a moment to respond I then asked slowly, "Why?"

She paused too and then, "I don't like my work. I think it's because I don't care the way the others do about the country. They're patriotic and I'm not. I care more about my grandfather and feel as he does about the West, and Germany.

"But Germany is part of the West, all of Germany is now", I replied.

Evette looked at me briefly and returned to her revery out the dining room window.

"No - not in the way I see it. We relate more to the Russians, my family and I. And while I don't like the way they eliminate their rivals I feel more like a rebel Russian than a settled Westerner." She trusts me, I thought, at least to some extent.

"What about the Chinese? How do you feel about what their government is doing?", I hazarded.

"It's like I said, I don't think about it much", she replied more quickly and looked at her glass, wishing it was filled with something stronger than water.

"Have you changed your mind? May I get you a glass of wine?"

Evette, looking at me and with pursed lips and an expression of disappointment in herself, said,

"Yes please. Thank you."

"I'll be right back", and headed to the kitchen. As I poured her a glass of white wine I wondered if we'd lost the chance for rescue. And I asked myself how can one not think about the complete loss of freedom? If the Chinese gain a full upper hand that will be the result.

Evette, with her gaze still fixed in the distance out the window said to me as she took the glass I offered,

"Why do you care so much?"

So she could tell. This surprised me. Yet why should it? She had been chosen, presumably by Roger, for his team. She was smart, quick, and aware. Was she calculating? Or even, cunning? Suddenly I wasn't sure. This was unusual. I almost always knew. Character was my study, my interest, and I had been practicing my whole life.

"It's who I am", I responded.

Evette removed her focus from the distance and brought it right back to the moment, fixing her eyes upon me. This was her power, in some way her charm, to be able to be very present with you in the moment. She smiled,

"Yes, it is. It's you." She took a few swallows of wine and continued, "My cause is a more equitable world. And yours, what is right and good?", she asked looking at me for confirmation.

"I haven't thought of my interest in the West's well being as a cause. I feel the West's well being is essential for life itself. Without a moral grounding which I believe the West still provides, there will be no well being for any one."

Evette was listening. "Go on," she said.

"Equitability must be clearly defined. While our souls are equally valued and sought for redemption, we are vastly different and with greater or lesser capacity for any particular field of human endeavor and for living our lives. To try and force a different reality denies reality. Human nature is fallen. Each makes his or her choice for personal responsibility, self control, discipline, perseverance, organization, thinking, readiness. Or, not. And life goes, at least to the extent we have control, accordingly."

Evette had alternated from looking at me to gazing out the window. She was quiet. Having answered honestly I stopped and waited.

She said, "So you think we have a decision, that our lives are ours to choose about, and if we are wise life will be good, or at least better than it would be otherwise?"

"As human beings gifted to be made in God's image our responsibility is great. Great is our potential power to control our circumstances and that of how we live. While it's true that many do not recognize this power, it exists."

At the word 'power' Evette's eyes were noticeably attentive. But her face did not convey agreement or acceptance of the idea before her. Was it the work required, the courage needed to take up the reins of responsibility that let one rest the reins? For endeavor too was needed to fight off the laziness that can easily set in.

"Yes of course, you believe in God", she replied, as in revelation.

"And you?"

"No. Or, rather I did, I think. But that's a long time ago. How can you believe with all the evil that exists?", Evette asked.

"It is all the more reason to believe. Good and evil coexist here. Who will I be is the question one must ask oneself. One chooses. Am I with God or against him? And if one is not with God one will be with Satan."

Evette's body stiffened. An uncharacteristic stiffness took over her normally relaxed self. She was noticeably uncomfortable.

"You don't approve then of the Wei and Greg Parsons's of the world?", she asked disparagingly.

"No. I don't."

"And I was thinking you might join us," her voice was reproving of her idea.

Without hesitation the question came to me and I gave it voice, "Who is 'She'?"

Evette stared, unbelieving, incredulous at the stark honesty of the question.

"How can I tell you?", her reply was an appeal, seeking the match to the honesty she had witnessed.

"You can."

With only an instant's hesitation she shot back, "I want to tell you."

I wanted to ask why but I made myself say firmly, "Then tell me."

Suddenly she rose from the chair and looking at me said, "I can't." Sweeping up her bag and moving to the door with her back to me I heard, "Thank you."

I presumed the thank you was for the invitation to my home, yet I wasn't sure. She was almost at the front door. I quickly followed my guest that I could offer a goodnight.

At the door she turned and facing me with tears said, "Goodnight Helena."

"Goodnight Evette", I heard my voice, low and soft.

As I tidied up and put the uneaten dinner in the fridge, nibbling a little on cold lemon chicken and bits of salad, I went over the evening in my mind. Evette had arrived reserved and reticent but open to me and our conversation. Her reserve and reticence seemed to stem from attempting to see her way to the path I walked. She recognized a complete change of view from where perhaps she had walked, not so long ago. Her view now, of luxury and power, contrasted fully with where I walked in clean air, air which felt good and soothed the soul. Jonathan Hill came to mind. Perhaps he could help. He would want to help a team member, and another human soul. Roger had said that Crispin would have to help us. Since Jonathan knew Roger through Crispin, Jonathan must be close enough to Crispin to get him involved now. Evette was scared and Wei Parsons had something to do with it. It was Evette's fear that made her reticent.

Jonathan happily agreed to meet for lunch. I sat waiting, people watching at the Ritz. People watching is one of my favorite things to do. New York is great for it. London is pretty good too. At the next table three business people sat, two men and a woman. I listened while taking in the well appointed room, sipping water from the crystal glass, spreading the beautiful white cotton napkin on my lap and sniffing the fresh table flowers. Apparently the neighbors were in advertising. Or rather, the one man who spoke more than the other two was the advertising man for the client sitting before him. He wore a suit with a drop of green in the material, it suited him. He was of about forty years and held himself with excellent posture. Most noticeably his confidence was the kind that comes from within, that which is not made from externals. This kind of confidence has a deep appeal. He liked himself. And it was obvious he liked his work too. And while he was pleasantly articulate, much more, his voice conveyed the depth of his interest in life which takes its natural course with others. And this confidence was doing just that at the table, permeating his words, his meaning, his person and so too his companions. I must have been intensely observing as he looked over at me and smiled. I laughed. Then he suddenly joined me at my table through his responding laughter. His two companions, startled, suddenly looked over at me. After a moment he resumed his attention at his table.

"What was that?", a familiar voice asked.

"Jonathan", I said and stood, facing Jonathan and Crispin Holtshire. I was surprised to see Crispin but suddenly felt glad of his presence. Crispin, thankfully, wore a noticeable smile.

"Crispin thought he would join us and this is why we are at the Ritz", Jonathan laughed.

"It is one of my old favorites", Crispin sparkled.

"It's lovely. And, great for people watching", I tilted my head to the next table where the unusual example of humanity sat. Both followed my indication, their eyes settling on the man with the green in his suit. Then Jonathan smiled and gave a wise nod. And when Crispin, after a good look, looked back, his eyes twinkled at me over the rim of his glasses in a shared recognition and delight.

A waiter arrived and gave us the specialties. Thankfully I had perused the menu and was ready when Jonathan indicated we would order immediately.

When the waiter withdrew Crispin began, "A friend lives in Sussex down the road from the Parsons's recent purchase. My friend was not pleased to learn of the new neighbor. They've been keeping a good watch for - any goings on. Tuesday night two black Mercedes limousines drove in just before dark and did not leave until the next day. My friend recently hired a watchman, an old employee of the firm's", Crispin chuckled. "He has a few special toys. The occupants of the cars were three men and a woman, all Chinese, except the woman. The woman was the sole occupant driven in one of the cars. He got the license numbers and because he caught them on the way in we had time for a few things. The check we ran indicated that the cars are owned by a holding company connected to the Chinese government. My friend then called in a couple of people working for us and they brought a few more toys with them. One of which is a long range sensing device for audio reception which can be operated from a car. The recording translated from Mandarin, offered discoveries on plans the CCP has to infiltrate and undermine not only our secret service, our way of life. This example is right under our noses. Getting hold of the mole, soon, is essential. The project we wish to launch with the Americans is to do with countering the infiltration, across the board."

Crispin had finished. The waiter arrived with our food, uncanny timing I thought. Once he left they both looked at me expectantly. I began between bites, explaining my experience with Evette.

"She wants to move off the course she has taken. She is scared and I think of Wei Parsons. Perhaps we can help her and help ourselves too", I said.

Jonathan and Crispin exchanged glances. And I heard Jonathan say under his breath, "… yes."

"Do you think you can continue with Evette?", Crispin asked me.

"Yes, I believe I can. I don't see how, quite yet." Crispin nodded.

Jonathan spoke, "Wiechert is too close to Evette. He doesn't look like an avenue for you. Ben Stillingfleet may be helpful again. Perhaps I can be', he ended on an enthusiastic note.

"That sounds good", I replied cheerfully.

Crispin laughed, and said keenly, "Let's think on that. In the meantime let's order our desserts."

The next day I joined Jonathan again for a walk along the wharf.

"Bye the way, that tanker we boarded was Monégasque," I said.

Jonathan, breaking into a smile said, "How did you know?"

"Simple. When we walked past the captain's office I saw Prince Albert's photograph hanging on the wall." Jonathan laughed.

Then spontaneously I blurted out my idea, "What if we included Evette, trusted her, and for example invited her to Crispin's friend's home and showed her, let her listen to, what we have on Wei Parsons from those toys our people used?"

Jonathan responded, "Do you think Evette can be moved to cross back over?"

"I don't know. What I did see the other evening was an unusual reserve. She liked being invited to my home. She seemed to register and appreciate something."

"Can you put your finger on what she was registering, appreciating?", Jonathan interrupted.

"She is not happy. My invitation seemed to jog her to something. My guess is that she is realizing that she is in trouble. A week ago I don't think she knew it. Now I think she does. Her tears at the door really surprised me."

"Tears?", Jonathan interrupted again.

"Yes, she was moving quickly to the door to leave. At the door she turned to face me and there were tears in her eyes. She thanked me."

"What was she thanking you for?", he asked.

"For inviting her to my home. And, I've decided for the conversation we had where a few things were named. And, I think, she was then able to see that things which have been secret can be spoken of."

". . . yes", Jonathan paused. Then he said, "So you think that further conversation along open lines could help her open up, perhaps share what she knows in an effort to clear her conscience?"

"Yes, that's what I'm thinking."

"Alright. Maybe Crispin's friend can help. Evette will enjoy the luxury of his manor house and perhaps recognize that not all such luxury is ill gotten. You made a good impression on Evette perhaps we can too. I'm glad to tell you that there are some very good people on our side", he smiled at me.

"I know, and one of them stands beside me right here", I said.

A handwritten personal envelope was on my desk the next morning. I wasn't expecting anything, and opening it immediately went to the signature. Crispin had written me a brief letter.

Dear Helena,

Where Evette thought to invite you into her web of intrigue, your idea to invite her out and over to your circle may be just what is needed.

Please invite her to join you for the seventh for 8PM to Montague Manor.

Crispin

That was quickly decided, and managed, time must be of the essence. I looked across to Evette's office, there she sat. No time like the present and I walked across the hall.

"Good morning", I said smiling.

Evette looked up from her desk, her eyes far away.

"Hello", she replied.

"Would you join me at a little party at Montague Manor on the seventh?"

"Oh . . .", the invitation was unexpected. But she addressed it, "The seventh . . .", she glanced at the calendar by the phone. "That's the day after tomorrow", she looked at me. I smiled. She seemed to decide,

"Alright. Thank you."

"Good. We'll go together - for 8PM."

Evette nodded and a little smile crossed her lips.

As I crossed back to my office I thought, she is still open to rescue.

Henry picked us both up. Evette was in the car when he arrived for me. She still does not want me to know where she lives.

It's good to see you again Henry", I said after greeting Evette.

"Thank you. It's nice to see you. Are you still enjoying London?", he asked.

"Yes, very much. I'm getting a bit of time in to experience your great museums and, the West End. It is often better than Broadway, but not I must say better than Off Broadway."

"Oh?', Henry replied. "Next time I'm in New York I'm going to test your Off Broadway", Henry laughed. And I joined him.

Evette looked bewildered by our easy banter. I think she was surprised we were talking with each other. She was quiet the entire trip not even asking about the party.

As we drove the private road in to Montague Manor Henry said, "I will be picking you up to bring you home."

"Thank you Henry", I replied and Evette seconded my response.

As expected Evette was taken in with the grand house and the prospect of grand guests. It was the beauty of the ancient trees, the serenity of the setting, and the history of the old architecture which captured me. Evette must have realized that Parsons' estate was in the neighborhood but she said nothing and seemed to be anticipating a view of the interior of the mansion. A butler answered the bell.

"Miss Madison, Miss Eliot, please come in. May I take your wraps?", the old gentleman asked.

I handed him my overcoat and Evette gave him the lovely chocolate brown cape she wore.

"You are expected in the farther drawing room. Please follow me."

We followed along the long wide entry hall that led into the depths of the house. Along either wall were beautifully framed oil paintings. Some must have been portraits of old family members for as we went further down the hall the apparel of the painter's subjects spoke of long dead ancestors. One landscape I noted was stunning in its capture of an idyllic open sunlit meadow of greens and yellows with horses and two walkers. I wanted to stop and spend some time there. We turned down another hall. Evette was not interested in the paintings, the tapestries, the vases or any of the classic objet d'art which so beautifully and tastefully adorned the halls. She seemed anxious to get to the party. I hoped she would not be disappointed as I knew our numbers would be few and though I did not know who exactly would be attending our little party I was excited for its possibilities.

The butler opened a dark oak door midway down the hall,

"Miss Madison and Miss Eliot", he announced and retreated.

Everyone rose. Closest to the ancient stone fireplace was Crispin, directly across from him Jonathan, beside whom stood a young man I did not recognize. Beside Crispin another man stood facing us, the owner of Montague Manor I surmised. The party was small, just six of us.

Crispin spoke, "Evette, Helena, thank you for joining us this evening. May I introduce Montague Astwell, our host."

Our host, a tall slender man similar in bearing to Crispin, perhaps fifteen years his younger, bowed his head slightly and looked at us most directly. I glanced at Evette standing beside me. There was uncertainty in her face. This was not the kind of party she was expecting. And it looked like she no longer held expectations for enjoying herself.

"You know Jonathan Hill of course", Crispin said.

Jonathan stepped forward and took Evette's hand in a friendly gesture. I saw a small smile come to her face. Then he squeezed my hand and turning to the young man said,

"May I introduce Jeremy Williams. Jeremy works for the firm. Please take a seat."

Mr. Astwell pulled the bell chord and said, "What will you have to drink?"

Evette's face lit up, "I'll have a whiskey and soda please."

"If you have it, may I have a sparkling non-alcoholic drink?", I responded.

"We have it", our host genially replied.

The butler arrived, spoke unobtrusively with Astwell and silently retreated.

"You must be wondering why we asked you here", Crispin said looking at Evette. He continued immediately, "Montague's family have lived here for centuries. He is therefore invested in who his neighbors are. The Parsons purchase was not ideal."

Montague Astwell took up the baton from Crispin who sat back into the depths of an enormous burgundy leather armchair which looked designed for him, as did the room.

"Upon confirmation of the Parsons's purchase we hired a watchman", Montague paused momentarily to let this register with Evette.

The drinks arrived and none too soon as Evette had begun fidgeting with her fingers. Now she firmly grasped the crystal glass and took a good swallow of whiskey and soda.

Once the butler had left Astwell continued, "Recently the watchman observed four suspicious visitors to the Parsons estate. A few others were called upon to help uncover more about these people, and about their activities", he stopped and looked to Jeremy Williams.

"We gained interesting information from the conversations they had Tuesday", Jeremy said as he pressed a panel by his chair.

A moment later what I knew to be the audio of the translation of their conversation began to play.

A British male voice began, "You will hear five voices representing the two women and three men who partook in the conversation translated from Mandarin. The first voice represents Wei Parsons. The others we are calling agents 1,2,3, and 4."

Then a different voice, a woman's representing Parsons began, "Two and Eight are well situated at Cambridge to help us recruit, and they work doubly well together."

A man's voice (agent 1) responded, "The recruitment is key. We have a lot of ground mapped out."

Parsons' representative continued, "The property purchases allow us the close access we need to the coast for orchestrating the planting of receiving devices along the coast, both on land and in the sea."

Evette and I were sitting together on a love seat sofa and I felt her shift and stiffen beside me.

The Parsons representative continued, "Would you explain further what the potential for these devices is?", she asked someone.

The other woman (agent 2) spoke, "The devices plot in detail the surrounding land and waters for a three mile radius including beneath the surface up to half a mile. This means we will know what the British, and anyone else, is doing, what resources will be available to us, and how to prepare to - remove any obstacles - when the time comes."

Another man (agent 3) continued, "Our new navy has opposite receivers. Submarines will be able to approach the shore once the devices are in place. Because their signals will be countered by the shore and sea devices we will be silent and invisible."

The woman (agent 2) said, "Of course the British will seek to counter with new technology but we believe they will be too late."

Agent 4 spoke, "With the help of the navy we will plant signaling materials which will attack U.K. and European communication systems without their knowing who or what hit them. The navy is ready now, - once the devices are planted we can act."

Parsons representative asked, "When will we have the devices for planting?"

The woman (agent 2) replied, "Next month. We will give you good notice. All your time will be required for this. And you will have help."

The initial British male voice came on again, "Once they broke up after dinner we were unable to record any further conversation. We do not believe the five spoke together again as a group. Any individual conversations, if they occurred, we do not have."

Crispin's voice brought us all back to our own company,

"Evette, we are asking for your help. Helena believes you can help us uncover Parsons' contact in the Chinese government. Who is the mole with whom you are in contact within our own government?"

There was a deadly expectant silence. Evette was motionless beside me. Suddenly she stood, hunched and trembling, and with her whiskey glass clasped in both hands began a slow movement around the room. She began to speak but her voice cracked and it was too low to hear.

I said, "Please come back and join us, join me here on the sofa."

She turned and looked at me, her face that of a lost child. She stood still, seemingly unable to move. I stood and went over to her. Taking her arm in both my hands I felt the coldness of her body. Slowly we moved back step by step toward the other four. Would she sit again I wondered. She stopped close to the fireplace, she seemed to need the warmth.

"They will kill me", she whispered. I heard her and so did Crispin who was close enough.

Jonathan leaned in toward us, his face indicating that he had not heard her words.

"You will be under our protection, and the safest you can possibly be", Crispin responded in low voice and with a warmth that offered comfort.

Evette shivered. Then she moved about a foot, seeming to will herself toward the sofa, but not letting go of my grasp. I directed our steps and when we arrived we sat down together, Evette perching herself on the edge of the chesterfield.

After another minute of dead silence Evette managed, "She works in administration", her voice was still a whisper but now she could be heard by all of us.

"Do you mean in our building?", Crispin asked, his voice slow, steady, strong.

"No. At Scotland Yard."

"At Scotland Yard?", Crispin asked, double checking, seeming uncertain as to the credibility of her statement.

"Yes", she replied.

"Who is it?", he asked.

Evette, alarmed, looked at him and then at Montague Astwell and said, "A pen and paper."

Montague rose, moved to the far end of the room and lifted the pen from the pen tray on the writing desk. He opened a drawer and removed a piece of writing paper, returning, he handed them to Evette. Unable to speak the words, Evette leaned forward to use the wood table in front of us in order to write. In the dead silence the crackling of the fire in the hearth suddenly seemed loud. She wrote two names, I could not see what they were, and handed the sheet to Crispin. He took it, read it, and slowly looked up at her, double checking again, with eye contact. Having read the paper he turned his face to the fire. It must have been five minutes. No one spoke, no one moved. I felt Evette's body begin to relax from its long stiffened posture, and she let herself slide to the back of the sofa for support. Handing over the sheet with the name seemed to lift a great burden.

Crispin, finally, said, "Thank you. You were right to write the name. He looked at Montague, Jonathan, and Jeremy and said, "it is better you did not hear this name." Then he looked at me. There was a decision forming in his mind but I could see by his face he had yet to decide.

"Evette, do you have someone you can trust, to stay with you? A cousin perhaps?"

Evette shook her head. Then she turned to me. I could see that she was asking silently, could you stay with me? I nodded.

Crispin was observing me with a very serious expression of concern.

Then he said, "Henry will take you home, and perhaps Evette should be with you at your house, for the moment."

CHAPTER FIFTEEN

EVETTE

Either Henry's instincts were far above regular fare or the firm's training was superb. Henry knew immediately upon receiving us not to say a word. The moment we entered the Mercedes Evette collapsed in exhaustion as from an immense emotional burden. She sank into the seat close beside me, leaning into me, and if I had not been there I think would have slipped to the floor of the limousine and lain prone.

I exchanged eye contact with Henry in his rear-view mirror. He kept a regular watch on as he drove us toward London and then through the London streets to Putney. The entire time Evette remained motionless, her eyes closed. But I knew she was not asleep.

When we arrived he drew up to the house on Dolby Road and spoke silently to me via the rear-view mirror, looking at me as he turned off the ignition. I gave him a slight nod. He came round to our door to help us get inside the house. I took Evette's hand and her instant response of a strong grasp came from a desperate need for support rather than from any self sustaining energy. She accepted Henry's arm around her. I got the door open ahead of them and pointed the way upstairs, following behind them to the bedroom. As soon as Evette saw the bed she collapsed in a heap, immediately closing her eyes, this time I knew it was to sleep. I took off her shoes, tucked the duvet around her, placed her cape on the chair and closed the bedroom door.

Henry and I moved silently back down the stairs. At the bottom we looked at one another, not sure as to what to say. Henry, again sensing the situation with his finely tuned antenna, said, “I will check in on you. We’ll bring you some breakfast in the morning”, and he gave me a most reassuring smile as if to say you’re not in this alone.

I smiled back, “Thank you. That sounds good.”

The moment I closed the door behind him I felt my own energy drain. Perhaps the full recognition of all that was now set in motion came upon me. Evette’s peril, and perhaps now my own through association, sapped my own capacity.

Since I hadn’t outfitted another bedroom I decided to sleep downstairs. The sofa I’d found, an enchanting and substantial 1920’s parlor sofa in heavy crewel work cotton of a deep red with a faint flower pattern in violet, now offered a practical invitation. With a half smile I tossed a large white sheet over it and brought out a wool blanket and two pillows from the main floor linen closet. The imagined coziness of its recesses beckoned me.

I washed my face in the main floor’s half bath. What about pajamas? Did I leave my nightie in the dryer? As I moved to the maid’s room off the kitchen I thought - yes I think I did. For once procrastination, not a trait I normally exhibit, rewarded. And while now the dryer contents were cold, the full length white cotton nightie was most welcome. As I dropped my clothes in the laundry basket, slipping the white nightie with tiny pink and violet flowers over my head, I sighed, and thought tomorrow morning has already been taken care of thanks to Henry. Cuddling in on this adorable chesterfield I thanked God for a clear conscience and dropped off to sleep.

Evette slept late. When I heard her in the upstairs bathroom I’d been up for five hours. This had provided the opportunity to think about what next steps might present themselves. I was praying that the new day would fortify her resolve to quit her authoritarian task masters. And, that the consuming fear they had inspired during yesterday's ordeal, if not yet vanquished, had been mitigated.

The breakfast delivered, though not by Henry, I could tell had been ordered by him, his careful consideration evident in the thoughtful details. It was a full English breakfast; eggs and bacon, kippers and English sausages, orange juice, scones with Devon cream and strawberry preserves, a lovely and varied plate of fresh fruit and an organic mix of berries. Brazilian coffee had been added along with a delicate and fragrant arrangement of flowers in a small vase fit for the breakfast table. All of this, including the kippers and sausages and the eggs and bacon in a warming pan now adorned the little breakfast table I had moved this morning to the end of the dining room. The sun poured in on this corner of the room and made for a cheery ambiance from which I hoped Evette would benefit, and then from which we all would.

"Good morning", I heard Evette's voice and came out from the kitchen.

"Good morning", I replied, noticing that she looked well rested.

A slow sad smile came to her face as she stood at the bottom of the stairs.

"Are you alright?", I asked and added, "You look well rested."

"I slept soundly", Evette said evenly. Then with a note of uncertainty added, "For what seemed a very long time." She remained unmoving at the foot of the stairs.

"We have a nice breakfast waiting for us", I said encouraging her and looking to the dining room.

Evette's look told me she was unable to lead but could follow. I led the way to the table. I was hungry and set to, with portions of everything. Evette began slowly. If I did not know it was Evette I would not have recognized the woman sitting opposite me. Her movements, slow and uncertain, did not speak of the worldly woman I knew. Perhaps the experience with Crispin, and with us as witnesses at Montague Manor, had caused a catharsis and here before me was a new woman.

"Would you have some juice?", and I lifted the carafe of orange juice to pour for her. She nodded.

Evette ate and drank. It seemed to revive her. After many minutes she said,

"Thank you for letting me come here."

"Of course. I'm glad you were able to sleep."

"Where did you sleep?", she asked and the note of real interest in her voice surprised me.

"Down here", I gestured to the sofa in the living room.

She smiled again, a small smile, but a smile not as sad as half an hour ago.

"You may have noticed I don't invite people to my home. I try and avoid letting anyone know where I live", Evette shared.

"Yes, I noticed."

"But they are experts at finding that sort of thing out", she added in a low voice.

"I think Crispin will have already arranged for a new place for you to live."

Evette was looking steadily at me. Was she absolutely decided I wondered. Her face was expressionless.

"Have you decided? Are you going to fight with us?", the two questions came to me and I gave them utterance.

She continued to look at me. Was she waiting for something? Was she looking for something in me? Something to hold on to?

"Doing the right thing seems automatic to you", she said.

I was listening and kept her eye contact. There was a long silence.

Then, in a very soft voice she said, "I want to too. I want to do the right thing."

I smiled at her, tears welling up in my eyes. Then, Evette laughed.

"How is she?" Crispin looked directly into me over the old and elegant frames of his glasses. He sat in his chair - which is what I now called the enormous well worn chocolate brown leather chair close to the stone hearth of his drawing room. This was only my second visit to Wellington Fields. The first had been just two days ago, the day of my breakfast with Evette in my house.

Today Crispin had rung me directly and suggested Henry come by to pick me up and deliver me for a short visit. While initially surprised to be delivered to Crispin's country home, I had been delighted. I was coming to like Crispin more and more and it was a fine treat to learn more about him through visiting his home. The house was built in 1720 as Henry informed me and the grounds were populated with the immense old thick trunked oak trees I had come to love and which are only to be found in England and Scotland. I sat across from him on a small settee meant for such interviews.

"She is much better", I paused a moment, " . . . in all regards. She is able to laugh again."

His brow rose ever so slightly. I continued.

To his question I replied, "She is quite recovered from the direct election you gave her to the truth." A half smile appeared on Crispin's face but the intensity of his expression altered not a jot. Again I continued, "Also, she is not the same woman she was. Having been brought face to face with reality she has not turned away. I believe she began to reckon with it that night, collapsing into the car on the drive home, and overnight as she slept. At the breakfast table the next day she made her decision to live with the truth."

"And now?", Crispin inquired with an eye to the future.

"And now . . . she wants to work with us. Finding her another house, a new place to begin, was a very good idea. It will help her organize for her new start." I finished. Crispin nodded.

Then after a few moments he said, "Would you fly with her?"

I didn't understand his meaning and it showed in my face because before I could ask an explanation Crispin said,

"It is an expression used by fighter pilots. Would you work with her when your life may depend on her actions?"

"Yes", the quickness of my response surprised me. But there was no regret in my responding as I did. It had come so quickly because it was true.

He said, "She knows our mole", again he was giving me his intense look. " . . . and we can use that. This likely means you will be working with the mole."

"Are you going to tell me who the mole is?"

Immediately Crispin shook his head, "No. Not before you need to know."

I remained quiet, listening.

Crispin asked, "Are you able, and I should ask, wanting, to remain with us for some time? I cannot tell you how long."

"Yes. I am happy and challenged here. And I am growing fond of old England."

Crispin chuckled, and his smile was his appreciation for my interest in what I knew was his beloved homeland. His verbal response was one word,

"Good."

"What is our plan?", Roger asked Crispin.

"Helena has helped lead Evette out. And now Evette is the main target, open season. But Helena, while in the cross-hairs, is indirectly a protection for Evette because they won't understand that she is not with the Americans. They will see her working with us and assume too she is working for our American counterparts. This will give Helena added protection because they will have their own to protect in both the U.K. and America. We've brought Trillian Wortley in. He has been quietly and effectively side lined. Have you ideas for the Parsons?"

"We could lead Greg Parsons away and astray through our business channels," replied Roger.

Crispin nodded.

Roger added, "Wei Parsons is a more difficult item to tackle." Crispin was listening.

Roger continued, "We will have to play her game, get in to her game for a time and then having amassed enough marbles zing it to them through her."

"By them you mean?", Crispin inquired.

"I refer to the side players that come attached to her. And, perhaps a higher up or two," Roger's voice lowered on the last note.

"Yes", Crispin said introspectively gazing into the fire which had been lit for their conversation.

Crispin in his chair and Roger in another of the large deep brown leather chairs which populated the drawing room of Wellington Fields looked a pair of solemn kings determining outcomes for their subjects.

"And what of our mole?", Roger asked slowly, bringing Crispin back from the recesses of his thoughts.

"Do you know him?', Crispin asked.

"I have met him only once", Roger replied.

Crispin said, "He is formidable. Beyond his steely determination, his inordinate capacities, both intellectual and personal, and his superb management of people, his connexions are legend."

"Yes . . . meaning we will rock any number of boats", Roger responded.

"The night of Evette's disclosure I made a phone call. I had to determine as certainty if he could be the mole. When I saw his name on the paper a great number of things began to coalesce. And I realized that though that name was as a sudden attack, it was not an assailing shock. And the response I received from my call told me it must be true."

Roger thought to himself, Crispin cannot tell me who he called, and I can only imagine who it might be.

Crispin continued, "It will be his connexions which will work against us unless we can get a couple of them to work with us. Amongst these connexions are the leads to the Chinese lead player. Wei Parsons is in that web."

"They will be working against us, pulling in the opposite direction", Roger said.

"We're in for a battle", Crispin replied.

Roger called.

"Helena, I am sorry I've not been in better contact with you. How are you?"

In the warmth of his voice and with the genuine interest he conveyed I recognized comfort. And only in that moment did I realize that I could use some comfort. I relaxed into it.

"Thank you Roger. Your call makes a difference."

"I'm glad. Hugo tells me that you are superb at asking good questions. Has one arisen as you think about the mole in the yard?"

I laughed, "Good pun. Yes. Why is there a photograph of the old Scotland Yard hanging in the hall of your offices?"

There was a pause on the line. Then he replied,

"Right outside the elevator - on the wall of the hall leading to our meeting room. It is a bit out of place there and I haven't thought about who had it placed there. I will inquire."

"I have another question. How does Scotland Yard work? Is it functioning these days?"

"To answer your last question first, yes it is a finely tuned instrument with nary a mistake made. And, the best way to learn how the Yard works is to work there."

"She has been placed at the Yard", the voice was low and strong.

"She is there for one reason. To confirm what Eliot has already divulged and to learn anything that will provide the final evidence for stopping us", the response was firm and confident.

"How will you dispose of her?"

"I don't think we can," he replied.

"What then is your plan?", she asked.

"I don't see what she can learn. She will not gain any evidence against me, and if your people have been careful, you should be free and clear as well."

There was a pause.

"You should get rid of her", her voice was steely, decided.

"I will take care of her in my own way", he said.

Henry picked me up at 7:25 PM for an eight o'clock dinner at Crispin's home in Belgravia Square.

"Good evening Miss Madison", Henry's blue eyes flashed in the rear-view mirror as his smile lit the front seat of the limousine.

"Good evening Henry", I laughed. "Has Mr. Holtshire moved to his city residence at this time?" I eyed him in his mirror and received a nod.

"You are climbing quickly it would seem, and in exalted circles. Enjoying yourself?", Henry inquired with energy.

"It is a whirlwind that is for sure. How often are you taking new recruits to Mr. Holtshire's home?"

"This is my first time taking anyone. I received specific directions just an hour ago."

"Hmm", I responded under my breath.

Henry and I waited in the limousine eleven minutes in order to time my bell ring for precisely 8PM.

The same grave old butler responded to the bell as at Wellington Fields, he silently ushered me in to the foyer.

"May I take your coat?", he asked.

"Yes, thank you." As I stood unbuttoning and taking in my surroundings I recognized a revered and earned way of life that was too quickly passing away. A Turner and a Constable met my eyes in a surprisingly well lit foyer. History. Perhaps Crispin's ancestors were collectors.

"This way please Mamam", the very British butler, with my coat well secured across his arm, made one step into the hall indicating that I should follow.

Immaculate mid brown hardwood led us further into the house and I scanned the walls to catch a glimpse of the works of other great artists should they too reside here. While two oil paintings caught my fancy I did not recognize their origin. Then I caught a glimpse of a Velasquez just as the butler stopped in front of french doors, bowed his head almost imperceptibly and opening the doors, announced,

"Miss Madison Sir", and retreated.

Two men, already standing, stood at one end of an enormous wood dining table. Crispin smiled directly into me. Jonathan, smiling, bowed his head slightly. Their warmth was a silent invitation to join them. Not knowing what to expect, I was simply happy and strangely relieved to be in their company.

"Are you hungry my dear", Crispin looked at me over the rims of his trademark spectacles. His look, which I first had found slightly unsettling in its charm, I now found endearing. Taken aback by the great and simple humanness of his query I broke into a laugh as an expression of relief.

"Yes, thank you. I am famished", I responded fervently.

Crispin and Jonathan laughed and Jonathan added with equal simplicity, "Me too."

Dinner was sumptuous, from the elegance of its presentation to the delicious food. A Waldorf salad, a scrumptious vegetable soup, roast duck with grilled asparagus, a fine wine of what vintage I knew not, was much enjoyed and appreciated.

"Evette is in Ireland, working for us there", Jonathan offered.

"Oh", was all I could say.

"They will have greater difficulty in . . . reaching her", Crispin added for clarification. And then continued, "They know Evette has informed on them, that she has informed us of the mole's identity."

I listened.

"How are you liking being at the Yard?", Jonathan asked rather cheerfully.

"I do like it. You are keeping me much stimulated."

Crispin laughed. "Yes my dear, and you are a great sport."

"A sport? Now that is a compliment from a Brit", I said.

Crispin, again intensely eyeing me, nodded twice.

"Are they aware of you yet?", Jonathan asked.

"I'm not sure who 'they' are. However while most of my colleagues are welcoming and helpful, a couple have looked askance at me."

"They are aware of you", Crispin asserted. "They are trying to figure out what to do with you", he said while keeping up his close observation of me.

I was listening.

"What work are you actually doing? With whom do you have contact?", Jonathan queried.

"I've been going round to the offices on my floor asking if I can be of help."

"Good idea", Crispin offered and added seemingly as an afterthought, "What floor are you on?"

"The fourth floor."

Jonathan looked quickly at Crispin. Crispin kept his gaze on me.

"Have you seen the Chief yet?", Crispin asked me.

"I saw him briefly when his secretary opened his door to bring him in some papers." It may have been my imagination but I thought Jonathan started at the word 'secretary'. Crispin remained unflinching.

"I would like to see him up close." And I instinctively added, "and his secretary."

Crispin, nodding, said, "Good idea."

CHAPTER SIXTEEN

SCOTLAND YARD

I awoke with an idea and a powerful drive to give my full attention today to the Chief's personal assistant, Caroline. Listening to one's instincts is always a good idea.

As I traveled the more than thirty five minutes by tube to Greater Scotland Yard I set about envisioning what to do. How would I make myself useful to Caroline? What would she think of my interest and overtures? Crispin said they are aware of me. And then, echoing clearly in the back of my mind were Crispin's words "Good idea" to my instinctive response to see Caroline up close. In the same sentence I had included the Chief but it was my decision to add 'and his secretary' to my statement that had solicited Crispin's "Good idea".

"Good morning Caroline", I smiled my greeting, after purposely passing her office.

"Morning", she replied looking up only for a moment. Was that a wisp of a faint smirk on her lips? What next? I headed slowly toward my desk.

"Helena," someone called my name. I whisked around to see Clare waving me down from an adjoining hallway.

"Good morning Clare. How may I help?", I asked in my finest volunteering American style.

"Oh good. You're available?," Clare responded with some relief.

"At your service."

"Oh good", she repeated, with further relief. She must be inundated I thought. "If you would help us organize the police brochures which have to go out today" . . . she took a breath, ". . . along with the signage which the officers are coming to collect today for placing in their precincts."

"Yes", I said firmly, smiling cheerily for her benefit.

"Brilliant. Come this way."

She led me down the hall from where she had come looking for willing hands and flung open two doors onto a huge room. Metal sign posts lay on the floor and brochures were piled high all along two enormous conference tables where also lay any number of pamphlets which looked like instruction sheets for how these materials were to be distributed. Clare thumped the instruction pile with her hand as she continued her way amongst the clutter,

"Read these and try and sort out a way to organize the signage and brochures for the seventy officers who shall be trooping through here today. I'll bring you another recruit." She seemed to finish as she made her return around the tables toward the door. And then she added, "Everything must be signed off by Caroline, the Chief's secretary, before going out," Clare finished as she exited the room.

Perfect, that's my way in, I said to myself. I set to for two hours with the revolving question in mind, how best to approach Caroline for maximum gain. A recruit appeared.

"Hullo, thanks for coming", I said to a dour faced long timer.

"Well what can you do? I was recruited. I'm Felicity", she said looking depressed as she surveyed the room.

"I'm Helena. I think I've got a hold of the tail of this one." She perked up a bit, I had her attention now.

"If you would gather the brochures entitled 'Look Alive Count Five' and place them at this end of the table in boxes of two hundred each, that will be a good start. You can use the empty boxes along the walls."

"Okay", Felicity replied and began.

"These sign posts are heavy but together we can shift them against the walls in their groups when you are finished there", I said.

"Okay", Felicity replied a tad more brightly.

Before I can okay the removal of any of this by police officers I need Caroline to sign off, I said to myself. Aloud I said to Felicity over my shoulder as I headed to the supply room,

"I'll be right back."

With paper and pen in hand I sat down at the conference table and created a list of the ten different types of brochures and the five different signs and how they were to be distributed.

"All done with this brochure", Felicity announced. "It looks like there are other kinds of brochures", she said, indicating some interest to work.

"Yes. There are nine other types. Would you like to organize them?"

"Yes, I can do that", she replied with a little bit of pride and surprising energy.

Felicity was a surprisingly good worker. I guessed she usually doesn't have enough to do. But given a job to get done, she sets to. By 4PM our job was done and just in time too because the officers were due to arrive.

"Hello Caroline. Clare asked that I ask you to sign off on the distribution of these brochures and signage", I handed her the description of the materials and their distribution, "as well as the list of the seventy officers to whom these are to be distributed", I said handing her the second list.

I watched, she seemed to be reading and not merely scanning the paperwork. My eyes scooted over her desk and its environs. It is a tidy and uncluttered desk. She is organized I said to myself. The phone on her desk rang and she picked it up.

"Yes, Caroline Worthington", she responded to the call. I could linger without suspicion as she had not yet signed the two papers.

"No", she spoke firmly, perhaps more firmly than a secretary might normally respond. Then, "No. Absolutely no. We will not be bullied", her manner was of one used to being in command, again not that of an average assistant. To whom was she speaking I wondered and what was the reference? "Not now", she ended the call and hung up the receiver.

For a moment she paused, reflecting, oblivious to me, and to all but her own thoughts.

Then she said, "Would you do something for me? Go down to the Chief Inspector's office, Room 301, and ask his secretary Dorothy for the file on Charlotte Parsons."

I was aghast. If they were aware of me - for whom I was working, why would she send me for something which I presumed was important? And who was Charlotte Parsons? Was the name merely a coincidence or was she related to Wei Parsons?

"Yes", and I turned to go.

"Hurry back. I'll be waiting", she said, again with a commanding tone in her voice. It was, I decided, the tone to which she was habitualized.

I took the stairs to ensure myself a few moments alone to think. A file? Wouldn't something important be on a computer? But then that is what anyone looking for it would think.

Room 301, one flight down, was at the end of the corridor and emerging from the stairwell it was on my left. The door to 301 was locked. I knocked.

"Yes", came a male voice from within. Was that the Chief Inspector?

"I am sent by Caroline on the fourth floor to ask for a file", I replied.

There was a silence within and then heavy footsteps coming to the door. The door swung open and a large man in his sixties with horn rim glasses examined me at close range.

Satisfied, he said, "Alright . . . come in. My secretary is not here. What file do you want?"

"Charlotte Parsons."

The name didn't seem to mean anything to him and he began to talk to himself.

"Now where would she have filed it?', he mumbled as he walked over to an old and well worn metal filing cabinet and fingered the letters of the alphabet on the exterior of the drawers. "P, Paine, Palowski, Parsons, here we are. Charlotte Parsons", he said as he pulled out the file folder from the drawer, turned, and handed it to me.

"Will you be returning it?", he asked.

"I think so Sir."

He nodded, and turned again, this time in the direction of his office and walking in, closed the door behind him.

"Whew", I whispered to myself as I closed the door to Room 301. He doesn't know anything about Charlotte Parsons. But I'm going to find something out. Swiftly opening the door to the stairwell I planted myself on a step half way between the third and fourth floor. There were three pages, some typed, some handwritten. The first page read 'Charlotte Parsons (Wei Parsons). The address attached was Golden Bundside Garden 300 Zhongshan S Road Shanghai. I fingered the file in my hand and looked again at the file folder name, Charlotte Parsons. Anyone seeing the file would assume, a Brit. Yes, that's why the

'Charlotte'. What did Caroline want with the file? I quickly scanned the rest of its content. "Suspicious activity: purchase of property by the water, Kent, Sussex, and Northumberland, husband in business in China." The notes seemed to be mere sketches. Parsons had been caught on Scotland Yard's radar but they weren't quite sure what to do about it. What was Caroline going to do? Somehow now I didn't think I would be returning this file.

"Here it is", I said simply, proffering the file in hand to Caroline.

"Thank you" she said, taking the file from me and going directly with it to the Chief's office, she closed the door behind her.

In that moment as I watched her move from her desk to his door I felt déjà vous. It was more a feeling, the image of her back registered. Outside, the terrace, only a glimpse, like a ghost, Parsons's party. It had been her. She. Then my mind snapped back to the present. Was he in there? Well I would wait. She had not dismissed me and now I could espy her office. Caroline's desk looked slightly less organized. Why? What was it that had not been there before? There it was. A small black notebook lay by her telephone. It looked to be a personal notebook. I snatched it up, quickly flipping through the pages. And there under the 'S' something jumped out, the same address I had just seen in Parson's file but the name at Golden Bundside Garden was different. Quick a pen. No paper. My hand. I put the notebook back in place. The door to the Chief's office opened.

"Oh, you are still here", she said, having completely forgotten about me. "Let me sign those sheets." I had completely forgotten about the sheets.

Without another glance at them she signed the sheets and handed them to me in dismissal.

"Are they protecting Wei Parsons?", I asked Crispin.

"That is most likely", Crispin replied.

We sat in his study. I had left my office at Scotland Yard early after calling Jonathan to report the 'Charlotte' file. He had called back minutes later telling me that Crispin asked, it was always asked not wanted, that I come to his home.

"Did Caroline come out of the Chief's office with the file?", Crispin asked me now.

"No. And I don't think he was in his office."

"He was not. He was on Parliament Hill all day." He paused. Then he continued, "He is not in it with her. She may be setting him up or arranging to disperse blame."

"Is Caroline the mole?"

"Yes and no. She is working for her husband, he is the mole working with Wei Parsons."

"Who is he?", I asked.

"He is the Chancellor of the Exchequer."

"Do you mean . . . that Britain's finance minister is in league with the communist government of China?", I sought to comprehend.

"Yes", Crispin replied simply.

"What can we do to stop him?", I immediately responded, and realizing both my boldness and presumption, bit my lip.

Crispin laughed, "Your attitude is exactly what we need. And by 'we' I mean the entire country. They, the Chinese communists, have set out to silently invade the free world. An Australian professor wrote a book on this silent invasion in 2018. What we need is an advertising blitz to educate the public", Crispin paused, thinking.

"I agree. We need one in the States too."

"Worldwide", he said in a low voice, still thinking.

A few minutes passed in silence.

Then Crispin said, "At the moment we must gain access to all communication between the Worthington's and Wei Parsons. And find a way to learn their communication with the Chinese government. We have a few of our people in Parliament and a couple of our men in the cabinet. But we need one person to coordinate", Crispin looked at me over his glass frames in that way he does.

"Me?", I could barely believe my eyes, for he had not asked aloud.

"Jonathan is one of them."

"Do you mean he is in the cabinet?"

"Unofficially, yes. You will have someone you know with whom to work."

"Does Worthington know Jonathan?", I wondered aloud.

Crispin nodded but said, "He does not know where Jonathan really works."

"Are you hungry my dear?", he suddenly changed subjects.

"Yes, I'm famished", I replied.

"Again", Crispin laughed. He saw the relief on my face. He seemed to know that a little of the ordinary, that sitting down at a meal together, was much needed at this moment. Crispin stood and walked over to the bell chord and gave it one tug.

"We will have some dinner brought to us", he smiled upon me. He gestured to the study door.

"We will repair to the dining room and eat there. It is a room made for enjoying one's meal."

The door opened.

"You rang Sir?", the butler asked.

"Yes Hampstead. Ask cook to prepare us something delicious. We will eat in the dining room."

"Yes Sir", Hampstead retreated.

Crispin said, "Jonathan will have some ideas to share and to discuss with you on strategy. Our objective is to lay a bit of ground work to prepare the PM, and a couple of others, for Worthington's demise. Then we will pounce."

The headline in the London Times read, "WORTHINGTON RESIGNS". Crispin's ability to "lay a bit of groundwork" was extraordinary. In less than twenty four hours he had plowed fields, including the PM's, and, I imagined, created a dust storm to cloud Parson's field of vision to bar any action for a self orchestrated exit. Now we pounce. My curiosity peaked as to how the pouncing should occur, I put the paper under my desk and walked down the hall to Caroline's office. There was no sign of her. The door to the Chief's office was, as I had always seen it, closed. For some reason, instinctively again, I turned and headed for Room 301, the Chief Inspector's office. As I came out of the stairwell I could see his door was open. I approached slowly. There he was rifling through the old metal filing cabinet. Apparently his secretary was still away.

He looked up, "Oh hello, it's you again. Did you return that file you took the other day?"

"No Sir."

"It was Caroline who wanted that file wasn't it?"

"Yes Sir."

"Where is it?"

"I'm not sure Sir. I handed it to Caroline and the last I saw of it was when she went with it into the Chief's office."

"Let's see if we can find it", he said firmly and strode down the hall to the stairs.

I smiled to myself. Now things were turning in the right direction.

The Chief Inspector knocked firmly on the Chief's door and called his name. When no answer came in reply he opened the door. The office was empty of any person.

He turned to me, "What is your name?"

"Helena Sir, Helena Madison."

"Well Helena let's see if we can find that file. Parsons wasn't it?"

"Yes Sir, Charlotte Parsons."

"Charlotte? Bollocks. Wei Parsons is the name."

"Right Sir", I could barely contain a huge smile that wanted to erupt upon my face.

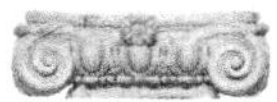

I rang the bell at the Belgravia Square address. The old butler opened the door.

"Miss Helena", he greeted me.

"Good evening Hampstead", we were on a personal name basis now.

Crispin, Jonathan, and myself were now regular dinner companions.

"The action at the Yard today was a clean out of the cover up by the Parsons brigade", I offered.

Crispin, chuckling said, "Yes, good ole Stanley, he knows what to do once he applies himself. "He knew instantly that Bertram was not in on it, that it was Caroline's doing."

Jonathan said, "The conversation in Parliament today was entirely on Worthington, the reorganization of the cabinet, and the potential impact on the economy. Of course, most do not know that Worthington was a mole working with the Chinese. What next Crispin?"

"Wei Parsons. The problem, while we have blocked her from leaving the country, is learning who her Chinese counterpart is."

We were quiet, silently eating.

Then I said, "Evette may be able to help us. It is a man on the other side, we know that much."

"Do we?", Jonathan responded.

"Yes, it would seem so", Crispin replied.

Jonathan looked surprised.

"I remember from that tape of their conversation at La Scala, Evette asking when she could meet him. Evette may know something she hasn't thought about", I finished.

"Yes. Go ahead and contact her. I think she will be glad to hear from you", Crispin said.

"And what about Wiechert? He must know something", I said.

"Wiechert is back in Germany", Jonathan replied. "And the door is closed."

I took this in. "The Russians?", I suddenly asked. He nodded.

"Dear", Crispin addressed me. "Go to my study and call Evette. See what happens", he said with an energy in his voice that stirred one's insides. Excited, I left the room.

"Evette, it's Helena. I'm glad to hear your voice", I said to her greeting over the phone.

"Helena. How are you? Thank you for calling."

"We need your help", I said directly.

"Yes. How can I help?", she responded in earnest.

I breathed a silent sigh, she is with us.

"What can you remember or think of that will help lead us to Wei Parsons contact in China? The big one."

There was a pause, silence on the other end of the line.

"I'm thinking. It is a man."

"Yes, we know that much."

After another few moments Evette said, "I think he is quite close to Parsons."

"What do you mean? Why do you say that?"

"I'm not sure . . . Sometimes I got the impression - when we were purchasing the properties - while we were at the property - that she was calling someone with a detailed description, she was always, every time, able to reach him immediately. It was as though she had his personal line, and he was there to answer her."

"We've got it!", I said breathlessly having fairly run down the hall of Crispin's Belgravia Square home.

"He is a relative of Wei Parsons. And it just came to me, he may go by the name, Charles Parsons."

"Charles. . .", Crispin, reflecting, repeated the name.

Jonathan's brow furrowed.

Crispin, talking to himself more than to us said under his breath, "the file, 'Charlotte Parsons'. Yes. I think you are right."

Without another word he stood and moved to the door. Over his shoulder he said, "I'm going to my study. You may follow."

I jumped up to follow. Jonathan must have sat for another couple of moments because he was paces behind me down the hall. I reached the study door as Crispin reached his desk. He seemed to press a button there. Then he sat down in his chair.

After only a moment a female voice said, "Head Quarters."

"Crispin here. Get me Clive."

"Yes Sir."

Jonathan arrived and we two moved noiselessly into the study. I closed the door and we remained stock still near the door. Crispin concentrating on his thoughts was in his own world.

In about fifteen seconds a man's voice said,

"Crispin, Clive here."

"Clive, we think the Chinese treachery is in the control of one code named Charles Parsons."

"Charles eh?"

"Yes. Will you run with that?"

"Right. Will do."

"We will be waiting to hear from you", Crispin finished.

"We are on it."

A little click could be heard and we three were alone again. Jonathan and I remained standing still by the door. Crispin was still with his own thoughts.

I tingled inside in a way I had not known before. Crispin had said "we think …" Crispin had included me in his deductions. Being in Crispin's study and hearing 'Head Quarters' announced and Clive being gotten in moments. Who was Clive? Someone with a very important job. All this was adding to this high emotional state in which I found myself. Exhilarated, I thought how interesting to learn that treachery, high treason, and threat to the national, the Western, well being would make me want to jump up and take a stand. And to be able to stand with Crispin Holtshire made me feel very humble indeed.

Perhaps this is what I have been seeking. Injustice, which as a youth bothered me, as an adult upset me, and now as a thinking person infuriates, was now grasped by its ugly tail. And I was part of the hold on this devil. Years, yes years, have come and gone and I remained infuriated with our fallen nature that allows, abets, and even instigates, injustice. Perhaps part of my outrage was not having a way to address injustice where I found it. Now, here, this wrong, this wicked violation of all that is right and good, this invasion into the God given rights of others, was to be rightfully addressed to the best of human ability. To use and abuse the openness a democracy offers, to come to another country under the cloak of deception for the actual purpose of undermining another peoples way of life, to act in an arrogance of power, to seek unprovoked to destroy, to be so deeply ignorant of the laws of nature, of Nature's God, is to be wholly deserving of being vanquished. And here too is where the arrogance and ignorance turns back upon its purveyor. For they will not have believed nor thought that they could be stopped.

Already the British and American naval intelligence were taking their people, along the shores in Kent, Sussex, and Northumberland.

I received an early morning call from Head Quarters,

"Mr. Holtshire asked that you be called. We have succeeded in camouflaging signals and expect to capture a number of submarines and other reconnaissance vessels. We have already two of their submarines. They were mightily surprised."

"Brilliant", I exclaimed spontaneously.

I heard a low chuckle on his end of the line,

"Good day Mamam."

"Is this the end of our project?", I asked Roger as we sat at the same board room table where I had first met the team, though this time it was only Roger and me.

"I cannot say it is the end of this project, as we call it. There is work yet to be done. But our work with our American ally is underway now and that was our immediate main objective.

"And Wei Parsons, what of her, what will happen there?"

"Wei Parsons has evaded us."

"What? Do you mean you don't know where she is?"

"That's right. She succeeded, against our better efforts, in leaving the country. We don't think she has returned to China", Roger said.

"And her husband?"

"He is here. And there has been no contact between them for more than three weeks."

"Where do you think she is? And what do you think she is doing?"

"She may be almost anywhere. And as to what she is doing - she will continue her nefarious work. She cares for no one and nothing but power. She will be unable to relinquish it. And so she will find a way to remain in touch with Charles Parsons. I believe that the evil intentions she holds will neither dissolve nor dissipate. In fact I think she will see our having stopped her and having stopped the landing of their work on our shores as further fuel for her unholy fire. Wei Parsons will pursue her purposes with an even greater fever."

"How strange it is . . ." , I reflected aloud.

"What is strange?", Roger asked.

"I have felt a fury against injustice and she is in a fever for an injurious, immoral, wicked destruction of order. She would undermine civilization."

We looked at one another. And in a moment of seeing through eyes which reflect the truth, we looked upon the future. Roger nodded.

CHAPTER SEVENTEEN

LEAVING LONDON

"I am glad that you are back dear", Mom said. "It's good to see you again."

"I've missed knowing how you are, seeing the little details of the day that tell me how you are."

Mom grinned, "Well we'll have more of that now." But then she asked with hesitancy, "Will we?"

"Yes . . ." , I replied slowly. "It was all rather thrilling, it all seemed to happen very fast – our project. But somehow it didn't seem to finish."

"Do you mean you didn't complete the job?"

"Yes, that's it."

The schools were calling again and yet I had little enthusiasm for the jobs. Something else was being asked of me.

"Will you join us on the school board then?", Tom Herring asked over the phone. "If you are not employed by the schools there is no conflict of interest", he added hopefully.

"Thank you for your encouragement. But I think I am supposed to be doing something else."

"Yes . . .", he wouldn't let me off the hook.

"I'm thinking of what it should be. You know that I dialogue with my clients", I paused then finished, "the children may benefit from this dialogue."

"I know they would", he responded emphatically. "How can I help?", Tom asked.

"That would be great. Why don't we start with a dialogue circle with one class. Can you recommend a particular class?"

"Let me think about that. Off the top of my head I have an idea that Doug Dalwan's fourth grade class at Ebon Park Elementary would really benefit from such good attention. They are an underprivileged group and he has been looking for something extra for them.

"Fourth grade", I said, thinking. "Why not?", I was already enthused.

Principal Dalwan was pleased to receive my call. Tom Herring had paved the way and Dalwan was open to a conversation on dialogue.

"Your dialogue sounds like a way to get children to open up, participate with their classmates, potentially air concerns, and generally exercise their gray cells", he sought to summarize our conversation.

"That is a good summary. Let me add that the dialogue is based in inquiry and the questions help one organize thinking and clarify what is most important. The overall effect is encouraging one to think for him or her self, to make connections in thinking and to learn to develop a habit of reflection."

"Alright", he said with enthusiasm. "When can we begin?"

"What is most important?", I asked the twenty two fourth grade students as we sat together in a large circle in their classroom. Hands went up.

"Yes Josiah?", I smiled at the little tow haired boy across the circle with his hand in the air.

"My family, and that includes my dog Rufus", he said cheerily with a big smile.

"Hannah?"

"My best friend Josie. She is important because we play together. I go to her house and she comes over to my house."

"What about you James? You have put your hand up every time. What is most important?"

"I don't know. I have to think about it", he replied, and quite a serious expression appeared on his face.

"Good for you. It is important to think."

Principal Dalwan had sat quietly in our dialogue circle and not said a word. Afterward he said,

"This is the one class I teach and I have known most of these children for four years. I learned things about them today which I did not know. I can see this is a very good chance for them to consider who they are, and to exercise themselves in reflection, and practice speaking their thoughts. Will you come for the rest of term?", he asked.

"Thank you. I'm very happy that you feel this way. I would like very much to be here."

"How many candidates are running and do you know them?", my colleague, Amy Bansard, from a previous maternity leave assignment, asked.

We sat together in the school auditorium where the election for School Board President would soon take place.

"There are three candidates and yes I've read something about each of them. I know Tom Herring who is a concerned parent", I replied.

"What did you learn about the candidates?", Amy asked.

"Susan Erickson has nothing original to say. She repeats the latest progressive nonsense one can read in any rag newspaper or hear on any tow the line television network. Lyle Bradley isn't much different. Tom Herring is a concerned parent who has educated himself on the education system's agenda; a progressive script of social justice, racism, sex education, politically correct speech, gender neutral language, and anything they can conjure to overturn the pillars of Western civilization," I said. Amy was looking a little bewildered.

"You're voting for Tom Herring, the concerned parent?", she asked.

"Yes", I said firmly and smiled.

"How do you know what they each stand for?", she inquired.

"Other than Tom they don't stand for anything, which means they will tolerate anything."

"What?", Amy replied.

"If you don't stand for something you'll put up with anything. In other words you will never put your foot down and hold the line because you have not drawn the line in the sand to say this far and no farther."

Amy was starting to look concerned. Good, I said to myself.

The candidates were introduced and each took his and her turn to speak. True to type, Susan Erickson and Lyle Bradley sounded much the same, using popular phrases and much repeated rhetoric. Tom, thank goodness, sounded the warning bell with a call to action against the dangerous trend to removing control of education from parents and handing it over to the enormously powerful directives of the national education system. By the end of the evening Tom had won by two votes. I couldn't help but wonder if mine and Amy's were the deciding votes.

"Congratulations Tom", I said with energy as I shook his hand with vigor.

"Thank you for your support. Your vote was important", he responded.

"You have my support. Thank you very much for running for President. Now our school board has a chance to begin to counter some of the policies that ill serve our children."

He nodded silently as he looked around the room. Then he said, "There are many here who are none too pleased with the result tonight. I will continue to need your support."

"You have it.", I said firmly.

"Helena, do you have time to meet me for a quick dinner tonight?", Tom Herring was on the other end of the phone and he sounded concerned.

"You sound concerned. Is something the matter?"

"Yes. A few things have occurred and I'd like your perspective", he replied.

"Yes, of course. Where shall I meet you and what time?"

Tom chose an eatery attached to an old bowling alley. It was out of the way and unlikely to be frequented by any school board members nor anyone either of us knew. As I drove up I thought to myself he must want to be sure we are neither seen nor overheard.

"I'd like to share with you three incidents that have occurred and I'd like to learn your response", Tom said seriously. He began, "Last week a school board member, Daniele Idendower, came to me to relate a rather disturbing incident. We have a vote coming up on which text books we will use next fall. I think you are aware that the Tandeman text books have only gender neutral examples for all grammar and vocabulary work." I nodded.

He proceeded, "Daniele was approached through email and phone calls to vote for the Tandeman text books. Someone from Tandeman emailed and two different people, a man and a woman, from the Secretary of Education's office called her. She felt pressured. She was surprised to receive a call from

Washington and while the man who called was business like the woman was, according to Daniele, downright aggressive and was trying to intimidate", Tom stopped, waiting for my response.

"Apparently they want the Tandeman text books in our schools", I summarized. Tom nodded.

"Do you know whether any other school board member has been approached?"

"I called them all. Apparently not", he replied.

"Does Daniele tend to vote non-progressive?" He nodded again.

"Strange that they should know this. But unethical that they should come after her vote."

"Yes it is", he retorted sternly.

"This matter is worth contacting our senators about. What are the other two incidents?"

"I've been receiving a lot of communication from other school board presidents, most of which has been encouraging me to reconsider my direction. I have had about a dozen calls, only two of which have been supportive. It looks like I may have to take up a campaign to get more non-progressives to band together", he said.

"Were any of the calls threatening?"

"I cannot say there were any threats but about half of them were strong and directing. Let's say they were unpleasant, and unwelcome", Tom related.

"And the third incident?"

"At first I thought it was just coincidence but most of my Board members are becoming cold toward me. Up until about two weeks ago, while we don't always agree, we were collegial and worked together quite amicably. But, as I think about it, perhaps a week prior to the calls Daniele received, the other board members turned away", Tom's voice held disappointment.

"Do you think they are afraid?"

"I'm wondering if they are afraid", Tom said, thinking aloud.

"Do you think they may have received communications too, pointing them in the direction they should vote?"

"I don't know. I'm beginning to think that may be the case", he responded.

"You said most of the members. Who is still with you?"

"Danielle and Joe Wharton are solid. Sally Artsem is something of an independent, sometimes she votes one way and another time she votes the other way."

"Your idea to begin investing in learning of other board presidents who believe in independence of thought and who may have the courage of their convictions is a good idea."

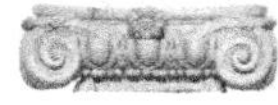

"Is this the discerning Helena Madison, adventuress extraordinaire?," it was Hugo Wentworth's warm rich toned voice over my home landline.

Laughing I replied, "Hugo, it's very good to hear from you. Thank you for calling."

"Well I'm glad to speak with you. It was that I daren't call whilst you were happily, I hoped, busily I know, ensconced in London. I had a chat with Roger about the problem of Mrs. Parsons."

I was surprised to learn that Hugo knew of Parsons. I listened.

"Her husband was into, still is into, big business in China. He seems to have managed to keep himself out of trouble, sticking to business although not infrequently with corrupt underpinnings. Mrs. Parsons is quite a different story. Her connexions go all the way to the top in China. Her family is in the military and the military and the controlling elements in their communist government are so inter-meshed one can not discern a separation. Their U.K. property purchases, made through Mrs. Parsons, were set up to house their engineers, and their naval intelligence officers, and as a base for their shore surveillance and maneuvers and clandestine coastal operations. These operations were intended to inflict serious damage to our defenses and to gain access to our American ally's intelligence. It was American technology they stole to help them establish these naval operations. It would seem that just as the world has depended upon a good and strong alliance between the British and Americans, the efforts of the citizenry of all free people is needed if any one would remain free." Hugh paused and then said, "An education is in order. Since my little group of contacts in the citizenry are CEO's I thought to start there, and you, Miss Madison, know a few."

"And you know a lot about the workings of the project I was on", I chuckled.

"Well Roger and I go back a long way", he replied.

"Are you - with the firm too?", I ventured.

"No - but I know a few of them, Crispin for example."

"Oh", I replied.

"I have called not only to let you know I am familiar with the upshot of the project but to ask if you would join our soon to be team."

"Oh", I said again in surprise.

"In other words we; Roger, Howie Hedrin, Mitch Orin, Wendell Sommersby and myself, have decided to join forces to educate our people, and others, on the threat to our way of life posed by the Chinese. We have been woefully undereducated as to the nature of their intentions and who they are. You can be of significant help clarifying the who question, and helping our people and others clearly see the threat. Do you know any other CEO's, those with large numbers of people we can reach?"

"Yes I think I do", I replied.

"Very good. Would you contact them, see if you can recruit for our team, and let me know any ideas that occur to you?", Hugo asked with such energy in his voice that I almost started up right then and there.

That afternoon I went over in my mind those whom I knew had large numbers of people for whom they were responsible and who would consider this project. Wynton Crane and Gerald Tucker came to mind. What would I say to them? 'I'm calling to ask (or invite?) you to join our team of international CEO's for the purpose of educating your people (and others) on the threat China poses to our way of life.' Will I be believed? I have to try. To my great surprise Wynton Crane agreed to join. And as I thought about it after the phone call, his initial hesitancy and his questions were a good thing. It made me think that he would stick with us. Gerald Tucker's response was unique.

"Hello Helena", he said simply and with I thought some warmth.

Then I gave him my little speech.

"Who has initiated this team, as you call it?", he asked straight out.

"Hugo Wentworth. He is British working out of New York."

Before I could continue Gerald Tucker stopped me, "I know Hugo." There was a pause on the end of the line. Then, "I will think about this. To do a thorough job time and a lot of attention will be required." There was another pause then he said, "And . . . it will cause a lot of trouble because the Chinese will come after us. This of course is all the more reason to engage in this education objective. I will call you back tomorrow with my decision. Thank you for calling me."

As I hung up the receiver I thought, his response is most refreshing. He is concise, and importantly he is a thinking person, he is considering the whole picture.

The next day I received his call,

"Helena, Gerald Tucker. I'm in. May I suggest a meeting of the team. We should not delay. I'm in New York in two days, if Hugo is in agreement we, and the others can meet there. We have got to do this thing in person."

"I will call Hugo now. I think Hugo will be back to you shortly. Thank you very much for joining us."

Hugo was pleased. His first response was,

"Tucker is an excellent man. He has steely determination. When his competitors wanted to bankrupt him they got the government involved. They got the IRS to audit him, they got the EPA to block his permits for drilling, and they got the FDA to stall on his pharmaceutical company's approvals for new medicines. He dug in. And he wouldn't give in. Finally the government let up because of some seriously bad publicity they were getting before a senatorial election in his home state."

"How do we begin?", I asked.

"We are going to start with you. I think we can start with you opening a few dialogues for our employees. We'll get Tucker and the rest to sit in on them and see how it can work in their companies."

"Wow. Thank you for your confidence."

"It's your confidence, and your discernment for asking the right questions that will make it happen", Hugo said.

"How many employees are we talking about?"

“I’ve got seven thousand. You have to tell me how many and who to begin with. I know you like small groups, is fifty too many?”

“I think we can start with fifty. I’d like to mix them up, a few executives, ten or twenty middle managers, and the rest from the shop floor. I’ll keep my eye and ear open for anyone who could lead and run with it.”

Hugo laughed, “I thought you’d do that. And I think you’ve probably got it just right. Have a chat with Charlotte, she will arrange it for you. This means another visit to New York.” I could here his smile over the line.

CHAPTER EIGHTEEN

NEW YORK

"Why are we here together in this dialogue circle?", I asked the group of fifty Fielding Enterprise employees as we sat together in a spacious room overlooking Rockefeller Center.

A man of about sixty years, one of the Fielding blue collar workers spoke up,

"Because the Chinese have taken our jobs, stolen our technology, and they have been infiltrating our country these last two or more decades."

A few people were nodding. This was a good start. A woman executive put her hand up and I nodded to her.

"As I understand we are here to educate ourselves on the China threat to our way of life. I agree with Jeff", she looked over at the man who had just spoken. "Should we be seeking to learn how many of us are familiar with this infiltration and to what extent, and let that guide our next step?"

"That's a good idea. With a show of hands, who would agree that infiltration is a good description of China's action in America?"

Three quarters of the group raised their hands.

"Someone who did not raise his or her hand, how would you describe any concern you have about danger from China?"

A woman from middle management said, "In the last couple of years I became aware of the Chinese theft of our research and technology. And it seems that China and Russia have an alliance of sorts. My husband is incensed by their treatment of the Uyghurs."

"Concentration camps", a man interjected.

Someone added, "And the Falun Gong. The live organ harvest sanctioned by the CCP."

Another man said, "Yes, and I've heard friends speak of the stories their kids have of experiences with Chinese classmates at university. If it weren't for the number of stories one would think it is all too strange and write it off. But when you hear similar stories again and again you can't ignore them."

"What stories please?", I asked.

"One kid went to a free Nepal protest and his Chinese classmate was so angry that he blackballed him socially and academically. Another kid had invited a Chinese friend over for dinner and while others were talking the Chinese girl began using the friend's computer, going online to a Chinese site. Afterward the kid's computer would suddenly bring her to a propaganda site or when she was writing her essays it would take over and write profanities. After a small gathering my nephew had, which included one Chinese classmate, he found strange sparkle glitter all over the bathroom floor. Before he had a chance to vacuum them up, while using the toilet a piece of the glitter nearest him lit up as like a camera flash for an extended time. Later in conversation he learned that others had experience with this spying too and the connection between them was a Chinese one. One fellow said he'd been on the dark web and seen a friend exposed inflagrante delicto in his bedroom."

Another man spoke up, "Yes, their intention is to undermine our society in order to make their objective of world supremacy easier. A Chinese communist convert has explained the effect of their mass brainwashing and how many people either forget to think for themselves or never have the chance to learn to do so. Our own government has taken on these Chinese tactics in so many ways including; managing our education system from the top, Washington, down, mandating masks and would be mandatory vaccinations, enforcing their will on millions of people and in so doing cutting away our freedom and reducing our very humanity."

"May I suggest that we break into smaller groups. Would you", I indicated five of those who initially raised their hands about Chinese infiltration, "lead a dialogue for your colleagues who may want to learn more about your thinking."

Immediately the five moved to create groups for their colleagues who readily joined them. After over an hour of lively dialogue I asked everyone to rejoin the whole group.

"What do you think? How can we take this dialogue to the whole company?", I asked.

One woman stood up, "If the other groups are like ours the interest and energy for this endeavor is overwhelming. One of our group said he felt that this is a cause of ultimate importance. Our future depends upon it, and specifically a future of freedom or as a people who lost their freedom. And we all sensed the same spirit. Not only do we have to bring this fire to the rest of the company we have to share it with our families, our friends, our neighbors and communities - our country." As she sat down the room burst into applause as confirmation of full agreement.

The next day I heard from Howie Hedrin, Mitch Orin, and Wendell Sommersby.

Mitch Orin said, "Hugo called to tell me that seven leaders stepped up to lead groups of fifty each within his company. That's four hundred people who have or are about to have a lot more knowledge and insight into the China threat and then who will be able to speak to it."

"We are starting Friday with our first fifty", he laughed and a deep throated sound of satisfaction could be heard.

About twenty minutes later Wendell Sommersby called.

"I imagine you have the feedback that our first foray worked very well?", Sommersby asked.

"Yes and Mitch Orin called just twenty minutes ago to say he was beginning Friday", I replied.

"Good. We're ahead of him, we begin today", he said emphasizing his lead. "Would you like to hear back from me as to how we do?", he asked.

"Yes I would. Thank you."

"Good", and he said goodbye.

"Hello Helena, I am happy to make your acquaintance if only over the telephone", Howie Hedrin introduced our call, that evening.

"Thank you. I am very happy to be a part of this team."

"Our people for the most part know something of this threat to America. Some know more than any one else I've met. We have been voicing our concerns for years. We had opportunity to go into China in the early eighties. I took a look with our then CEO. I was a youngster really but lucky enough to be working under a most intelligent and insightful leader. Most importantly he was also a most principled gentleman. He saw the opportunity and he also saw the cost. And the cost he saw was not only to our proprietary rights but extrapolated, to the proprietary rights of all Americans to their privacy, property, and sovereign well being."

"Ohh", a whispered gasp inadvertently escaped my lips, with at once surprise and appreciation for such foresight.

"Well you should gasp. Richard Neville was an exceptional person, a rare human being. As you may have guessed we never got entangled in China. We have no regrets. And we have nothing to reproach ourselves for, as many of my chief executive colleagues do for the help they have given China in undermining the fabric of our great country. I want you to know that I am at your service if in any way I can help you or this endeavor of which we are both a part."

I paused, collecting my thoughts.

"Thank you. Thank you for your generous offer. But most of all thank you for sticking to the task your predecessor set. America needs more people like you", I responded.

"And you", he said with warmth.

That night before bed I reflected on the team and our endeavor. I hadn't heard from Roger I noted. I wonder about his task. He certainly has a pertinent example to offer his people, in Mrs. Parsons. I should be in touch with Wynton Crane and Gerald Tucker. Mr. Tucker, I had a feeling, would be the example to follow. How he and his people faired would be a fair predictor for the entire endeavor.

"Mr. Tucker please", I called and requested of one of his assistants, a woman with whom I had not before spoken.

"Is he expecting your call?", she replied.

"Not specifically. However he knows of me and I think will not be surprised at the call."

"One moment please", she said. I waited.

A booming voice came on the line, not a minute later, "Helena."

"Mr. Tucker. My call is to ask how our battle goes on your front."

A laugh, full, and resonant echoed back at me, "Your call is most welcome. I don't think I'll be able to stop my people now. I may be calling you for help to rein them in and get them back on company task."

"I'm thinking that how goes Tucker's battle, so goes the war."

"That is a compliment I hope is deserved. All I can say is the entire executive team took off like greased lightening with it and they were immediately matched by the managers and their people. It looks like a battle royal to see who is first across the finish line. I have my bets on the blue over the white."

I laughed, "Then I'll bet too on the blue, the red white and blue", I chorused.

That night I was just getting into bed when the hotel phone rang. Charlotte had booked me into the Exeter again. While it wasn't unheard of for a CEO to call late or even on a Saturday, I could not imagine who it might be.

"Hello", I responded.

"Miss Madison", a hissing male voice on the other end of the line fairly spat out my name. I could hear other voices and general noise in the background. It sounded like he was calling from the lobby phone.

"You must stop your unjustified actions against China. Now", he hissed in demand, emphasizing the last word in an ugly tone, and hung up.

Rather than upset me, which I knew was their intention, I was angry at this intrusion. Quickly I put on a loose pullover to cover my pajama top and pulled on my jeans. Luckily the elevator came immediately and I was in the lobby in little more than three minutes. The lobby of the Exeter is open and one can see at a glance the entire area. There were six people. I did not see an Asian male, which the voice had betrayed.

I went to the hotel lobby desk clerk and asked, "Did you see anyone use the hotel phone just now to ring up to a room?"

"Yes. A few minutes ago I saw an Asian man pick up the hotel phone there", he pointed to the small alcove visible from the front desk. "He rang a room and was on the line only moments. When I looked over again he was gone."

"Did he ask with a name for the room number?"

"No", the clerk replied.

"Could he have asked anyone else here for the room number?", I gestured across the whole of the front desk.

"No. I am the only one on at the moment", he said.

"Thank you."

He knew my room number. Would he have gone up to the room if I had not answered? What would he, or someone else, try next? I will call Hugo and Roger first thing in the morning. These were my thoughts as I took the elevator up to the tenth floor.

"We will move you", Hugo said.

After I told Hugo what had occurred he immediately called Roger.

Hugo called back within ten minutes, "Roger will have one of his own here within twenty four hours. He will be stationed where you are living. How are you Helena?", Hugo's voice held kindness and concern.

"Thank you Hugo. I am very well. I'm not frightened by their tactics. I know they want to frighten me but they won't succeed."

"Good for you. You should know that this call was a minor tactic. They will continue and not just with you, with other team members, with our employees. They will continue until we stop them. And the closer we are to getting them, the more they will turn up the heat. Crispin will pick the right person. The heat may be on but we will provide you air conditioning."

We laughed.

Angus Solwater met me at my new abode. Instead of an hotel Roger's team got a hold of a townhouse on the upper east side.

"How do you do?", Angus, about 6'3, twenty eight or thirty years of age, very fit and muscular, offered his hand. His grip was very firm, always a good sign. "This looks pretty posh", he said as we both looked up at the three story townhouse.

I nodded, taking in what was to be my home, at least for the time being.

"Apparently they could purify this one", he said.

"Purify?", I asked bewildered.

"Yes. You never know who has lived here. That is, while we know their names and something about them one cannot be sure if the place is bugged, if the Chinese have already got their grubby hands on it. But when we do the first go through we can get a good idea. And this place was clean. So we took it, and went through it with a tooth comb. Spotless", he said the last word with a finality and a certainty that I found reassuring.

"That sounds good", I replied.

"You probably want to get settled in. I will too", and he touched his temple, where a thick mop of blond red hair lay, as in a casual 'so long'. Walking to the next door townhouse he pulled out a key and opened the door.

Seeing my stare he said, "I'm right here."

"You mean you are right next door?", I asked for confirmation.

"I'm your neighbor", he laughed as he walked inside.

"Goodnight", and he closed the door while I stood staring.

The next morning I heard a lovely bell ringing, like a church bell.

"Oh that must be my doorbell", I said aloud.

I opened the oak door and there stood Angus on the stone stoop.

"Good morning. May I take you for a spot of breakfast?", he asked in a lively voice with lovely Scottish accented English.

"Oh . . . thank you, yes. Come in while I get my shoes and sweater."

Angus stepped across the threshold and began making what I could only call an in-depth examination of the entryway and immediate interior of the townhouse.

I laughed, "You are used to casing the place? Or, what is the term when the intent has the reverse operation in mind, when you wish to protect the place?"

"It is not so much the place as the person in the place whom we seek to protect", he said as he looked at me sideways. "Let's go around the corner to Le Pain Quotidian. A bit noisy – which is good, and the food is healthy and tasty", he smiled as he held the door for me to go through first.

As we walked seventy eighth street toward Madison I noticed Angus's intensity of awareness. His eyes took in the entire street as a whole. He seemed to observe everything; the cars, the dogs, the windows, and most specifically the people.

"What are you looking for?"

"That's hard to say. But when I see it I know. Something or someone out of place", he replied.

"What did you see as we left the townhouse? Something across the street."

"You are observant. Good. It's the brownstone across from your townhouse. There were two different tenants there until yesterday. At the moment it is empty. But not for long we anticipate."

"Who is moving in?"

"Officially, no one", he responded.

"Unofficially?"

"Let's just say someone we don't want as your neighbor. Here we are", Angus adroitly changed the subject as he led me to the door of Le Pain Quotidian.

At a communal wood table with benches four people sat eating their breakfast. Angus chose a table for two people and we sat down on chairs.

"What do you know of the project?" I asked. I wasn't sure how much Angus knew of what we were doing.

"Roger talked with me. He called me to his office for half an hour, just before I left London for New York." I nodded, expecting to hear more.

Angus said, "From what Roger said it's going well. The key team members have reached between twenty and thirty percent of their employees so far and the word is moving outward from the center. People are now talking to family, friends, and community about the threat. The numbers are currently in the thousands, but the exponential effect is soon to reach a million and will continue to balloon. And this is happening in Britain and America simultaneously. They are not going to like that."

"I am wondering about Mrs. Parsons."

Angus stopped eating his breakfast bowl of kale, black beans, blueberries, and chia seeds and was paying close attention.

"Where is she? And what is she doing?"

Angus lowered his voice, "That's also a reason I am here. Roger says Crispin is quite certain she is on the move. And likely right here, in New York."

"Why is she elusive? You got Mrs. and Mr. Worthington - and he was the Chancellor of the Exchequer."

"You hit on it right there. We got someone so high up because he was part of our democracy. She is not", Angus responded.

"Do you mean that she is protected by the totalitarian oligarchic regime of which she is a part?"

"Exactly", he said and changed the subject.

"Have you explored your new neighborhood?", Angus asked.

"No, it's as new to me as it is to you."

"Well there's fun to be had on Madison Avenue my sister told me. Shopping", and he laughed. "I have to meet someone midtown. Enjoy yourself. And keep an eye out", and on this note he lowered his head and looking intently at me gave a slight nod. "See you later", my good neighbor said and picked up the check.

I walked south along Madison Avenue to begin the tour. Angus's sister is right, one could shop for everything from top quality hairbrushes and combs and scrunchies, to $5000 handbags, incomparable leather boots (except for the handmade ones in Florence) and designer dresses. But the real treasures are in the long established little specialty shops including the pharmacies. A tiny pharmacy on the north west corner of Madison and seventy sixth has The Mason Pearson hairbrushes and French made, Camila, hair clips and pins. A lovely little shop on the same side of Madison further downtown has exquisite house slippers. While I went in to these two shops I stayed mainly on the street window browsing. As I stood admiring a display of good leather shoes for men something drew my attention away from the window and further down the street. A woman was gazing into another shop window four or five stores down. I stared. Had she been looking at me? What had drawn my attention? She had a lovely scarf, likely Channel, wrapped around her hair and neck and wore sunglasses in the signature Audrey Hepburn style. Suddenly I realized, it was Wei Parsons. I could not believe that this was coincidence. In spite of myself a shiver ran up and down my back and arms. Angus had warned me, though indirectly. I made myself stand still to think for a moment. Then, again in spite of myself, I walked toward her and put a smile on my face. As I approached she looked up and turned her head toward me.

"Mrs. Parsons", I greeted her with energy and with my smile.

"Helena", she replied.

"The last time I saw you we were both in London."

"Yes. What brings you here?", she asked in her even tone.

"Work. This is a rare time out. I'm exploring Madison Avenue. Are you quite familiar with it?", asking a question while I tried to think of what to do.

"I've been here a few times. Some of the shops are well worth a visit", she spoke in a typical American style. She was obviously more than capable of adapting to her surroundings. She said, "Why don't you join me for lunch? My plans to meet an old friend fell through and I'd be delighted to take you."

There was that phrase she had used before, old friend, when introducing me at her party to the worker bee woman, her cohort in crime and deception. What would she try to do? Try, was not a good choice of word. Anything she tried was most likely to succeed. But she wasn't going to succeed with me. Her attempt is likely intended to lure me into following along with her. Would she try to physically detain or capture me? I think she is certainly capable of it. But how was I to try, no I had to succeed, and get her, or more accurately get her for Roger and Crispin?

"Will you join me?", she stood before me, and while I could not see her eyes I knew they were as cold as steel and beading upon me. To myself I said, what kind of an interlude will this be? Two people speaking in code, and different codes.

Aloud I said, "Yes, how can I refuse your offer?"

She managed a smile. But it was not real. And in its falseness, was ugly. For a moment after I had agreed, while we still stood together in front of the shop window I sensed she wanted to hail a car which idled close by. But she apparently thought better of it. We walked the few blocks to the The Carlyle.

"Have you been to The Carlyle before?", she asked as we entered the lobby.

"No, this is my first time. And I've wanted to see it as I know Roger Federer stayed here during the U.S. Open."

She turned to me, smiled, and nodded, seemingly knowingly. I had the distinct feeling that while she knew who Roger Federer was, because he had moved a main sponsorship to a Japanese company, and given the Japanese Chinese deep animosity, she chose now to ignore any reference to him. The clerk at the desk saw her, smiled and nodded. Then he looked at me expecting to recognize me, but not recognizing me immediately looked away.

"I think you will enjoy it. The food is very good here", she said matter-of-factly as she led us into the boutique restaurant.

Over lunch she regaled me with stories, stories in which she played the major role, stories all about money and power. These were stories she had likely told many times and from which she expected to gain the same wide eyed interest and sheep-like following she had likely most often gained. The Carlyle is where she was staying and I thought where she is comfortable. This is where she likes to be, in moneyed surroundings where she is being served and waited upon, where she is recognized. But I wasn't giving recognition to that which she valued. Suddenly I saw in her eyes and by a slight movement of her chin that she realized this. She was at a loss. But only momentarily. She was disappointed but she would take a new tact.

"You are unmarried, is that right?", she said.

Here it comes I thought. "Yes, that's right."

"You met my husband briefly at our party. As I think you know", she paused, was this to emphasize her knowledge of me?, "he is always at his business, traveling, meetings, we seldom have time with one another", she ended with a commiserating tone.

Did she think I was lonely? Was her intention to make friends? If so she knew nothing of who I am. I had thought of her as a sharp, astute, aware, woman, but her cunning nature did not include any understanding of character. Of course, it could not. She had never thought about character. Her focus on money and power had consumed her time, her life, and precluded any understanding of character. Now, there was no room, and perhaps no time, no life left for the substance of character. We had finished our lunch. At this moment I could excuse myself, I could extricate myself without rudeness.

"Oh goodness, look at the time. I must be off. Thank you for our meal. Are you in town long?", I made a little foray.

"I'm not sure," she said and paused.

This did not sound like Wei Parsons. Perhaps she was trying to determine my plans.

Confirmation came. "What about you? Are you here for sometime?", she inquired.

"For a while I believe."

"We shall meet again then", she ended with certainty.

As I walked back up Madison the air felt fresher. It was not fresher, it was later in the day and the day was without a breeze. It was the escape from Parsons which refreshed. I was no longer confined, under restraint, having to put up a resistance to a falseness which poisons every moment. And there was something more. I recognized a heaviness in the time with Parsons, like an unnatural weight that pulls down the spirit. I'd felt it in China when my father, invited to attend a physicist's conference, had asked Mom and I to join him. The communist squelching and killing of freedom also can and often does kill the human spirit because the evil is palpable.

Turning the corner on to my street I studied the brownstone across the street from the townhouse in which I was living. Nothing covered any of the windows. It was the normal three story New York brownstone residential building. Comparing it to its two neighbor brownstones flanking it either side, one with well tended flowers in the window boxes and the other with a small fountain and statue in a miniature courtyard, it looked empty. As I climbed the few stairs to my front entrance my mind went back to Parsons. Were her spies already out watching me? I went back to the moment I recognized her. Yes, I had known it wasn't a coincidence. That car, she had wanted for a moment to take, was it her car? Did they see me leave my house, the restaurant? Where were they now? I no longer felt I was breathing fresh air. While I was not in her presence she was nearby, or would be. She and her worker bees were buzzing me.

I called Crispin's office directly. As I heard the ring I wondered why I had immediately dialed his number instead of Roger's.

"Helena", that intelligent, kind, deeply confident, and very posh British accented voice greeted me. And I was comforted.

"Hello Crispin."

And before I could say anything else he asked, "Have you seen Parsons?"

"Yes. How did you know?"

"I didn't know. I guessed. You called Hugo for the nasty phone call so if you are calling me, it was likely Parsons. And because having suspected she was on the move again, the two things went together."

"What else are you thinking? Why does she care about me?"

"I think her view is if you are valuable to us, you could be dangerous to her. And, she got wind of you coming to New York for us."

"Dangerous enough to . . . ?"

"Dangerous enough to try and rid herself of you", Crispin replied.

"And that means?"

"It means we are not going to wait. There are a few developments of which you should know. Wiechert contacted Evette. The Germans are thinking if she could be corrupted once she could be again. Evette contacted us immediately, she is willing to be a double agent."

The church bell rang. I opened the door again to Angus.

"This just came for you", and he handed me a rather official looking sealed envelope.

I looked at him and asked, "It is from . . . head office?"

"Yes. It has come via me to ensure they do not get it", Angus replied.

"Do you want to come in? And am I to give a reply?"

"Thank you", he said stepping across the threshold, "I'll come in just for a moment. No reply is requested."

My brow raised, "You seem to be in the know."

Ignoring my response he said, "I'd like to try a little test. Would you go up to the third floor and let me know if you hear my knock?"

"Yes", and I proceeded upstairs.

"Ready?", I could clearly hear Angus's raised voice.

"Ready."

In a moment I heard one firm wrap of the knocker on the front door.

I said loudly, "I heard it. I'm coming down."

"You heard one loud wrap of the knocker on the front door, is that right?", he sought confirmation.

"Yes that's right."

"Good. Going forward when I come to your door I will first give the knocker one firm wrap and then I will ring the bell. I suggest, firmly", and he paused, "that you do not answer your door unless you know who it is, even if you are expecting someone, or a delivery. Either ask who it is or call through the door and ask them to leave a delivery."

"I will do as you suggest."

Angus gave an almost imperceptible sigh, "Good", he said.

"Why? What exactly is your concern?"

Angus looked down at me through intelligent hazel eyes and taking his time in reply said slowly,

"Because we don't know what they will try, but they will try."

The sealed envelope contained a missive directly from Crispin, hand written.

Dear Helena,

Your voice sounded calm and confident. We would not have blamed you if you had been agitated and frightened. Parsons is a formidable enemy. As we are sure you have discerned, she cares for nothing and no one but herself, specifically for her power. She believes in the ascendancy of China, probably for the reason that it suits her will. She may try anything. They have tried the following: hallucinogens or noxious vapours through air vents in homes and in vehicles, capture and torture, sudden murder (dark alley attacks), slow poison, high frequency wave pressure which can seriously injure and lead to death.

Be aware my dear. We understand you may wish to leave us. In fact we ask that you consider what is best to do. I will call you in the next twenty four hours to learn your response.

Best and warm regards,

Crispin

I went to bed that night and lay awake for over an hour. Over and again I retraced my times with Parsons; first at the house in Sussex, her party, and yesterday. At the house initially she was silent watching, then she watched Evette and me while we were unaware. At her party she was purposefully friendly, leading me to her worker bee friend whom she certainly would have questioned about our conversation. And yesterday she had been watching again, decidedly. Had the purifiers done their job? Are Parsons' people in position to place their surveillance tools here? Were they watching now? Somehow I managed to get to sleep.

A church bell rang in the distance. I'm late for church. I started to run, but it seemed an endless distance up hill and down hill, jumping across streams, and I seemed to be running in slow motion. This is a dream I told myself and woke up.

The doorbell rang. Was this the second ring, had my subconscious incorporated the bell to my front door into my dream? As I flung on my robe I glanced at the clock, 7:18AM. I had not heard a knock. Trundling down the stairs I thought I have slept two hours longer than usual.

"Hello, who is it?", I called from behind the oak door.

"Delivery", a female voice answered.

"I'm not expecting a delivery. Who is it from?"

"I dunno", and I heard a thump as the person dropped something on the stoop.

I waited and then I heard a truck drive off. Unfortunately one cannot see the front stoop from inside the house. I opened the door and a medium sized box sat where she had dropped it. There was my name and address with a return address of Carlton Corp, 2166 Avenue B, Oakland California 94604. Who is Carlton Corp.? And what do they produce?

I called Angus.

"I'll come right over and take a look. Just leave it on the stoop. I'll take care of it", he responded.

I got dressed, ate a piece of toast with tomatoes on top, drank some orange juice and went out for a morning walk. Descending the stairs, sans package on the stoop, taking my time I gained a good look at the brownstone across the street. It still appeared to be empty, but there was something. I paused and sat down on the steps feigning the need to retie my shoe lace. Was that a dark curtain on the upper floor left side window? If so, it had not been there before. I casually studied the window. I would look again on my return.

Other than a minute with a very friendly Doodle dog the entire walk my mind was agitating on that brownstone and its potential occupant. I bought a Mars bar on the way home so I could stop and eat it on my steps. Leisurely I unwrapped the top of the bar and let my eyes roam the street, lingering on the brownstone. Definitely, that was a curtain on the upper left window where none had been before. What or who was behind that curtain? Had Angus noticed the curtain? I scanned the front exterior, nothing had changed there. It would appear Angus was right, no ordinary tenant now occupied the brownstone across the street.

I knocked on Angus's door. No answer. Isn't he supposed to be here? I rang the bell. I heard something within, and then the door opened. So, the code was the same for requesting entry.

"Angus?", I could not see him.

"Yes. Come in quickly."

The door opened and then quickly closed behind me.

"Angus, I couldn't see you from the stoop."

"That's the idea. Why are you here? I would have come over shortly", he said.

"Why?"

"I've checked the box and dispatched it to your, our, people", he offered.

"The FBI or CIA?"

"Not exactly. Our own people, so to speak", he finished.

I raised an eyebrow but said nothing more on this question.

"What was in the box?"

"Various product. Did you order anything?", he asked.

"No."

"I didn't think so. We're checking it out", he said.

"Have you noticed a change at the brownstone across the street?"

Angus shook his head but asked, "What?"

"There is a dark curtain now in the upper left window."

Angus looked at me, unbelieving, and began to shake his head but looking at me again he stopped, and said,

"Stand away from the door. I'll be right back."
In one swift motion he opened the door, was outside and closed the door behind him. In another moment the door opened and closed and Angus again stood before me.

"You are right. I missed it", he said looking apologetic and sounding angry with himself. Then, as he guided me to a sort of sitting room off the foyer he said, "This is anticipated but perhaps more quickly than expected", he stopped, waiting for me to sit down. Then he continued, "An old and experienced communist party member has moved in there."

I interrupted, "But how do you know that? You didn't know until a moment ago that anyone was there. Ohh. . .

"Yes. We knew they were coming and we know who they have sent", he replied.

"Who? Exactly, please."

"He goes by Joe, Joe Hu. He is smart, very smart, and he does not involve himself in violence. He will watch and decide about you. But we are moving in on Parsons, and that means Joe too."

"Please explain."

"Parsons is in charge. We stop her, Joe and his people cease operation", Angus said.

"And his people . . . are they nearby to possibly grab me?"

"Possibly", Angus said slowly, frowning.

"Do you have any advice?"

"Are you staying?", he asked.

"Crispin will call, and I will let him know."

Angus nodded. Then he said, "In the mean time I'd like to be your boyfriend, so to speak."

To my raised brow he responded, "I mean, sticking close to you. Going for dinner together. And I should sleep over - in another room."

"Oh, I see."

"Okay?"

"Okay."

One firm knock and the church bell told me my boyfriend had arrived. Angus stood on the stoop carrying one small bag.

He asked, "May I check out the accommodation?"

"Be my guest", and I ushered him in.

Crispin called while Angus was upstairs deciding on what room was best for his purpose of my protection.

"What have you decided?", Crispin asked directly.

"I'm staying."

"I thought you would." There was only a very slight pause and Crispin said, "Evette is arriving tomorrow. She is staying on their side of town, which is also the east side but further downtown. To all appearances she is with them. She will be contacting you in the old manner asking you to lunch, to parties, to be her confidant. She will teach you the code language you are to use together. She will be reporting directly to me, and to Parsons. Do you have any questions?"

"Is Parsons your counterpart on their side?"

"Not exactly. They have a different system."

"I hope I didn't insult you", I said rather sheepishly.

A wonderful laugh, full and alive with joy of living, came across the line to me, "No my dear. I don't believe I could be insulted by you, only delighted."

"Oh, good", I said quietly, quietly very pleased.

After the call I went upstairs to learn how Angus was making out. He had decided on the room next to mine and had begun to transform it.

"I will cut into the wall here", and he placed his hand flat against a section of wall. "So I can get into your room from here, not just the door."

"I see . . . not just the expected way."

"Exactly", he replied.

"I'll leave you to your work."

I called John.

"I know I should have discussed this with you but I've decided to continue with them."

"Are you safe?", John asked.

"Well . . . they are doing everything possible to protect me."

"That is not fully reassuring. What exactly is happening?"

"They sent a fellow over from Scotland to take the townhouse right next to mine, Angus, a very capable and responsible fellow."

"Why did they decide that was necessary?", John asked.

"Parsons. She may think it valuable to get rid of me."

There was a long pause.

"You need to think seriously, very seriously, about getting out. You can't be playing with your life", and his voice was as I had never heard it before, almost commanding.

"I believe we are all playing with our lives, in fact with life itself, by doing business with China. And that is just what I am not doing. We are playing with our lives by letting them attend let alone hold the Olympics, by allowing them in the U.N. let alone having them on the U.N. Security Council, and these are but two of myriad examples of Western wrong thinking. They are laughing at us as we give them the rope as well as the gallows to hang us."

"Alright, point granted", he replied and paused to think.

"I must do my part. I believe every one should."

"Yes. Are they after her then?", John asked.

"I pray they will get her and that China will receive a most serious message."

"Yes", John said and was silent. Then he said, "I will pray too."

CHAPTER NINETEEN

ROOMMATE AND NEIGHBOR

Angus slept on the floor in the next room. He was still asleep or at least still in his room when I went for my morning walk.

There was nothing new that I could see at the brownstone across the street. But as I descended the steps its front door opened. An elderly man stepped out closed the door and took the steps slowly. I reached the street before he did. Strangely, as I studied his face my response, rather than revulsion at character lines permeated with the evil that communist thinking would likely ingrain, I saw life, a love of life, and a calm spirit. I did not see him look my way. But as I paused on the sidewalk he slowly crossed the street toward me.

"Good morning", he said to me, in a low, calm, voice.

"Good morning", I responded.

Whenever I pass someone in the morning, invariably I offer this Christian greeting. The response one gets varies; Good morning, Morning, Hello, Hi. But it is almost always a response, rarely an initiation. Of course if this is China's representative he has a purpose in mind. I waited.

"You are going for a walk too?", he asked.

"Yes", and I smiled.

"May we go together? Perhaps you will show me the neighborhood?"

I liked his voice, serene, in no way pushy. He was taking his time. He seemed simply happy to be out for a walk, with no particular end in mind. He was as unlike Parsons as one could be.

"Alright", I replied slowly, taking my time too. But I added a smile.

He smiled back, and there was warmth in his smile.

"Shall we take Fifth Avenue, along the park?"

"Yes, good idea", he had a Chinese accent but it was not thick, his words were clear and well spoken.

"Have you just moved in?", I asked, honestly, innocently.

"Yes", he said and turned to me with a slightly raised brow and a wee grin.

I checked myself. Was he the most charismatic person I had ever come across or did this man who was close to three times my age and I have an instant rapport? I decided on the latter.

"Are you working for Parsons?", I blurted out.

"No", and he turned to look at me again, his face showed a seriousness that sprang from extensive life experience.

I waited. We had crossed Fifth Avenue and were walking north along the park.

"It is beautiful here, I like walking next to the trees", he offered.

"So do I", I answered him.

We walked silently for many blocks.

Then he asked, "Where are we going?"

"I think we should go to the secret garden."

He turned his head to me and said, "That sounds just right." We chuckled in harmony.

"I discovered the secret garden by chance, as I imagine many New Yorkers do. It is up ahead at about one hundred and fifth street in the park. One can easily miss it, and probably one most often would, because it is down from street level. It's sunken. You'll see, we have to take steps down into it."

When we arrived we both stopped at the black wrought iron gate entrance and looked down into the garden. I sensed his appreciation for this offering of quiet and calm immediately adjacent to the cars and traffic of the street. We took the steps and once in the garden he looked to me to lead.

"Let's go left here, to the more private and secluded part of the garden." He nodded.

We came to the children's part of the garden, the fairy fountain with the little piper boy and the lily pads. He sat down on a wooden bench under a huge tree. I paused nearby. When he looked up at me he signaled silently for me to join him.

"It is special here. Thank you for bringing me", he said.

"You are welcome."

We listened to and watched the sparrows and robins, and attended to the quiet of nature.

After a few minutes he said, "I do not work for anyone. I am here because I love China", he stopped speaking, seeming to take in the beauty surrounding us, the greens of the trees and the blue of the sky. Then he spoke again, "We have been much brainwashed to believe that China is under attack or will be if she does not step out and over or on others. And in particular one other, the United States. While I moved in across the street yesterday, I have been here three months. In that time it is shown to me that Americans love America the same way my fellow countrymen love China. They don't want to bother about too much other than living their own lives. Parsons asked me to watch you. She knows you work with the British and you were involved in stopping the coast project set up to help eliminate British defenses. That made her, and many others, very angry. I am sorry for them, they do not see far." He stopped and looked at me for a moment and then back to the trees where the birds and squirrels were playing. Then looking up into the trees and sky he said,

"You see far."

We walked from the secluded enclave through the main part of the garden where the large fountain pool is in the center. Now we were in the third part, furthest north by the three laughing girls and the fountain where they play.

"What are you going to tell Parsons about our meeting?"

"I will tell her that you are not a threat", he said simply.

"Will she leave me alone?"

"I don't know", he answered.

"My people are after her. What about you?"

"They are not after me. I will disappear. I will not cause them any trouble", he said, placidly enjoying this cheerful place.

"Will you continue being my neighbor?"

He smiled but did not look at me. Then he said, "For a little while."

"What do you think of New York?"

"I like it very well", he replied.

"Why are you connected with Parsons?"

"Our families are both in the government, her's in the military, mine, long time CCP members."

"Do you like her?"

"No. I detest her", he said simply.

We were quiet again. We seemed to enjoy the beauty of the garden in the same way. God's nature was delighting and our delight grew with each breath of air in the secret garden and with each gift it presented.

After many minutes he said, "Why are you involved?"

"I love the good and the true, just as I love the beauty here."

Slowly he nodded, "Yes."

"Why did you say, ""You see far"?"

"I also said the Parsons's of this world do not see far. Their minds are blinded - as in second Corinthians." He dipped his head to me. Then suddenly he stood. "You must go back, Angus will be worried about you. I must go on alone", and his last note held sadness.

I made my way down Fifth reflecting on my neighbor and our conversation. How did he know of Angus? I suppose it was the same way that Angus knew of him. Angus was right in that this man was no ordinary person. He was, most likely, a Christian. What an accreditation, especially in China. He was a gentle, and most intelligent human being. He must be a student of human nature.

As I walked beneath the huge trees extending into 5th Avenue from Central Park a revelation arrived. He had wanted to come to America to see for himself. He had not allowed himself to be brainwashed. He was his own person, under God. Parsons, in her purely pragmatical thinking had assumed from the surface of things that as a CCP member who loves China he would have the same motivation as herself, to further oneself and China. He had allowed her to continue to think this and had come to America, not to further her cause, to learn the truth. And this was the defining difference between people. In seeking the truth one meets reality face to face. If one is not seeking the truth one does not get to see reality. In the end, the truth will bury the lie and unbelievers will go down by their own design. I was home.

The phone rang. It was Angus.

"How was your walk?", he asked.

"It was enlightening. Joe crossed the street", I paused, "and wishing me a good morning asked to join me."

Angus was silent, listening.

"He is not with Parsons, though Parsons thinks he is. He is his own man", I stopped.

"Go on", he said.

"I think he will help us get Parsons."

"He would be signing his own death warrant", Angus responded.

"He will know how to help us, if indirectly."

Angus, ever a changer of subjects said, "Evette is here. She will call you today."

"Do you think I should tell her of our new friend?"

"Speak for yourself. I do not know him, and I certainly do not consider him a friend," Angus replied.

Evette asked me to meet her in Central Park by Bethesda Fountain. I saw her first. She was sitting on a stone ledge off to the side of the fountain. Observing her face, I saw a steady calm I had not seen there before. Doing what is right has a salubrious effect.

"Hello Evette. It is good to see you again."

She looked up and took me in for a moment.

Then a simple smile came to her face and she said,

"I am happy to see you Helena." She stood and stretching out a lovely hand touched my forearm. "Shall we walk?," Evette asked. I nodded, smiling at her genuine warmth.

I began, "You've chosen a difficult and treacherous road."

She said, "Crispin has been very good to me." There was a long pause and I saw much thinking making expression on her countenance. Then she said slowly,

"I want to help. I had been fooled by my view from the past, an unrealistic view. And one which did not include an understanding of human nature nor consideration for the value of our Western substance and all that has been given and that which has been required to create and to maintain this way of life. Crispin has helped me to understand. Now I want to help save it," she shared the thinking which had brought us to the moment.

Tears welled up in my eyes for this redemption. After a moment Evette continued and on the subject at hand.

"This is the only time we can speak openly like this. After this meeting they will have our meetings on their radar. We will have to speak in a manner that will not register as an alert. You will get the hang of it. When I have something on Parsons to give you I will send you an invitation, preferably to a party. Parsons thinks I will entrap you and thereby she will rid her side of a connexion for the British and Americans which includes a number of important people."

"So I am valuable, indirectly?"

"You are more valuable than the Chinese can conceive. They do not understand the value of a free human spirit."

"Yes", I said quietly, thinking of my neighbor across the street.

I had decided not to mention my neighbor to Evette. I don't know why. Perhaps I wanted to see her again and then decide. However that evening I had not changed my mind. It would be interesting to learn if the Chinese would inform her of Joe. But I thought that not likely, they were more likely to keep all cards close to the chest.

Not much happened the rest of the week. Angus did not ring my bell and I didn't see him. He had not returned as a roommate and wasn't acting as a boyfriend either. Perhaps he too had learned from his sources more about our neighbor and it confirmed my view of him. And, if not, I decided I would not worry. I took advantage of the time left me and walked the city or at least the upper east and west sides and the Park. I walked from my little neighborhood across to the East River and up to eighty sixth and back across to Central Park. Thursday I decided to spend the day in the Metropolitan Museum of Art.

I stood on Fifth Avenue looking up at the Metropolitan Museum of Art's beautiful Beaux Art facade designed by William Morris Hunt and appreciatively accepted Hunt's silent invitation to his entrance to the world's finest classical art museum. In the grand Roman domed entry I stopped and stood still, absorbing the gift genius and time shared. Directly in front of me was a large enclave planned that it should be built into the wall. It held an enormous and beautiful arrangement of fresh flowers. Something learned in the immediate moments of standing in the entry to the MET, something about symmetry and balance from the wisdom classical architecture reveals, had me turn one hundred and eighty degrees in the knowledge, unseen, that directly behind me and across from this enclave must be another identical enclave for a matching bouquet of nature's bounty. And there it was. I walked up to the enclave closest to me, 'A gift of Lila Acheson'.

I strolled in the natural light filled Great Hall, which from the marble floor to the center of the glass dome is sixty five feet. Then I took the stairs of the grand marble staircase to the second floor. I wondered at the immense imagination of American architecture schooled in Europe, of the financiers and the governors of the city of New York who had a grand plan in the latter part of the nineteenth century. Again I stopped, this time midway up the staircase and looked back. The grandeur and elegance of the staircase planned as center of the building was perfectly placed, as purposed, to offer the public beauty for one's betterment.

"It is truly beautiful, truly beautiful," someone spoke almost in a whisper by my left shoulder.

"Yes it is beautiful", I said as I turned in response to a young man of about my age who stood close beside me gazing, as on the message the museum imparted from this vantage point. We smiled at one another in like appreciation.

"Have you been here before?", he asked in a reverenced tone as we climbed the remaining stairs to the top.

"No, this is my first time."

"May I properly introduce you?", he asked.

"Oh - yes, thank you", I replied to one who indicated with this offer a familiarity and knowledge greater than my own.

He led the way I was already headed, into the European gallery. He walked us over to Rembrandt's 1660 Self Portrait and standing me in front of the portrait said,

"You stand here. I will stand outside your peripheral vision and speak to the painting."

And as he did and as I gazed upon a Rembrandt masterpiece I was introduced to Rembrandt himself. Here was Rembrandt the man. Here was a man who saw who a person is and held the capacity to share it with another, a man who sought to see life. He was before me in this very moment. The hair on my forearms stood up responding to this privilege. Rembrandt understood character and, therefore could see the interior man, for all the external trappings. He could see the eternal and if it existed in the particular soul viewing his works, he could share it and in so doing offer revelation and inspiration.

"You have given me a key to a secret garden I did not know existed, another world. Thank you very much indeed", I said to Stephanos, my Greek guide.

"You are welcome. It is a privilege to share with another who can appreciate history, that which time and talent can tell", he replied, in a classically Greek manner.

I returned each day to the MET for the remainder of the week and into the next. Each time a different gallery offered its treasure. Having discovered the Temple of Dendur I returned to it each visit at a different time of day. In 1963 before the flooding of the Aswan Dam the Egyptians went to the world asking who would preserve the Temple as it was destined to be underwater. Only New York had the money and the will. At the time it cost $16 million just to disassemble the stone of the temple. New York City and the Metropolitan Museum of Art expanded the museum further into Central Park, building a new room to house the temple. One enormous wall of the room built to house the Temple is all glass and looks out into the Park. It is a simple and perfect space for the Temple of Dendur's proper display and appreciation. On each visit, arriving at a different time of day, the Temple, bathed in a different light, appeared anew; pink, beige, yellow tinged, or a pale brown to tell its story afresh. In different seasons I was sure it would show itself in another light entirely.

After a most enjoyable week exploring, enjoying, and learning of history and life at the MET, Evette called.

"This is a heads up for an invitation you will receive to Parsons's party on the fourth."

"They are not disguising that they know where I live", I said.

"Hmm", she murmured and then said, "You are right you will receive a written invitation. It's some big wigs and apparently invitations are hard to come by."

"You mean some people are clamoring for them?"

"Yes, so I've heard", Evette replied.

"Who will be there? Should I do some homework?"

"I don't know but there is someone, a man, she very much wants to meet, which is the reason for the party."

"One would think Parsons would have no trouble meeting anyone she wanted."

"Yes, you'd think. Seemingly, he dictates all meetings and he hasn't asked her. But she is determined. He has the ear of everyone at the top", Evette divulged.

"At the top of what?"

"The top of every tree", she said, and added, "wherever they grow."

"What's his name?"

"Henri John", Evette said.

"He is a Westerner?"

"I don't know but I would think so", she responded.

"He sounds interesting. Perhaps he reserves himself and only comes into society infrequently to keep up the mystery and thereby raise his status."

"That could be", she laughed.

"I look forward to meeting him, or at least seeing him", I said.

"If he accepts and comes", Evette replied.

I reported the invitation to Jonathan knowing he would pass it along to Crispin, though Evette perhaps had already done so.

Jonathan said, "I don't know this fellow. Let me know what you think of him. And in the meantime I'll see what I can learn about him."

I went shopping at Bergdorf Goodman, to their sale racks. Luckily a simple chocolate brown and deep green linen dress, at a third of the regular price, size six, hung alone amongst a clutter of trendy more flamboyant items. It fit perfectly and would work for the evening at Parsons's.

Parsons's New York apartment, or the one she had rented, was on Park Avenue at seventy first. The concierge rang up with my name and after the okay the elevator attendant conveyed me to the eighth floor. The butler, given his lack of assurance I guessed had been hired for the party, opened the door and took my coat. The living room was lavishly furnished bordering on garish. This was in stark contrast to the classically decorated Kent manor house. Apparently the impression was more important to Wei Parsons than her own personal tastes. Or, as per a previous observation, attention to character was not within her ken. Parsons liked spending money and showing that she had money to spend. As I stepped further into the room, keeping an eye out for Evette I tried to size up the guests. While mostly Chinese, about a third were Westerners. I heard some British accents though the Western voices were mainly American. There was Parsons smiling at me. She always seemed to spy me first. She was engaged in listening to an older Chinese man, or at least he was under the impression she was listening. I noticed Evette wafting down the hall toward me. She looked very pretty and her dress of deep green silk and cotton fit her to a tee. Parsons followed my line of vision. What was that tentative look on Parsons's face? Was it distrust? I must mention this to Evette.

"Helena, we're glad you could come. I'm sorry I was not here to welcome you. How long have you been here?", Evette said, speaking so Parsons could hear her. Then she gently and expertly guided me to the bar which luckily was on the other side of the room and out of Parsons's earshot.

"He is not here. Parsons is in a bad mood," she whispered.

"Oh . . . why is he so important to her?"

"Two martini's please", Evette smiled charmingly at the bartender.

"Only a guess, but," Evette spoke in an inaudible, to anyone nearby, voice. We were shoulder to shoulder and I could hear her, "He must be the lead on a major project to which she wants to be a major part."

"What kind of project?"

We had our drinks and again with a charming smile on her face, which belied the content of the conversation, she moved us to another corner of the enormous living room.

"A like project to the Kent, Sussex, Northumberland scheme, but likely even bigger."

"Do you mean another attempt to thwart British or American defenses?"

"Yes, but with much greater impact. High tech, AI, and incapacitating satellites", she said.

"This Henri is a traitor then?"

"One would think", she responded.

"We are going to become suspect if we continue in our tête-à-tête whisper."

"Alright I'll leave you now. I don't think he is going to show. You can go anytime. Just give it another ten minutes," Evette said smiling continually.

Perhaps it was Parsons's bad mood but Parsons did not make an attempt to speak with me. As Evette suggested, I left after another ten minutes.

As I returned from my morning walk and mounted my steps a voice I recognized called,

"Good morning Helena. May I persuade you to extend your walk? Would you join me?" It was my special neighbor. As I turned he was crossing the street again toward me.

"Good morning," I greeted him and as I did, wondered why I did not reciprocate with his name.

Then it dawned on me. He had not introduced himself, he had not given me his name, I had only been told his name was Joe. I descended the stairs and we stood before one another.

He gently repeated his request, "Will you join me?"

"Yes."

"Central Park please,", he said waiting for me to accede. I nodded happily.

Moments following our joining one another, and as we silently, comfortably, walked to Fifth Avenue and then into the park, I had that uncommon feeling of complete calm, of that rare rapport with a fellow human being which sets all at peace.

"I think you noticed that I did not give you my name," he said when we were well beneath a canopy of trees. I nodded again. He was aware of my thinking.

He said, "It is Joel Wu. Some know me as Henri John."

I started. "Henri John? Parsons wants to meet you. But I thought she set you up across the street from me," I said, really asking for him to explain.

He laughed and then said, "I am sorry. I do not seek to confuse you." He turned to look at me as we walked side by side. "Let me explain," he said, seeming to read my mind. "Parsons did set me up across the street. She does not know me and we have not met. There are many connections and much is interwoven in the Chinese network." He paused and we continued silently for some time.

"Parsons would have that I recommend we get rid of you. What I am about to say she would dearly like to know. We, two of my family members and two of my closest friends, were considering a major project to seriously undermine Western defenses. However I, and one of the friends, have decided to change course completely. And we have convinced our associates, two family members, my sister and cousin, and our other friend to do the right thing. We have decided this is what is better for China in the long run. That is, to rebel against the communists and show our people that they are far better off free. You see when I asked you to join me it was meant in a sense beyond the moment."

I stopped walking and turned to him, staring. He laughed and his laughter caught me off guard. I began to laugh too. We laughed and laughed until smiling passersby began to turn their heads.

Once we continued our walk he began again, "I will help you capture Parsons. She will be a good catch because she leads the pack of those who care nothing for doing the right thing, and therefore nothing for China. When others who would follow her see her end they will be deterred from continuing down the dead alley."

"How will you help?", I asked the simplest question.

"I, as Henri John, will give a party and invite her. You can inform your people that the opportunity exists to get her," he said simply.

"Alright. When?"

"Next week," he replied.

"And how do you see me helping you bring freedom to one billion four hundred million Chinese?", I asked a complex question simply.

"That is not what I see. The Chinese people will be given the opportunity to help themselves. What I see is your example. You can help teach our young people how to think, and how to think about freedom", he said.

I went immediately to my desk as soon as I was home and began to write. It was as though a power beyond my own capacity pulled me on. I wrote of freedom; of what it means, what it feels like, and the life it opens for us. My pen marked the page with words about the finger of God in the American founding, how two thirds of the Founding Fathers were seminarians and how they related America's foundation to the principles of liberty under God, that Lady Liberty herself can only exist when people are subjects of God and understand what it means to serve. When I noticed my writing hand becoming sore I left my desk to wander the townhouse upstairs and down, reflecting.

What did I think I was doing? Someone would have to translate this writing into Mandarin and Cantonese. What medium would be used to communicate the message? Would native Chinese be able to speak these words to their fellow Chinese and be understood? Joel would have the answers and apparently the means. Is this, these words, how I would join Joel and his project? He said one billion four hundred million Chinese will be given the opportunity to help themselves. As I understand his meaning, they will be given the opportunity to help themselves understand; freedom, the personal responsibility required that freedom may exist, and the appreciation for life that sparks the fire to ignite souls to answer to God and not to their own will. How would all the underlying evil that arises when people follow their own will be pierced through the heart? Joel must be a Christian or how could he come to this determination for such a project? His faith had him see the light for this endeavor. And through his faith is how he must plan to see his way through. He must be very highly connected and at the highest level I thought, and not just in the CCP.

I sat down finally in the rattan chaise lounge chair I'd bought having noticed it on sale in a Brooklyn shop window. The chair, without a cushion, was hard, and the white rattan made it feel clean and simple, helping keep my thoughts organized. I'd positioned the chair for a fine view south out the back bedroom window. The bright outdoor sunlight entered, filling the entire room with brilliant light. One branch of the London plane tree that easily reached the third floor, nearly touched the window through which I gazed, day dreaming. My mind became attuned to the relative quiet the thick townhouse walls afforded and which the early afternoon offered. A chickadee sitting on the branch peeped. The London plane tree . . . London, back to New York, what a journey this was. And China? Something told me, no. Perhaps via video? No, too impersonal. If the Chinese were to engage with freedom it would be very personal indeed. It would require a lot of personal responsibility. Were people capable of taking personal responsibility for their lives when all they had known was government interference and control over all aspects of life? The clarity for the enormity of consequence of Joel's vision struck my own internal line of vision. One billion four hundred million free people . . . what a picture of a new horizon. The world would be a vastly different place. All of us would need be better people. Would the Chinese learn to innovate rather than copy Western product and ideas? The impact on competition would be staggering, and could be marvelous. A new or thoroughly revived sense of service for the customers of airlines, hotels, all market transactions, would come into being. Most of all, more than a billion people would have the chance to awaken to a new day where the light shining upon them would offer a new, a sixth, sense of possibilities. Spirits could come alive, like a new born baby aware of his mother's or father's face and his instinctive joy in the recognition of love and life in that face. The world would show a new face.

"Apparently Henri John is giving a party, a big party," Evette said as we ate lunch together at a west side diner.

"Why do you say apparently?", I asked responding to her comment. My neighbor, former neighbor for he had moved out of the brownstone across the street, had sent me a lovely invitation to his party.

"It's hard to believe. He barely appears in public. His reputation is for being a recluse", she said, with a note of excitement.

"Are you going then?"

"Yes, Parsons invited me. Her husband is away as usual and her invitation includes a guest. It will be interesting to meet him and to meet some of his guests. Can Roger get you an invitation?", she asked.

I smiled but did not nod, "I'm invited."

"Good. Parsons will finally get to meet him. I'm pretty sure she is working on persuading him to give her a significant role on his project," Evette said.

Parsons doesn't know that he is working on a wholly different project than the one she envisions and that, while as she desires she would be a part of it, it would be a very different part than the one she has in mind.

Tonight was dinner at the apartment Crispin had taken in New York. It had been weeks since the last time we had shared dinner and I was looking forward to being in his company.

"I think you would quite like Joel Wu," I said.

"Why do you think so my dear?", Crispin asked.

"While I only guess that your backgrounds and upbringings are very dissimilar, your characters share some fine similarities." Crispin smiled at me but if he was about to say something it was preempted by a servant entering at that moment with our meal. The table was set for three. Before the third person arrived I savored these moments with Crispin for I knew that it would be very hard to ever replace the place he held in my life.

I said, "I wish my best friend John could meet you, his character is as sterling and I think there would be a good rapport between you."

"We shall meet then", Crispin said as fact.

I flushed with a deep appreciation and my insides tingled.

The sliding doors of the dining room opened and Jonathan was ushered in by Hampstead.

"Helena", Jonathan said cheerily, and nodded to me. I was delighted to see Jonathan again.

He turned quickly to Crispin and said, "We've connected with him. All is now in place." Crispin nodded.

Over dinner the conversation revealed the plan. Jonathan was to be introduced to Parsons at the party as Henri's right hand man in America. Once the party was in full swing and the guests enjoying themselves with food and wine Jonathan would have her join him in a room apart from gathering guests. Then they would leave after a consummating visit from Joel. The firm's limousine would be waiting to escort her out of the country forever.

"Why is she not detained here?", I asked Crispin.

"We will detain her, for a time. Just enough time to help Joel get things moving in China. If we keep her they will seek the first opportunity to capture our people. Their methods are severe", Crispin replied. He continued, "But they will take note. She and her family are in the leadership ranks of the CCP and our capture of her puts a significant crimp in their plans. They will have to pull off, and may leave off their plans", he finished.

"Who is the mole?", I asked.

"You helped get the internal mole, Mr. and Mrs. Worthington. And the mole on the Chinese side? Parsons," Crispin said.

"Parsons? And Charles Parsons?", I asked, momentarily bewildered.

"There is a Charles Parsons or rather a person code named Charles Parsons. And he is a relative of Wei Parsons in China. While he is set up as the big fish, in reality he is a gopher for Wei Parsons. She is the mole. Once we catch her the game is up, she is finished and they are severely hindered, at least for a time."

"Goodness."

"Not too much of that", Jonathan added.

"What am I to do tomorrow at the party?"

"Enjoy yourself. Chat with Parsons if she is amenable. Otherwise be friendly with Evette. We don't want Parsons suspicious while we are about to pull her in", Crispin responded.

"Evette doesn't know?", I said simply. Crispin shook his head.

The next morning when I went out the front door and down the steps my eyes went to where the dark curtain had been. Joel had left no trace of his short sojourn. A sad feeling crept in as I walked into Central Park. Joel, like Crispin, was a treasure, a precious gem I had been given for a short time. Each was a jewel I had surprisingly, unexpectedly, come upon, like a shimmering sunrise that touches the dew of the morning making everything within its beams sparkle. I had been placed where all the sunbeams seemed to reveal all the possibilities of life. But when the sun sets the day is over, and one must have made all effort to live fully in the light. I felt that if I got a glimpse tonight of Joel that there would be no chance to speak with him. Our day was done. But perhaps a glimpse.

"This is it", Henry said in his energized voice. Henry had driven me over to Fifth Avenue to where, apparently, Joel Wu was currently residing. But I did not think that this was where he was staying. This place I thought is likely on loan for the evening party.

"Thank you Henry. Are you . . . returning?" As per his frequent habit Henry looked at me through the rear-view mirror. He nodded. I responded with a smile.

"Enjoy yourself", he said.

"That's what Crispin told me to do."

"You've been with us a while now, better take the opportunity for enjoyment whilst you can", he said wisely.

"You're right. Thank you. I will."

The Fifth Avenue building at seventieth was a posh pre-war residential building. I showed the doorman my invitation. He nodded and began to lead me further into the lobby. He stopped and gestured to the elevator man who stood waiting to take me up.

"Hello", I said to the elderly gentleman who waited for me to enter and who then joined me pulling the iron gate closed. The elevator door closed and he pressed the top floor button. Normally I would engage the person with whom I shared such close quarters. But somehow I felt it would not serve Joel Wu and remained silent. The elevator stopped and he pulled back the iron gate.

"Thank you", I said and smiled.

"You are welcome. Enjoy yourself", he said.

There it was for the third time. Alright I will I said to myself.

I rang the bell at the only door on the floor. And who should answer but our host.

"Hello Helena", he said in his gentle voice. "Thank you for coming. Please come in", and as he stepped aside I stepped inside.

I found myself doubly delighted, to have a moment with Joel and, in the atmosphere of the open foyer where we stood. The foyer was well and subtly lit, simple, and the only adornments a beautifully sculpted wood bench for sitting to put on one's shoes or boots and above it hung a medium sized oil painting in the style of Turner of a large English summer garden. This beauty along with the exotic hardwood floor gave warmth to the entrance and indicated that the owner was a Westerner. Joel Wu's warm dark eyes looked into mine and held my gaze. He gave a small smile, an acknowledgment that we both enjoyed this moment.

"Thank you", I whispered.

He gently placed his hand on my back to guide me into the main room. Everyone in our immediate area seemed to turn, if not their heads, their eyes to learn who Henri John was bringing into their midst. He continued into the room with me by his side and stopped midway.

He said, "May I introduce you to my cousin, James Li."

James Li was perhaps twenty years his younger and he stood as we approached.

"How do you do?", he said extending his hand in a Western fashion. I liked his voice, strong, yet kind. Was this the cousin he had persuaded to join him on his new project of educating the Chinese on freedom? As though in answer he slowly bowed his head and allowed for a small smile to crease his mouth. The doorbell rang.

"Will you excuse me. Another guest arrives", Joel said.

"Please join me", James offered. I sat down on the sofa next to where he indicated. I was beginning to enjoy myself.

"Do you live in New York?", I asked.

"No. I live in Shanghai. I am only visiting for a time", he said, looking at me without removing his gaze from mine.

"How do you like New York?"

"Like my cousin, I like it very much. I hope to be able to return . . . one day." His voice altered on his last words.

"I hope so too", I said, my voice low, almost as a prayer.

"Thank you", James replied in like timbre.

Joel came toward us with Wei Parsons beside him. If her perpetually expressionless face could look happy I would describe what I detected there as elation.

Joel said to her, "You know Helena, may I introduce my cousin, James Li."

"Helena how are you? How good to see you." She sounded authentic. Then she came and stood in front of James Li who had stood upon the introduction. They did not shake hands but she lowered her head ever so slightly as he kept eye contact. Just then Evette came over.

"Hello Wei, Helena", she said and nodded her head to Henri John.

"May I introduce Evette Eliot?", I asked looking at Joel.

"Please", he replied.

"Henri John, Evette Eliot", I made the introduction.

"I am pleased to meet you", he said graciously, extending his hand.

Evette looked excited, and by the look on Parsons face was winning kudos. But there would not be the time to have them amount to anything.

"There is someone else to whom I would like to introduce you", Joel said, he made his offer specifically to Parsons.

Parsons quick on the uptake moved closer to his side. I watched as she followed him across the room to where Jonathan stood by the fireplace. While I had not yet noticed Jonathan, this is where his agreed positioning must be for this introduction. It was strange to witness a wholly different set of operating tools come into play with Wei Parsons. How many times in her life had she followed anyone? Was this a wholly new experience she was having in this moment as she followed Joel's footsteps toward Jonathan Hill? What was it like to be Wei Parsons in this moment? I thanked God in the place where I stood that I was not Wei Parsons and that I am Helena Madison.

CHAPTER TWENTY

The Key

I watched their introduction, trying not to stare. Jonathan, absent his usual open warm smile, wore a considered smile offered as appropriate for one interested in business, the kind of business Parsons was in, making money and gaining power.

"I didn't know Jonathan knew Henri John", Evette said.

I had not considered how leaving Evette out of the loop on Jonathan's current role would work. But Crispin would have considered this. Evette will say nothing to Parsons about it.

And to help fortify this I said, "Best say nothing to Parsons about Jonathan." Thankfully she was right next to me and even as I lowered my voice Evette nodded.

Jonathan and Parsons must have chatted about five minutes when Joel returned and inclining his head slightly to Parsons ushered Jonathan away. This is likely a demonstration to Parsons of their closeness I thought. What would she do now? Parsons watched them until they were lost in the throng of guests and had turned down a hallway. Surveying the room and seeing someone she knew Parsons made her way over to him. I studied her as she moved across the room. Expressionless again, yet one could detect a buoyancy to her step. Drunk on power or the prospect of more power? I nodded.

"Why are you nodding?", asked Evette as she sipped, no more gulping, her drink.

"Oh you know, always thinking", I replied somewhat evasively.

I surveyed the guests. There must be over two hundred people here. And like the parties to which Evette had invited me, I did not see a face that beckoned further interest. Evette began talking with Joel's cousin and I found myself lost in thought. The education of the Chinese in freedom could not occur without an understanding and belief in God. Millions of Chinese had become Christians over the past decades. Would this be enough? It was a start.

"Helena" I heard Joel's voice. "May I speak with you for a moment?", he asked as he stood on the other side of a group of people who were parting to let him reach me. Evette's face broke out in a smile, she is excited for me I thought. Did Evette sense his goodness? Or was it a hold over from her former interest in power?

I moved toward him. He guided us to the hall at the other end of the living room. Then we moved down the hall to a door which he opened and waited for me to enter. Closing the door he turned to me with a serious face.

"I must leave now. It is of course rude for the host to leave his own party. However you and I know in reality this is not a gathering for the purpose of partying. All is arranged for Jonathan to meet with Parsons privately, shortly. This room, where they will meet, has another door", and he moved over to show me. "A strong man, I'm not sure what you would call such a person, will come through this door once Parsons is here alone with Jonathan. I must be on my way back to China before she arrives there. There are many with whom I must speak and convince of right action." He paused for a moment. We were standing facing one another. The moment was intensified by the enormity of the plan he shared with me - to change the world by helping enlighten more than one billion people.

He began anew, "I sense that I will call upon you again, that we will see one another again, and that it will be a happier time. At this moment I ask you for a little favor. Will you stay close to the other side of this door and unlock it when the strong man arrives?"

It was such a simple and funny request that I began to laugh. And Joel laughed with me.

After a few moments of laughter he said,

"This is the second time we have made each other laugh. It is good to do."

"Yes. It is good", I responded.

"This is the key," and he showed it to me. "The door must be kept locked until the last moment. It leads directly to the building stairwell and the back door of the building where your firm's limousine will be waiting. The strong man has access to that back door of the building. But I can give this key only to you. Once you have used it to open this door hold on to it and return it when you are contacted. He will do so in a way similar to the way I did when we first met", he smiled at me knowing I would understand, that I would do as he asked, and to tell me that he trusted me completely. He handed me the key. "I am sorry you will have to forego the rest of the party and wait in the stairwell," he said kindly.

"I'd far rather be of service in the stairwell that be back at the party," I said. "Won't Parsons hear the key in the lock?"

"No it is silent. It is a special door and a very particular key", he replied. "Go now", Joel said and opened the door for me. I left the room and turned to face him on the other side of the threshold. "I will go now", he said in that sad tone I had heard in Central Park when he had said "I will go on alone."

It was sad to hear the sadness in his voice. I made myself focus on the task at hand.

Waiting silently behind the door and grasping the key tightly I felt my palm begin to perspire. Opening my hand I studied the key. It looked like an ordinary key with a square head. But the serrated lower portion for fitting into the lock appeared to have a double edge. Would it fit simply, quietly, and quickly into the lock? Would I hear Jonathan and Parsons on the other side of the door? Would the timing work? I prayed that all would work that the whole picture could come together.

Then I heard Jonathan's voice beyond the door and felt my body tense for readiness. What would Parsons do when the other man entered the room? Then I heard what must be Parsons's laugh. It was startling. It was a sound that one knew to be a laugh but that should not be a laugh. It held no sense of fun, was absent merriment, and devoid of joy. It lived in the realm of a cackle.

I became alert to a slight sound below me on the stairwell and hoped to goodness that it was the strong man. Whoever it was was ascending as quickly as quietly for there at the base of this floor's stairwell was a man of medium build and extraordinary agility. In one moment he was at the bottom of the stairs and in the next he stood before me.

"Hello", he mouthed the word.

I nodded and tried to smile. And a small smile came as his presence reassured.

Then he mouthed the words, "The key?"

I opened my palm to show him. For a moment I thought he would take it and proceed to open the door. But he gave only one nod and then looked to me as if to say 'It is you who is entrusted with the key'. And I knew he was right.

The moment had arrived. Please work silently I said silently.

He moved to the door in readiness for his next move.

I took the key between my fingers and placing it in the lock angled it for turning and turned it.

As the door sprang open, flat against the adjoining wall, he sprang into the room as a tiger, silent, dangerous. I remained on the other side of the threshold opposite to where Joel had been minutes before. But now I saw Parsons instead.

She was momentarily stunned. In one moment the strong man leaped behind her pinioning her arms. The normal face she wore was now contorted in rage. Her eyes afire with malignity bore into me.

"How dare you", she screamed. "How dare you, you puny little upstart."

"Quiet", Jonathan said to her. "We have you now", he continued as fact and as he moved to the door with the strong man, who held Parsons in his grip, I jumped back out of the way. Then they were ahead of me descending the stairs.

"Close the door and lock it", Jonathan directed his words to me from the stairs below.

I closed and locked the door and again grasped the key tightly in my hand. What now? They had disappeared and I began to take the same stairs hesitating a few moments not wanting to be anywhere near that woman. Her twisted face and black eyes piercing through the space between us just moments before held me on the second stairwell. Then, releasing myself from further thought in her direction, I continued my steps to leave the building. Every step moved me closer to the source from which sustenance came, opposite of that which those eyes betrayed, life over death. I saw them drive off turning the corner onto Fifth Avenue and wondered what conversation, if any, Jonathan was having with Parsons. How long would he have to be in the same space with that woman? For I knew it would be an ugly place to be, all those operating tools of hers would be in play, at least in her mind, and their energy would be negative at very high voltage.

Another car, a black Mercedes, drove up to the building on seventieth street. The driver's window came down and there was Henry. I breathed a sigh of relief and realized I was releasing a lot of tension induced by thoughts of Parsons.

As soon as I closed the door I said, "Home James."

We laughed. And sensing my eagerness to be far away, Henry opened the windows for fresh air. As I breathed in deeply I knew Joel was right, it is good to laugh. We didn't say much in the few blocks to my townhouse but it was good to be in Henry's company.

A question arose and I asked, "Why did they bring you to New York?"

"I asked if I could be here for this assignment. And because I'd been driving you and Evette, they agreed."

Henry's smile was so full of love of adventure that I nodded and kept nodding, thinking how could they refuse him.

As he drew up in front of the townhouse I asked, "Is Angus still there?", looking at the neighboring townhouse.

"Yes, he is there", Henry replied.

I looked at him in his rear-view mirror. He nodded in confirmation and as reassurance.

"It's dark", I said observing all the windows.

"Of course", he replied and smiled.

I was in need of some familiar company. It was too late to call John or Mom. Their voice would have offered comfort. I put on Bach. Thank you God for the genius you instilled in Johann. Comfort came across the fields of time through Bach's music and his great contact with God. What man can do when free. What chains man binds his fellow man with when he seeks control and power, blind to who is truly in control and oblivious to any understanding of in whom all power resides. Hong Kong came to mind as I let Bach carry me. My favorite sweaters, were labeled 'Handmade in Hong Kong'. And the CCP had sought to destroy all that was good in Hong Kong. How they would pay. God had that justice planned. And I tried to think on it. But not knowing his plan the good people of Hong Kong came into view and a fire against injustice, forever kindled, ignited in a full fury against the evil. The little I could do here and now seemed too little. Joel Wu flashed across my internal vision and I knew that it was the Chinese people who must fight the evil alongside God.

"She is being extradited to the U.K. to face charges of spear heading intended crimes against the nation and its people", Crispin said as he passed me the roast beef and Yorkshire pudding. Hampstead had served the food and left the room.

"Did you arrange it?"

"I was involved", he replied.

"That sounds like some justice. Do you think it will be?"

"It will be the best attempt for justice I have witnessed in too long", he said. "We are working on getting as much as is appropriate into the papers and news outlets. That is, the sale of prime British property to the Chinese - a lot of Brits won't like that, the attempt to attack our defenses from within, and the general infiltration of the Chinese into our way of life. It will wake up a few people", he said. Then he slowly added, "But so many always seem to remain asleep."

"They remain in a fog in hopes of hiding from the truth. The truth is too hard for many."

"Yes", Crispin replied and I heard in his voice an echo of that same sad tone I had heard in Joel's voice.

I said, "You know though, the wisdom is that it only takes a few good men, just one if we take Churchill's example, to stave off a calamity and then others can get on board. Many want to do the right thing. They have to have a leader to follow."

The key sat in a small upper drawer of the roll top desk in the study. "He will contact you in a similar way to the way I did." Joel's words echoed in my mind. How can that be? From across the street? I kept my eye on that brownstone. And then one morning, a little more than a week later, as I was coming out for my morning walk the door across the street opened. Out stepped a young man - American I thought. He paused and looked over at me with a big grin, definitely American. I came down the steps a little more slowly than usual to learn what he would do. Sure enough he came down the brownstone steps and crossed the street.

"May I join you for a walk in Central Park?", he said, his voice held a warm, alive confidence.

Wanting to laugh, but not needing to, I smiled instead. We walked to the park. I said nothing. He silently obliged. Once we were walking along the bank of trees he spoke.

"Joel speaks very highly of you."

I looked down to the ground, a mixture of sadness and embarrassment, then changing the subject said,

"Are you from New York?"

"I grew up in Hong Kong."

" Hong Kong . . . I was wondering about your accent. I couldn't place it."

"My family is here, we're from New York, but my heart is in Hong Kong. So as you can imagine it is separated from me at this time."

"What can be done about all the evil which lives in the world?", I asked.

"You have a way of getting to the big picture", he said. "I think we are addressing it, you, me, Joel, Crispin, Jonathan and others."

"I'm glad to hear you say that. What are you doing here? Are you able to be in Hong Kong at all?"

"I'm going to get my key back for one thing", and he laughed the happiest laugh from what must be the most lovely place deep inside. All I could do in return was laugh along with him.

But then I blurted out, "What a wonderful laugh. How good to be able to laugh like that."

In another moment he said as discovery, "You're right." Then, "It mean's that something is working, that life is speaking." And a fine smile, full and warm, clean and happy, appeared on his intelligent face. Suddenly he stopped along the path beneath the canopy of trees before Bethesda Fountain and turning to me extended his hand.

He said, "I am David Wisden." And he grasped my hand with verve and might as though we were embarking on a fine and bold adventure.

Responding enthusiastically I replied, "I am happy to meet you."

"Let's go get that key off your hands", he said decisively.

"What can one do to help Hong Kong?", I asked as we headed to the townhouse.

"Speak about Hong Kong to everyone, speak about China's evil wherever you go and to whomever crosses your path. Be in contact with your congressmen and senators and be sure they know what you think of this evil. Don't support China in any way and tell everyone that it is their responsibility to do the same", he answered.

"And you?", I asked again, with brevity.

"I am supporting Hong Kong in every way I can. This means being here raising funds and support for them. And working to increase awareness of China's evils there. I know people there and I am in touch with them. They are very appreciative of others' interest in them and their plight. China is having troubles, lack of good food to eat, lack of clean water to drink, serious problems in the economy and people weary and angry with the crackdowns. We must be ready to apply pressure to the cracks in the walls."

We had arrived at the townhouse and David came in while I retrieved the key.

As I handed it to him I asked, "Is that apartment yours?"

"It is given me to use", he paused and then added, "by one who is supporting Hong Kong, and the cause of liberty and justice."

"Good for you for finding such a person." He did not reply but just kept looking at me.

After a few moments I said what came to me, "I think I've been in search of such people all my life."

Then David nodded, and said, "Sometimes it's just one person. One person may be all it takes."

David invited me for lunch to a charming little French restaurant off Madison.

"Did Joel tell you exactly how he arranged for us to meet?"

" . . . not exactly. I knew he was staying in that brownstone," David replied.

I waited but when David said nothing more I continued,

"This - business - should I call it the spy business? While I'm not sure it matters, I am wondering how others came to consider the role I play to be important?"

"You have managed to or happened to connect yourself with some important people", David replied.

". . . Yes", I hesitated. "I'm not sure how that happened."

David smiled giving the impression that he was dealing with a much younger person than himself, yet his smile was not condescending.

He said, his dark eyes sparkling, "I can see that rather than ambition, your motivation is that of interest. It is a good interest, one with depth. I would expect Crispin saw that right away – as did whomever introduced you to Crispin. And their interest in you caught Parsons and her crew's attention." I thought about this for a moment.

Then I responded, "Yes, you see I am interested in what is right, good and true."

"That is how you got involved with those good people with whom you now work", David said. He added, "What is right, good and true must be very clearly defined in your mind."

"Yes I suppose it is."

"I'd say you know it to be", he suggested.

"You are right. I do know it. And I am troubled by others not knowing more themselves about who they have been given to be."

"Why?", he asked.

"Why what exactly?"

"Why does it bother you that others are not interested enough in what they most value in order to put themselves in position to actualize these values in their life, and for life?", he asked.

"That's it. Life itself would be better if people would take up their personal responsibility to life."

The waiter arrived.

"May I order for you?", he asked.

"Yes. You know this restaurant", I said as a conclusion.

"I do", he replied.

After David had ordered I gave voice to my thoughts,

"I've been given that for which I've been asking, fine people to know, with whom to work, with whom to learn. I knew Crispin was exceptional immediately upon meeting him. And Joel. Goodness. The two of them, Crispin and Joel, are individual treasures. Two treasures in one place and time. I consider myself blessed to be able to be in their company. I can't say 'to know' them."

"You could get to know them, with time", he said.

The waiter arrived with our food and deposited it silently before us.

"Do you know Crispin?," I asked.

"Know, no. However I have met him on one occasion," David said.

I waited hoping to hear more.

He said, "I agree Joel and Crispin are as fine as they come. You know Crispin better than I do. And I suppose I know Joel better. But you've had more time with Joel than I have had with Crispin."

"I do feel very thankful. It's a gift that tells me life is very grand indeed, precious, and wonderful."

David said, "When one is fighting evil, when one sees through the fog screen put up by lying mouths, deceiving eyes, and false faces, one's succor is provided by the existence of such fine people."

"That's sort of it, isn't it? If one seeks to pursue what is right and good, and in finding a way to do so in the world, - fighting evil - as you say - then fighting along side the best and the bravest is a fine reward on earth."

" . . . on earth . . . you are a Christian", he said it as fact.

"Yes."

"I am a Christian, I am glad we have met", he said and he offered a beautiful smile and then bent his head to say grace.

"Character, human character is to be understood, and then reckoned with. This is what we fight, the world created by those who have not understood that human nature is fallen, those who would follow their own will without respect for God's creation. How does one live in the world when one does understand?"

"I think you have been answering this question. Finding work that engages one's values, and if lucky, finding too the people with whom one can join hands in this work, one finds the answers", David replied. "Do you pray?", he asked.

"Yes, all the time."

"Me too. That leads you to where you should be here. We were speaking of time. The question is what will one do with the time one is given," he said.

"We were also speaking of knowing oneself and discerning who another human being is. Is there ever enough time to know a fellow human being?", I asked.

"In marriage perhaps", David said.

"That is one's best chance. And how many see this opportunity and seize it?"

"Certainly far from all married people see marriage as this kind of opportunity. And fewer seize the chance to know the other well", he said.

"Having the chance to know another human soul, how sad to waste the opportunity."

"As you said, it is essential to know what is most important in order to live this life alive to it", he offered.

"Time must be invested, not spent. One must do the homework to be able to answer the question what is most important and learn to understand the value of time and life and, that life is a gift."

"And you are right to use the singular - 'it is a gift' - time and life - because time is life", he said.

"Though life is more than time."

"Yes. You understand", David said.

Chinese agents Two and Eight, having been removed earlier from Cambridge, divulged other links within Cambridge. And with some additional investigation a compatriot spy and two Russian plants were likewise removed shortly thereafter. A cleanup operation by British intelligence, or more specifically Crispin's operations, gained full approval from a parliamentary subcommittee. At the same time American counterparts, in particular, connections of Crispin's, successfully conducted a sweep of three of the Ivy League universities, toppling two Presidents and numerous less visible plants. Additionally, media networks, including social media were swept clean. It was apparent that the West or at least some if it's patriots were no longer standing by while China conducted its march to undermine the West from within.

"It's good that we got her, and perhaps only just in time", I said as Evette and I sat across from each other in a Broadway diner.

"Yes, along with her insidious placement of agents in our academic institutions, furthering her and her comrades plans for espionage and the use of the secrets discovered to undermine our defenses, she might have gotten me", Evette said.

"You mean . . ."

"I mean had me quietly killed," Evette replied.

"From something Crispin said I think she has done such things. Was she corralling you into something?"

"Yes, and I didn't realize it until the party where Jonathan got her. She had suggested we visit some friends of hers but this time in the country. In England the country is never very far away. But here it can be out in nowhere, where no one else is around. At the party Parsons told me that she had accepted an invitation on our behalf to join these friends Sunday afternoon", Evette's face showed fear. But in another moment a small smile replaced the expression of alarm.

Evette said, " I have you to thank for saving me. Without you, I don't think Crispin and Jonathan would have been able to reach me. I would have gone with her Sunday, and I believe not to return."

I paused a moment and then responded, "You saved yourself by being open to another way of living life."

We were silent for many moments. Then Evette nodded.

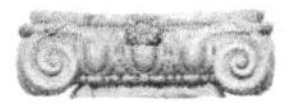

The education campaign was working. Though where progressivism had made deeper inroads it was slower going. Where people still innately love America, the Midwest and areas of the South and pockets everywhere in the country, it was more of an awakening that was needed. Americans whose families had always loved who America is were naive to both the fact of a motivation to destroy her and the extent of the damage already done. In the back of their minds these Americans were thinking we just had to wait for another election and get the right people elected. What they were helped to realize is that the right people, people who run for office because they love America, soon won't exist. If you remove history, the truth, God from the classroom, our children will not know who America is. They will not know who they are. The naïveté had not allowed for imagining that this destruction from within, of who we are, is exactly what the elites who dictate education policy want. Where progressive thinking is entrenched a re-education is required and this takes time, a lot of time. What will help is the addition of the tidal wave, the tidal wave that is coming from others whose love for America, and for what she has stood, is rooted in the soul, this will have others join the wave toward the truth. The truth, that cleanser of souls, that solvent which cleans away time and life wasting irrelevancies, distractions, all that thwarts one's simple movement to the natural rhythm of life must be valued to be recognized. It is the unction of the truth which anoints for the the discerning that clarifies, positioning one for appreciation of the good, offering one the acuity for recognizing beauty, and for a mind faithful for understanding.

Crispin was true to his word. An invitation arrived in my mailbox requesting my and John's company for dinner in his home.

"I have been wanting to meet you", Crispin complimented John.

"Thank you very much. It is very good to meet you. It is good to be here," John said and paused. Then he said, "There were times I was concerned for Helena's well being."

"These were concerns which I shared. Thankfully these concerns tend to arrive ahead of time, in good time to allow for the readiness", Crispin said raising a brow and looking over his spectacles he leaned almost imperceptibly forward toward John and me.

John smiled. I breathed an inward sigh of relief, knowing John had worried.

"Are you in New York much longer?", I asked Crispin.

"This is my last evening", he replied.

"Oh", was all I could say, appreciative of the privilege of this time with Crispin and sorry to know that New York would be without Crispin Holtshire again.

"Are you making New York your home?", Crispin asked me.

"Upstate. I need the quiet of the countryside."

"Yes, I often do. I have been spending more and more time away from London", Crispin replied.

"Will you ever retire?", I asked him.

"One who cherishes life and understands his personal responsibility to it can never retire", Crispin's voice was firm, and as always animated.

"Yes. That is the truth", John and I said simultaneously.

We three laughed in unison.

"And when ye see the south wind blow, ye say, There will be heat; and it cometh to pass. Ye hypocrites, ye can discern the face of the sky and of the earth; but how is it that ye do not discern the time?"

Luke 12 v 55-56

"Whoso keepth the commandment shall feel no evil thing: and a wise man's heart discernth both time and judgement."

Ecclesiastes 8 vs 5

Made in the USA
Monee, IL
03 April 2024

55660339R00152